# Too Many Secrets

# By

# Nina Guilbeau

Too Many Secrets

Book 2 in the Sisters Trilogy

This book is a work of fiction. Names, characters, places and incidents are products of the author's imagination or are used fictitiously.

Copyright@2013 by Nina Guilbeau
Edited by Barbara Ellers
Cover Design by Lynda Alfano

Published by Juania Books LLC
www.juaniabooks.com

Library of Congress Control Number 2013908406
ISBN 978-0-9818047-4-3

Printed in the United States of America
First printing 2013

Visit ninaguilbeau.com for other titles by the author and for book club meeting information.

*It was a knock on the door, a simple knock on the door that started unraveling secrets that would change the sisters' lives forever.*

## Chapter 1

Alise moved about the kitchen bubbling with excitement. Her son Anthony was coming home after seven months of combat duty overseas. For years he had talked about joining the Marines after graduating from high school, but Alise always managed to talk him out of it. However, this last time it was her idea for him to join, and she had been on pins and needles for approximately 210 days. It broke her heart, but she didn't have a choice if she wanted to get out from under Paula's thumb. The secret videos her older sister had made showed Anthony and her two other sons engaged in enough illegal activity to get them arrested, and most likely, put behind bars. Anthony was by far the worst offender, and it both angered and hurt Alise to find out about her boys' activities through Paula. Things were going on right under her nose, and Alise couldn't figure out if she was completely fooled or if she had let herself be fooled. Had she turned a blind eye?

Alise shook the thought from her mind. It didn't matter now. What mattered most was that those videos would be released if Alise didn't keep Paula's secret. It was straight up blackmail and Alise didn't doubt for one minute that Paula would follow through with her threat.

She hated feeling so helpless, but she couldn't take a chance with her children's future at stake. She had to stay quiet and let Paula stay in full control until she could find a way out for her sons. Alise had finally figured a way out, but she still had to be careful. When dealing with Paula, Alise knew she couldn't get ahead of herself.

She also knew Paula could do a lot of other damage with those videos too. If she wanted to, she could bring Terrance in on the blackmailing. It galled Alise knowing it was Terrance's idea to make the videos for leverage against her in the first place. He wanted to use the videos of his own kids to force Alise to sell the house that they jointly owned. Alise shook her head thinking about her small minded, stupid ass ex-husband. He didn't care about his own sons, only getting his hands on the equity in the house. It wasn't even the best time in the market to sell, but Terrance didn't care. He just wanted Alise out of the house. Unfortunately for him, their divorce agreement gave his ex-wife other options and Alise wasn't ever going to sell – not as long as those tapes stayed hidden. If Terrance ever got his hands on those videos, he would be blackmailing her too. The only plus for Alise in this whole mess was knowing that Paula had double crossed him. Terrance had made the big mistake of asking Paula for help and then the bigger mistake for actually trusting her with the goods. In the end, Paula simply did what she did best - lie. She told him she couldn't get anything of use on video and kept all the damaging tapes for her own purposes.

Of course, Alise knew Paula couldn't care less about helping Terrance get what he wanted. He was just a bit player in the game of wits between the sisters. Paula's angle was simple; the more she could put the screws to Alise, the more assurances she had for Alise's silence. No one but Alise knew that Paula had forged documents allowing her to fraudulently claim inheritance money. She was then able to manipulate everyone and get her claws into the successful production company that rightfully belonged to their younger sisters, Callie and Marlisa. Alise didn't like standing by while Paula lied her way into their lives again. She was the oldest sister who always felt out of place, and because of that she resented them all. However, very soon Alise would be able to push Paula out of their lives, but first she had to protect her boys. She had to get them out of the line of fire.

"Heads up, Aunt Alise," Vanessa, Callie's oldest daughter said from the doorway. "I'm about to send Mom in here because she's in the way out there."

"What's she doing?"

"Just being her bossy self. I swear the woman can run a multimillion dollar company, but can't hang up a Welcome Home sign."

Alise chuckled. "Ok, send her in."

"Do you have any tape?"

"Yeah, in the drawer by the fridge."

"Thumb tacks?"

"No."

"Good. I'm going to send her in for thumb tacks, but tell her you have them so she'll look for them."

Alise burst out laughing. "So you want me to lie?"

"If you lie to keep family harmony, then it's really a blessing," Vanessa said laughing along with her aunt.

"Oh, really? Is that in the Bible?"

"If it's not, it should be," Vanessa said, still smiling as she turned to leave.

Alise couldn't help but grin hearing her niece call out to Callie, knowing Vanessa was about to send Callie on a wild goose chase. However, as she thought about her niece's words she became somber. Was lying to Callie, Marlisa and her kids to keep peace in the family really the right thing to do? Alise had misled her family to buy time and to protect her boys from the uproar Paula had promised. Although she wasn't ready to say it was a blessing, it did look like it was paying off.

Jamal, Alise's oldest son, was doing very well two thousand miles away at UCLA and Jackson, her youngest who was still a minor, was about to get into a prestigious boarding school. After seeing for herself what her boys had been up to, Alise had clamped down on their freedom. She put Jackson in a program run by a local church group called Look Up. It guided young minority boys without a father in their lives towards positive living. The idea was to teach them that finding a prosperous future meant to turn away from the street life and to "look up."

Jackson had a great mentor who had worked wonders with him. In just a couple of months, his grades had improved and his test scores had gone through the roof! Alise wasn't ashamed that she had asked Stephen, her very rich and very powerful business partner, to pull some strings and get him a shot at getting into this private school. It's not like he couldn't keep up with the work, he was certainly smart enough. He just needed the opportunity that Stephen's influence was able to give him. With Jamal doing well on the west coast and Anthony a highly respected member of the armed forces, Jackson was looking forward to doing something worthwhile, too. He had learned to "look up" just like it said in the brochures.

Alise smiled. After Jackson was accepted into the boarding school, so what if Paula released the tapes? First off, all of her boys would be out of the state doing something good with their lives. What was the DA going to do, try to extradite them to give them a slap on the wrist? They weren't a danger to society, and the police had other things to do than try to "capture" a minor from a fancy boarding school, a United States marine recently assigned to a special task force and a college kid on another coast who had never been in trouble before. Plus, they weren't involved in illegal activity any more. Alise groaned. At least, she hoped they weren't.

Alise tried once again to shake Paula out of her head, but as she had already learned, it was nearly impossible. For months she had been focused on reaching the moment that was almost here. She was one letter of notification away from Jackson's official acceptance. She knew that with Stephen's help and influence, the school would let him in, but the waiting was making her nervous. So much was riding on this final piece falling into place so that all of her boys were out of Paula's reach. When that happened, Alise would be set free. She could do what she had been dreaming about for months and that was to shut Paula down. As soon as Jackson was in, Paula would be out. Alise thought back to one of her confrontations with Paula.

*"Your day is coming," Alise had told her, but Paula had only laughed at her.*

*"Maybe. But it ain't today, is it?" She had snapped back at Alise.*

"Well, it's almost that day," Alise said aloud as she began to put icing on her chocolate cake. "It's coming, dear sister."

"What's coming?" Callie asked entering the kitchen. "Oh, by the way, the kitchen looks great."

"Thanks," Alise said admiring her surroundings. The maple cabinetry, the backsplash and appliances were all sleek and modern. The cream and gold granite countertops highlighted the slate and stainless steel squares in the backsplash tiles. Alise had added a stylish wet bar between the kitchen and dining room. The piece was not only elegant, but with the extra counter space, it was also highly functional. The dark Brazilian cherry wood flooring, two beautiful chandeliers over the large island and the counter-to-ceiling glass cabinets, made the kitchen very worthy of the showroom design Alise had in mind when she started her redecorating project.

"I finally have my dream kitchen and now I'm too busy to even cook in it."

"Hmm....true," Callie murmured distracted by the cake. "Do you have any thumb tacks?" she asked as she reached to touch the icing for a little taste.

"No!" Alise yelled and slapped Callie's wrist.

"No to thumbs tacks or to touching the cake?"

"Both! Uh...no wait. Thumb tacks you need to look for. But absolutely "no" to cake touching."

"Why not?"

"Because I don't want you being all nasty coming in here and licking all over the cake."

"What are you talking about?" Callie asked laughing. "I was just going to put a little icing on my finger to taste it. How does that make me 'all nasty' and licking the cake?"

"First of all, I don't know where your hands have been."

"Want me to tell you?"

"Ugh! No, I do not want to know the filthy details of your sex-capades with Michael. I know he spent the night last night."

"Yeah, but we didn't do anything." Callie sighed. She sat down on the bar stool at the end of the high kitchen counter, seemly forgetting about her thumb tack mission.

"Didn't do anything? Is that because of Stephen?"

"No...no...it's because we...I want to take it slow. So, we're just dating."

"And Stephen doesn't have anything to do with you keeping Michael at arm's length?"

"The last I checked, Stephen didn't have anything to do with Michael sleeping with Marlisa. Out of all the women in the world, my husband chooses to sleep with my sister. I just have to learn to trust him again. I can't put a clock on it. It's going to take as much time as it's going to take. *But,* even though we're still separated, so far it's been really good between us. I know Michael is trying hard to work it out."

"So, Stephen has nothing at all to do with you dragging your feet?"

"*Nooo.* I told you no. Why do you keep asking?"

"Because I see the "googly eyes" you two make at each other every time we have a meeting. By the way, when are you going to let me buy you out of the restaurant? I keep asking and you keep dragging your feet on that too. I swear, sometimes I think it's because the restaurant is the only real excuse you have to keep in such close contact with Stephen."

Alise smiled at her sister, thankful that Callie, her little sister and best friend, had put so much on the line to help her open *Josephine's,* which was now hugely successful. Alise had brought in billionaire Stephen Russell for marketing, but he was also an investor and ended up being very instrumental in the restaurant becoming such a local sensation.

Callie had promised to let Alise buy her out, not because she wasn't proud of what the three of them had accomplished, but because Callie knew it was Alise's dream, not hers. Callie's "baby" was CM Music Productions, the company that she had started with their youngest sister, Marlisa. Everyone, including Marlisa knew Callie was the work horse behind its success. Unfortunately, now that Paula had wormed her way into the business with lies and blackmail, Callie's hard work was benefiting two untrustworthy sisters who were nothing more than dead weight. Alise let out a sigh and pushed the unnerving fact from her mind. The truth was, she had succumbed to Paula's blackmail and let Callie be manipulated by Paula. Callie didn't have two untrustworthy sisters, she had three.

"So Callie, what's the deal? Are you and Stephen…?"

"No, we're just friends. Um, you know business partners and friends…or… more like friendly business partners."

Alise had stopped icing the cake and stared at Callie. "Are you done? Because now you're just mumbling and making excuses like you're feeling guilty." Alise continued to stare at Callie as a new thought took hold. Stretching her eyes she asked, "Are you sleeping with Stephen and not Michael? *Oh, my God*, no wonder you're-"

"*Noooo* I'm not sleeping with Stephen! Or Michael. I might as well be a nun, 'cause I'm sure living like one."

"Shoot," Alise put a few more icing swirls on the cake, "then let me personally welcome you to the Sisterhood of the Holy Nuns Gettin' None."

Callie and Alise laughed as Alise exchanged the spatula and bowl for a tube of icing with a decorator's tip.

"But," she continued as she began to carefully write on the cake, "there's a big difference between me and you. I'm in the convent because I don't have a man or even a prospect of a man that I want to be with. You, on the other hand, have *two* men that you *choose* not to be with, even though it's clear that you want to. I'm not saying go full hoochie mode or anything, but I mean, I just don't get it. What are you waiting for? Just choose already instead of pushing both of them away."

Callie bashfully looked away just as Alise looked up from admiring her art work.

"What was that look?"

"What look?"

Alise gasped. "Oh, so you're not pushing both of them away! You *are* doing something!"

"I don't know what you're talking about."

"No wonder you come in here ready to be licking all over stuff!"

"Oh Lord, I cannot believe you're-"

"Which one is it?"

"Which one is what?"

"You know what! You're doing something with somebody 'cause otherwise you wouldn't be looking so embarrassed!"

"I am not embarrassed! You're blowing this way out of proportion, Alise."

"Oh, no I'm not, sister girl. It's Stephen, isn't it? That's why you've been meeting with him by yourself so much lately. Pretending that you're helping me out." Alise stuck her chest out to do her best sexy Marilyn Monroe impersonation. "'Don't worry, Alise, I'll get with Stephen and we'll handle it,'" she whispered. "Yeah I bet you did handle *it.*"

Alise grinned and Callie couldn't help but laugh. "I am not going to dignify that with an answer."

"I knew it! I'm right, ain't I? You don't have to give me all the details, but girl I need to know something. I mean, when you're fooling around do you …touch the parts that …your bathing suit covers?"

"Parts that my bathing suit covers? What are we, five years old?" Callie asked, clearly amused. "Anyway, it's not like that."

"Well, I know that you're at least smooching with him."

Callie rolled her eyes, but she didn't say anything.

"And Michael?"

"What about Michael?"

"I mean you just said that you're dating him, taking it slow. What do you think he's going to think if you're not….Oh, what a minute. You're smooching and extra stuff with him, too? *Both of them*? Oooohh!"

"Shh, Alise," Callie whispered looking towards the kitchen door. "Stop trying to put my business out there for the kids and everybody to hear!"

"What? You don't want your kids to know their mama got a little hoochie still left in her!" Alise said loudly and then laughed at the look of panic on Callie's face.

"Don't worry," Alise said lowering her voice, "I won't tell anybody, especially Stephen and Michael."

While still laughing, Alise covered the cake and carried it to the other end of the kitchen where she sat it down gently on the counter.

"What's so funny?"

Callie stiffened at the sound of Marlisa's voice.

"Alise, I'm going to go check on the kids," Callie said getting up from the bar stool. "I'll tell Vanessa you don't have any thumb tacks."

"You didn't even look."

"Yeah, well, she won't know that," Callie replied, and without even looking at Marlisa, she walked briskly out of the kitchen.

"What's her problem? Sometimes she's ok with me and sometimes she's just…I don't know…so cold. I still don't know what to expect from her, and it's been almost a year since all the sisters decided to work together."

13

"No, it's been almost a year since Paula showed up to force all the sisters to work together. Besides, I don't actually work there, so that leaves Callie having to deal with you two backstabbers alone."

"I have been nothing but good to Callie," Marlisa said ignoring Alise's insult. "I have supported everything she wanted to do with the business and I've gone against everything Paula wanted to even try! Plus, I'm sharing my office with Paula since Callie won't authorize any more real office space. Although, she's ok with putting a desk in the storage room."

Alise giggled.

"It's not funny, Alise. I'm miserable there, but I'm still bending over backwards to prove to her that I'm on her side!"

Marlisa ignored the fact that getting closer to Callie was part of her plan to get closer to Michael. Because of Callie, Marlisa was still able to see and talk to Michael from time to time. Staying connected with him was the most important thing in Marlisa's life, that and being patient. Marlisa knew that her chance with Michael would eventually come again. It took twenty years for Michael to turn to her the first time, but Marlisa knew that if things went according to plan, it would happen again very soon.

"Alise, I don't know what else I need to do."

"Can you "un-have" sex with her husband?"

"If I could, I would."

They both knew immediately that that was a lie. Alise sighed and studied her baby sister who was actually looking quite pitiful.

"Marlisa, a very wise person told me that learning how to trust someone again takes time. You can't put a clock on it."

"You seemed to have forgiven me."

"Well, you didn't sleep with my husband," Alise said thinking briefly about Terrance, "but then again, you always had better taste in men than I did. Besides," Alise opened her arms towards Marlisa who quickly walked into them for an embrace. Hugging Marlisa tightly she whispered, "forgiving you is not the same thing as trusting you."

Marlisa quickly pulled back in surprise and looked at Alise, not sure if her sister was joking or not.

"Oh, please don't look so surprised! You were in cahoots with Paula and you actually signed over a share of your business to her because of some secret deal that involved Michael. Don't tell me you don't remember our first official company meeting last year?"

"No, I remember it, all right," Marlisa said as she gently pulled away from Alise while carefully averting her eyes, "but my dealings with Paula like that are over," she lied.

"Uh huh, ok," Alise replied, raising her eyebrows.

"Honest, Alise."

Alise shrugged her shoulder and then continued, "Anyway, back to the subject at hand. You are Anthony's aunt and he wanted you here. And we're still family, so that's what I try to remember. Look, Marlisa, you made some bad decisions, a lot of bad decisions, a whole, whole, *whooole* lot of bad decisions. As a matter of fact, you probably made some of the worst, most horrific-

"Okay, Alise."

"-unthinkable and even sad-"

"*Okay, Alise!*"

"-decisions I've ever seen. But I still have a little hope for you because you're my sister."

Alise smiled genuinely at Marlisa, who had the same caramel colored skin and hazel eyes as Callie. They looked so much alike on the outside, but Alise knew better than most that on the inside, they were worlds apart.

"Hello?"

"You invited Paula, too? You're really into this sister loyalty thing."

"Oh, hell girl," Alise said pushing Marlisa out of the way, "you know good and damn well I did not invite the devil's wife into my house! Paula!" Alise yelled as she marched out of the kitchen. Finding Paula in the living room, Alise stood with both hands on her hips.

"Why are you here?"

"Anthony is coming home. He's my family too, you know. I'm not here for trouble. I'm just here to welcome my nephew home."

"That boy barely knows you. You've been away from this family most of his young life."

"That was before, Alise, I've been in town for a year now."

"First of all, it's only been ten months and second-"

"Alise," Paula held up the palm of her hand towards Alise while turning her head in the opposite direction. "I do not have time for your theatrics. I just want to welcome my hero nephew home from war torn Afghanistan."

"Oh, no, no, no, no," Alise said incredulously, "I must be in the Twilight Zone or something 'cause I know you don't really think you can disrespect me in my own house and get away with it! You gotta go!"

Alise stepped towards Paula just as Callie, Marlisa and Vanessa jumped between them. Paula stood with her arms crossed watching while the three of them forced Alise back into the kitchen.

"You got her?" Vanessa asked her mother.

"Yeah, make sure Paula stays out there!" Callie instructed her daughter and then turned to Alise.

"Callie, let me go! 'Cause I'm getting ready to put her disrespectful behind out of my house, even if I have to drag her by the hair across the doorstop!"

"I know, but Alise listen, listen," Callie grabbed her sister on either side of her face to force eye contact. "You can't do this now! Anthony's coming home today so this is a *good* day. Don't let her ruin it. You just have to take a breath and let her have her moment for now."

Alise focused on Callie and began to relax as the anger drained from her body.

"You know," Callie continued, "that when all of us are together, you've always been the grown up in the room. We need that now. But in the spirit of compromise, after the party if you still want to kick her behind, we can all go in the backyard where there's nothing but space and opportunity."

Alise smiled and leaned back against the counter as Callie released her. Settling next to Alise, she rested her left hip against the counter to face her older sister.

"For the record," Callie continued, now smiling too, "I really don't have a problem if you still want to have at Paula later. I'll just get a lawn chair and a bottle of wine, maybe fire up the grill. Oh, and I'm definitely getting some video footage to go up on YouTube where I can make some money off of it. Two old dinosaurs like you two fighting and both of y'all wearing dresses? You know that's going viral."

"Dinosaurs?"

"Yep, T-Rexes."

"Is that the one with the little arms?"

"Yeah and the big butts," Callie added grinning and watching carefully as Alise laughed. She could tell the storm was over, at least for now.

"You're ok?"

"Yeah, just give me a minute."

"Ok," Callie said not moving.

"Alone."

"Oh, sorry," Callie responded and moved quickly towards the exit, "leaving now."

Alise took a deep breath and chided herself for letting Paula get her so worked up. She realized it was probably because Paula had never been very far from her thoughts for the last ten months. Almost everything she did was fueled by her need to expose Paula and her lies.

Because of Paula, Callie and Marlisa think that Phillip Elliot, the man who raised all four sisters, was not their biological father. Everyone knew that both Paula and Alise were fathered by their mother's first husband, even though Alise wasn't aware of that fact until Paula let that secret out the bag. Until then, Alise believed she was Philip Elliot's daughter, but the truth didn't change how she felt about him. She still loved him the same and she still carried the Elliot name. However, she looked like an Alexander. She and Paula had the same fair skin and dark eyes.

But Callie and Marlisa were Phillip Elliot's biological daughters and according to the details of his will, they inherited the bulk of his estate. That is, until Paula came up with her big greedy scheme to get a bigger share. Never mind that Paula and Alise got insurance money from their biological father, and never mind that they both also got some inheritance from Phillip Elliot. None of that was enough for Paula - she wanted more. So she unceremoniously appeared after being out of touch with the family for years with "new" information on the legality of the will.

According to her forged documents, one of the sisters, Callie or Marlisa was not a biological daughter and would lose everything to the other. Paula skillfully used the rift between the sisters to manipulate them into an agreement. After telling each sister privately that she was not the biological daughter and heir, and arranging bogus DNA tests to "prove" it, Paula then suggested a solution. Agree to keep the results of the DNA test secret in exchange for signing over shares of their successful music production company, which happened to be the biggest product of their inheritance. Each of the four sisters would then have equal shares within the company and neither Callie nor Marlisa would lose it all to the other.

Alise was anxious to give back all the shares of the company that Paula stole from Callie and Marlisa, but more importantly, Alise needed to give her younger sisters their father back. She needed to set things right. For some reason, Paula didn't understand how much it hurt Callie and Marlisa to lose their father and their identity. She didn't seem to care how painful it was for both of them to feel as if their entire life was just a big lie. Alise understood, that's why she couldn't let Paula get away with her selfish, deceitful plan. She was confident that, in the end, she would beat Paula at her own game.

Being at odds with Paula was familiar territory for Alise. They've been opponents in one situation or another since Alise was a young teenager. Even if Alise wanted to make peace with her older sister, she wouldn't know how. Their twisted competition was a part of her now. It was the only way they communicated with each other. Alise was incensed that Paula had managed to bring her to her knees and keep her there for months with blackmail.

She reflexively balled her hands into tight fists and then instinctively relaxed them again. Her strength was that she could remain calm and think. She would fix the mess with her boys, make things right for Callie and Marlisa and then get Paula out of their lives forever.

Hearing movement at the counter, Alise looked behind her to see Marlisa cautiously watching her from the corner of the kitchen.

"I'm pretty sure I said I wanted to be alone."

"I thought you were talking to Callie," Marlisa answered softly.

Alise couldn't help chuckling a little. Marlisa. She was a tough one to explain.

"I was talking to Callie because I didn't see you standing there like a mouse in the corner. But when a person says- oh, never mind."

"Callie was right, though. You've always been the sensible one."

Alise nodded her head a little, understanding how important it was for her be calm now more than ever.

"Except that time you threw my favorite Barbie out the window and onto the neighbor's roof."

"You destroyed my Jermaine Jackson posters I got from *Tiger Beat* and *Right On* magazines!"

"I did not!"

"You did so! I *saw you* drawing a moustache and raccoon eyes with a black magic marker on my absolute favorite poster that hung right over my bed."

"Oh, I did do that one."

"I know you did because I saw you with my own eyes! And to add insult to injury, you were standing on my pillow with your ol' dirty tennis shoes still on!"

"But I only did that one. And that was because you threw my Barbie out the window onto the neighbor's roof."

"No, no, no you got it backwards. I threw the Barbie on the roof because you destroyed almost all of my posters."

"No I didn't! I don't know why you don't believe me!"

"Well, if you didn't, who did? The evil elf that "tinkled" in your bed?"

"Oh, my goodness," Marlisa said letting out an exasperated sigh. "You will never let me forget that, will you?"

"Nope."

"I was five."

"You were eight, but I just brought it up to remind you that you've always had issues with a little something that I like to call the truth."

"I'll say," Callie said walking back in the kitchen.

"She's trying to say she didn't mess up my Jermaine Jackson posters."

"Not this conversation again," Callie said opening the refrigerator and reaching for a bottle of wine.

"I didn't do them all. *For real!* After all this time I would admit it if I did. I only did the one over your bed, Alise. I didn't go through your so called secret trunk with all the magazines in it."

"Well, you're on the hook until you can give me another suspect."

"What about Callie? You never even questioned her, Columbo. Remember? You felt bad because she wasn't speaking to you after you made her take down her artwork from the bedroom wall."

"Artwork?" Alise squinted thinking. "Oh that foil over cardboard junk?"

"That "junk" got an A," Callie said whirling around quickly with a bottle of Pink Moscato in her hand. Standing in front of the open refrigerator she pointed to Alise, "and you threw it out the window onto the neighbor's roof." Callie closed the refrigerator door with her foot before continuing. "Where it stayed for only a moment before a gust of wind blew it into the neighbor's backyard. And then their dog snatched it up and chewed it into itty, bitty pieces."

"She sounds bitter," Marlisa whispered.

"So you decided to destroy my Jackson 5 stuff?"

"I thought we already established that Marlisa was to blame for that? And it wasn't all of your Jackson 5 stuff, it was just Jermaine stuff."

"You did it, didn't you? Boy, I sure am uncovering your dirt today!"

"Why are we even talking about ancient history anyway?"

"I cannot believe this! You pulled off the crime of the century right under my nose!"

"Crime of the century?" Callie laughed. "Crime of the century? Really, Alise?"

"Yeah, as far as I'm concerned it is. Then you managed to blame it on somebody else for over twenty five years. Oh my goodness," Alise said laughing, "I should punch you in eye. I loved my posters! I was supposed to marry Jermaine, you know. He was so cute and-"

"*Was* cute."

"- had that big 'fro."

"Bush wig."

"Huh? You think he wore a wig?"

"I think they all did sometimes."

"Well, he could use one right now. Have you seen his hair lately?" Marlisa asked making a face.

"I know right," Alise said shaking her head from side to side, "that stiff, shiny hair makes him look like he's wearing a helmet all the time. No," Alise added pensively, "he didn't age that well. It's a shame 'cause he started off so cute!"

"Makes you wonder what people who knew you when you were a

lot younger think when they see you now. Like if a guy who had a crush on you in high school sees you at the 7-11, would he be like 'you haven't changed a bit' or more like 'what was I smokin'?"

They all grew quiet, lost in their own thoughts.

"I think we all basically look the same," Callie said after seriously considering the question.

"If anything, I've gotten better looking," Alise added just as seriously. "But you know who else did *not* age very well? Patricia Atwell. Remember her? She used to live across the street from us?"

"Oh, yeah she was kind of heavy set?" Callie asked.

"Yep, that's her. I just saw her in the grocery store yesterday. She lost a lot of weight on one of those quickie diets, but now everything just sags. Even the bags under her eyes are long and saggy. She looks like the old cartoon character ...um, you know, the one that talks really slow..."

"The one that says 'I say, I say' all the time?"

"No that's a big rooster, I'm thinking of a dog."

"Deputy Dawg?"

"Tom and Jerry," Marlisa chimed in.

Callie and Alise both stared and Marlisa.

"What? You said cartoon."

"I also said a dog. Tom and Jerry were a mouse and a cat."

"Oh, yeah, that's right."

"Droopy!" Callie shouted.

"Yeah, that's him Droopy! She reminded me of Droopy, but scary looking. Her face looked like melting wax or something!" Alise scrunched up her nose. "Honestly, if your skin is going to be drooping all over the place and making you look that terrible you just need to stay chubby. And she's the same age as us!"

"No, she's the same age as you. I'm younger. Where's your wine bottle opener?"

"Second drawer," Alise answered pointing to an area next to the stove. "And not to mention that while she's looking like Droopy her

22

hair is a mess! It's half grey and not styled 'cause she says she's going natural. Like natural means how your hair looks when you roll out of bed in the morning."

"Well, technically…" Callie said shrugging her shoulders.

"Technically nothing! You didn't see her! She really thought she had it going on. But let me be a witness – she was only fooling herself. I think somebody needs to send her a reality letter."

"Reality letter?" Callie asked with the beginnings of a smile. "What's this reality letter supposed to say?"

"It's going to say..uh…just.. 'You ugly, the end.'"

They all laughed and Alise opened the dishwasher to begin loading the dirty dishes from her cake project.

"That was a little mean, Alise," Marlisa said now taking a seat on a barstool at the counter.

"So, what else is new?" Callie replied uncorking the wine bottle.

"Hey! I thought you said I was sensible?" Alise asked poking Callie on the shoulder.

"You are… until you're not. Like throwing people's valuable art stuff on roofs! And chewing up all of those Barbie dolls' feet. You chewed so many that-ow hey!"

Alise had jabbed Callie with her elbow before turning quickly to face her sister. Leaning towards Callie, who was still holding her side, Alise whispered with clenched teeth, "Not now!"

"You chewed my Barbie dolls' feet? You said it was the dog!"

Alise spun around to look at Marlisa, "It was the dog," she answered while taking a big step sideways to block Callie from Marlisa's view. "The dog always-"

"It was not the dog!" Callie yelled over Alise's protests. She was peeking over Alise's shoulder while her sister tried to block her.

"-she would get into the room-"

"Alise was the chewer!"

"-and go right to your stuff because-"

" Alise was the chewer!"

23

"I can't believe you are such a turncoat!" Alise said giving up the charade and whirling around to face Callie.

"Hey, if I'm busted you're busted! You chewed up stuff and blamed the dog! 'For over twenty five years now,' Callie said mocking Alise. "Talk about the crime of the century!"

"Yours was worse than mine. You blamed our little sister."

"And you blamed our little dog."

"Well, a sister is a person."

"Who could at least say she didn't do it. The dog couldn't defend herself."

"It was your baby sister."

"It was a baby dog when you first started blaming her. A defenseless little puppy. Why didn't you just kick her, too?"

"Well, if I hurt her she couldn't be the fall puppy for the other stuff."

"What other stuff?" Marlisa asked.

"But I still think a baby sister outranks a puppy."

"What other stuff?"

"I'm not too sure about that. I mean, a tiny, little puppy, Alise? She couldn't even say 'it wasn't me.'" Callie scooped her hands together and began a rocking motion like she was holding a baby. "A teeny, tiny, little pup. With puppy breath and everything."

Alise let out a long sigh. "Alright," she said dryly, "it's a tie."

"What other stuff?" Marlisa said loudly finally getting the attention of her two sisters. "Is there something else I should know?"

Callie and Alise looked at each other, looked at Marlisa and then slowly looked back at each other again.

"Nooooooo," they said simultaneously and quickly turned away from each other. Both were chucking as Callie busied herself with the wine and Alise went back to the dishes.

"You know, after blaming me all of these years for something that I didn't even do, do I get an apology? No. You two have a contest and I end up in a tie with the dog."

"Well, you're not tied with the dog anymore," Callie answered pouring herself a glass of wine. "Right now the dog is winning."

"Yeah, and she's dead," Alise added.

"I hate being the youngest sometimes! You people get on my nerves" Marlisa snapped as she slammed her hand down on the counter.

"You people? Did she just call us 'you people?'" Alise asked looking at Callie.

"I think she did."

"What do think she meant calling us 'you people?'"

"I think she meant 'cause we're black."

Alise and Callie both burst out laughing while Marlisa frowned.

"Ha, ha, ha, you two are so funny. You should take your hilarious act on the road."

"We should," Callie said while nodding her head.

"Yeah," Alise picked up a dish towel and flung it over her shoulders like a cape. "We will be called," she said in a deep announcer's voice, "The Great Alise and the Other One!"

"Oh, so I don't even get my name on the marquee? That's messed up!" Callie said laughing.

"That's just business," Alise said still using the fake announcer's voice. "If I have to replace you, I won't need new business cards. No offense."

"None taken," Callie said before taking a sip of her wine. "Mmmmm, this Pink Moscato is delicious. Ohhhh." Callie sighed and closed her eyes.

"Ew, sounds like something sexual is going on over there," Alise said looking at Callie.

"Well, one of my senses is having a satisfying moment. Maybe it is a little like sex," Callie replied, her eyes still closed. "This wine has a full bodied taste. It's sweet, but not too sweet, with just a hint raspberry and a dash of pomegranate, so the flavor just *rolls* off the tongue."

"Oh, my! Do you need some privacy?" Alise asked.

"Wow, you really do know your wine," Marlisa said laughing at the look on Callie's face.

"Yeah, you're like a ....umm, what do you call them?" Alise asked snapping her fingers.

"Connoisseur?" Callie suggested opening one eye to peek momentarily at Alise before closing it again.

"I was going to say drunk or wino, but ok, you're a connoisseur if you say so."

"Well, they are sort of the same thing," Callie said pensively.

"Ok, whatever," Alise said holding up her hand in surrender.

"But just on different levels."

"If you say so."

"And for different reasons, I suppose."

"Whatever helps you sleep at night."

Alise began humming and Callie opened both her eyes and looked at her. She couldn't help but laugh as Alise danced around in her plaid "cape."

"So you're the Great Alise," Callie said giggling as she watched her sister, "and I'm the Great Connoisseur."

"Well, what am I?" Marlisa asked smiling, getting into the silliness of the moment. "The Great what?"

"Don't you ever, ever, ever, ever, *ever* ask me that again," Callie said dryly. "Trust me; you do not want to hear the name I have for you. And I have one for you, too. How about The Great-"

"*Okaaay*," Alise interjected and then looked at Marlisa. "You walked right into that one, but we are not going down that road today," she added referring to Marlisa's sleeping with Callie's husband and all the fallout that occurred because of it. "Today we are celebrating, having fun and trying to be family. If I can fake it with Paula, the least you two can do is avoid fighting, right Connoisseur, or wino or drunk? I hear they're all the same anyway."

She nudged Callie, who begrudgingly nodded in agreement and

smiled, lifting the mood again. Soon the three of them were laughing as Alise poured wine for Marlisa and herself. She didn't see Vanessa standing in the doorway until her niece called out to her.

"Aunt Alise?"

"Yeah," Alise answered looking up with a broad smile on her face. However seeing the expression on Vanessa's face immediately gave Alise a cold chill.

"What is it?" She asked, her smile fading from her face. "Is Anthony here?"

Vanessa shook her head as fear shone brightly from her eyes.

"Is this about Anthony?" Alise asked, panic rising in her throat.

Vanessa nodded imperceptibly. "I think so. There are two people from the Marines here to see you."

Out of nowhere Alise heard a ringing in her ear. It started low, but got so loud that it blocked out all other sound. She could see Callie's mouth moving, but she couldn't hear the words. The ringing was so shrill that she couldn't hear Vanessa's sobs or Marlisa's gasp or the sound the bottle of Pink Moscato made when it slipped from her hand and smashed loudly on the floor.

*Chapter 2*

Alise sat stoic on her living room couch. To cry or even to think anymore was beyond her comprehension, especially when she was finding it difficult to simply breathe. Anthony was dead. The details didn't register with Alise, nor did the comforting words of bravery and thanks for her son's service. Those were things Alise knew were said by military people all the time to mothers like her. They said it, but not because they knew Anthony. They didn't hold him as a baby, help him with his homework, or calm him when he was scared. Alise wondered if he was afraid in those few moments before he died in the ambush. She didn't want to be angry thinking about her child dying on foreign soil helping people, some of whom didn't even want his help. However, she was sure that the anger would come, along with the guilt, but at this moment Alise felt nothing. She was just numb.

There had been a whirlwind of activity around her for the last few hours. Callie and Marlisa had herded the stream of friends and relatives arriving for the welcome home party on their way, blocking them from even coming into the house. They completely shielded Alise and Jackson from all of those eyes filled with pity. From all of the, "I'm sorry for your loss" comments and the, "Is there anything I can do?" questions.

Jamal was the only one Alise had spoken a word to since the official notification. He was supposed to fly in tomorrow morning to surprise Anthony. Jamal had convinced his younger brother that he couldn't take time away from school and a new internship to visit. Anthony had been disappointed, but that was going to make Jamal's surprise appearance even more special. Vanessa was supposed to pick Jamal up at the airport and meet them all at Callie's house for a dinner with just the two families. Callie and Alise had always been very close and so had their kids. Alise was not sure how much dwell time Anthony had before his next deployment, but she had planned to savor every moment they all had together as a family.

Vanessa had helped her mother as best she could before falling apart, so Callie sent her, along with her younger sisters Maya and Ashley, home with Michael. Now the house was quiet. The food was packed up and put away and Callie and Marlisa could only hover, enveloped in their own grief. Alise knew that she should feel grateful for her sisters' help, thankful for their strength, but she couldn't waste energy caring about something so insignificant. Anthony was dead.

Her baby boy had been so happy the last time she spoke with him and his letters were full of hope as he looked towards his future in the military. He wanted to be a career serviceman. Alise could already see the difference in him. He had matured, he was focused and he was determined. Alise smiled sadly remembering how he had told her that he finally knew what it felt like to have honor. He had grown from thinking like a boy to acting like a man in such a short time. His pride in the person he was becoming was obvious. Alise took a deep breath, only slightly comforted by the knowledge that her son had died doing what he wanted to do. The problem was that Alise was to blame for his death. She had put him in harm's way, and there was no comfort in that knowledge...there never will be.

"It's my fault," Alise said aloud, her voice cracking. Callie and Marlisa looked at each other, not sure if they should respond. "I should have never let him go."

"You couldn't stop him, Alise." Callie moved closer to the couch where Alise was sitting before continuing. "This is something that he was always going to do."

"No," Alise said shaking her head. "You don't understand. He only went because I told him it was okay. See, he promised me he would never go, but I let him out of his promise."

"But you did it for him. To make him happy."

Alise slowly shook her head again. Callie didn't understand. How could she? It had nothing to do with his happiness or with her doing the right thing. It was all about one upping Paula. Alise could have let Paula release the videos and deal with the fallout. She could have let Terrance sell the house and she could have made her sons face the consequences of their actions like any decent mother would have done. Instead, she played the game that Paula had set in motion. She let herself be blackmailed to keep Paula's lie going until she could figure out a way to win. She wanted to see the look on her sister's face when she claimed victory, so she pushed her sons in certain directions to strengthen her position. She didn't have to go along with any of it, but in a strange way, it was like she couldn't help it. Paula always seemed to be able to pull her into a game of wits and this time the lives of people she loved were at stake. This should have never been about getting the best of Paula. Why did her baby have to die to make her see everything so clearly?

"It's my fault. I practically killed Anthony myself. It was my decision and I did it for the wrong reasons."

"What do you mean, Alise?" Marlisa asked coming to stand next to Callie.

Alise looked up at her two sisters. They were innocent in this competition she had with Paula, too. Alise had to come clean with them. Tears welled up in her eyes as she looked at Callie, her little sister and best friend. Would Callie ever forgive her?

"Alise? You shouldn't blame yourself," Callie said gently.

Alise closed her eyes for a moment, but then opened them suddenly. "Anthony's cake! I have to finish it!"

Jumping up from the couch, Alise hurried to the kitchen with Callie and Marlisa following just as quickly.

"Alise, you've already finished the cake," Callie said, puzzled by her sister's actions.

"No, I have to put the candles on it. It's not done until you put the candles on."

Rushing to the cake that she had set aside earlier, Alise uncovered it and sat it on the kitchen island.

"Now where are those candles?"

Callie and Marlisa looked at each other and unspoken concern passed between them. Neither knew where Alise was going with this.

"I've got to light the candles. You know how much Anthony loved blowing out his candles on his birthday cake. He always used to say 'The cake ain't ready Mom until the candles are lit!' He liked these." She held up three unopened packages of large, colorfully striped candles. "He's going to love this!"

Alise began sticking the candles in the cake one by one. She emptied the entire first package and then opened the second pack and started placing those on the cake, too.

"Alise," Callie whispered.

"He's going to love this! So many candles!" Alise admired the cake, now overly saturated with candles.

"I think we need more," she said looking up at her sisters.

Opening the third package she began to frantically put candles on the cake until Callie gently grabbed her hand. Alise froze and stared down at the mess she had made of the cake. Slowly pulling her hand from Callie's, she walked over to a kitchen drawer and opened it. Picking up a large knife, she stood with her back to her sisters, staring at it and contemplating.

"I think we should cut the cake, don't you Callie?"

"Ok," Callie said softly. "If you want to, we can."

Alise felt her shoulders sag. She couldn't do this. She couldn't let her mind drift so far out in her grief. Closing her eyes, she slowly turned to face her sisters. She needed rest. She needed to be alone and maybe sleep – dream about her baby boy. Alise shook her head. No dreaming. It would be better not to dream at all, but just to lay there in a black hole, not having to speak or listen or think or remember. Taking a long, deep, breath she opened her eyes and froze. Paula was standing in the kitchen doorway.

"You did this!" she snapped, banging the knife on the nearby counter. The kitchen utensil broke in two, cutting Alise's hand before it noisily clattered to the ground. "How could you stand there with tears in your eyes when *you* did this!"

"You think I wanted this to happen?"

"Didn't you? What did you think would happen when you came to town to tear up this family with your lies and blackmail?"

"Alise, I just wanted to say I'm sorry." Paula's eyes darted anxiously from Marlisa to Callie. "I just stayed to shoo away the late comers. You know your cousins, they're always-"

"Shut up, Paula! No more! I'm not letting you steal from us anymore! You took away Callie and Marlisa's father, you took from their business and you took my children away from me! You just take, take, *take!* But not anymore because I won't let you!"

"Alise, I know you're upset," Paula said nervously eyeing the blood oozing from the cut on Alise's hand, "so let's just all calm down."

"Don't tell me to calm down! Don't you tell me to calm down!" Alise was screaming so loudly her voice was cracking.

She tore her eyes away from Paula and looked at her younger sisters. Callie and Marlisa looked both afraid and confused. However, it was time for the whole truth to be revealed. Paula didn't deserve to be protected any longer. Alise wavered momentarily. Even though she was angry with Paula, she knew how much she was going to hurt her other sisters. She wasn't looking forward to the moment when Callie would know she was betrayed by all three sisters; Marlisa by going after her husband, Paula by concocting a scheme to get her money and Alise by keeping the big, hurtful secret about her biological father.

Callie had been devastated when Paula showed her the fake DNA tests "proving" Philip Elliot was not her father. Alise swallowed hard knowing how painful it was and still is for Callie not knowing her parentage. Her younger sister had been deceived for almost a year, and for almost a year Alise had known it was all a lie.

"The paperwork has been done," Paula said quickly, taking advantage of Alise's hesitation. "No matter what you say, you can't undo that. You can only make things more complicated for everybody."

Alise looked back at Paula and tried to mask her reaction, but it was too late. Paula had gotten Alise's attention and Paula knew it.

"Think about it, Alise," Paula added calmly, "take some time and *just think.*"

"Get out of my house, Paula," Alise ordered sharply, "and don't you ever darken my doorway again!"

Paula, happy to escape, fled the kitchen grabbing her purse from the dining room table as she headed towards the door. Alise looked down at her bleeding palm. She hadn't even felt it.

"I guess I should see to this," she said in a shaky voice, looking at her hand. She stared at the blood dripping from her trembling hand and then realized that her entire body was trembling. She wanted to explain everything to Callie and Marlisa, who looked at her with expressions mixed with confusion and concern. Later. She would have to face everything later.

"Thanks for being here tonight," Alise said wearily. "I'm going to …I'm going to bed. Can you lock up on the way out?"

Both Callie and Marlisa nodded. Alise hugged both of her sisters and then kissed each gently on their cheeks. Looking at them for a moment longer, she sighed loudly before turning and leaving them alone in the kitchen. The sisters continued to stare at the empty kitchen doorway that both Paula and Alise had just walked through.

"What was that all about?" Marlisa asked.

"I don't know," Callie answered pensively, "but I'm going to find out."

*Chapter 3*

Paula sped along the beltway with the windows cracked open to let in just enough cold air to clear her head. She was in a place mentally and emotionally that felt foreign to her. For almost a year she had been in complete control of her sisters, but now she could feel it all slipping away. Alise was not going to keep quiet for too much longer. Why should she? Jamal was on the other side of the country, probably for good. Jackson was in a good program, which had kept him out of trouble while turning him into a poster boy for how to turn your life around. Then there was Anthony....

There was no other way for Paula to look at her situation. She had lost power and needed to figure out what to do about it. Alise had no incentive to keep quiet except for what it would do to Callie. Right now Alise was fragile and needed Callie in her corner. If Alise revealed the secret nothing would initially change for any of the sisters legally, but everything would change between Alise and her loving sister and BFF Callie. Paula rolled her eyes thinking about how close those two were. It made her sick sometimes. The only good thing is that Paula knew Alise would think long and hard about the best way to break the news to Callie about the paternity secret. Alise would have to explain her part and Paula sensed with Alise's hesitation that she wasn't ready to confess, at least not yet.

Paula's mind was racing trying to figure out the best way to set up a defense against whatever Alise was planning to do. She knew the secret would be out, but she also knew that that would not be enough for Alise. Her son was dead and she blamed Paula for setting everything in motion.

Never mind that if Alise had to pick someone, she should look at herself in the mirror. Paula just didn't understand her younger sister. She was smart, but allowed herself to be vulnerable through her kids and through Callie. Paula didn't have kids, but she couldn't imagine allowing herself to be brought to her knees the way Alise had fallen to hers. However, she did have sisters and while she didn't want to see any *real* harm come to them, being blackmailed and getting all caught up trying to protect their feelings seemed silly. Alise always tried to be too noble and come to everybody's rescue. Well, now that she's gotten herself all tangled up in her Super Woman cape she had to find someone to blame.

"Don't think I'm taking the blame, Alise," Paula said aloud. "That'd be your biggest mistake."

The ringing phone pulled Paula away from her thoughts. She looked at the caller ID on the dashboard of her car and grimaced. As if she didn't have enough to deal with right now.

"Answer," she said, engaging her voice activated phone system. "What do you want Marlisa?"

"What was that all about?"

"What are you talking about?"

"You know what I'm talking about. That cryptic argument between you and Alise."

"Why don't you just mind your business? That was between me and Alise. So now, I'll ask again. What do you want, Marlisa?"

"I'll tell you what I want," Marlisa said tersely, "I want to let you know that with every day that passes, you're becoming less and less valuable to me."

"What do you mean, 'less valuable' to you?"

"You're supposed to be helping me get Michael. That was our deal for me signing over more of my shares of the company to you! You have the extras shares, so help already!"

"I am helping you!"

Paula could tell Marlisa was getting all worked up and was about to starting acting like a big baby. Soon she would be pouting and throwing a temper tantrum. Paula knew she had to quickly defuse the situation and settle Marlisa down.

"Listen Marlisa, we have to bide our time so that—"

"You *promised* Paula. And if you're not helping me, then there's no reason for me not to turn you in to the police for what you did in North Carolina, *Pastor*!"

"Oh, for heaven's sake! It was only a little bit of embezzlement of church funds!"

"And bank fraud and faking your death to disappear with the money!"

"Oh, please! It's not like it's a federal offense or anything!"

"Actually, Paula, it *is* a federal crime."

"I meant, nobody got hurt!"

"Except all those people who trusted you and lost their personal property, money, and the church grounds!"

"*Anyway*, what do you want from me?" Paula was getting irritated. While it was normally exhilarating to spar with her sisters, having to deal with both Marlisa and Alise's unprovoked attacks was getting to her today. What she did to deserve two scheming backstabbing sisters, she'll never know.

"I want an end date."

"An end date?"

"Yeah, I want to see some real results."

"Just stick with our plan and–"

"Well, I don't have as much confidence in your plan anymore. Not with Alise this mad at you. She'll get you and then where will that leave me?"

"She'll get me?" Paula scoffed. "I am so insulted that I can barely speak! First of all Marlisa, don't worry about Alise. She has nothing to do with our deal! You are so–"

Paula stopped abruptly. There was no need to get upset or even burn too much grey matter on Marlisa. She could handle her baby sister in her sleep, but Alise was different. The last thing she wanted to do was to get Marlisa so upset that she would turn to Alise and hand over the evidence of Paula's "business" dealings in North Carolina.

Paula took a deep breath to help her focus. She had to pacify Marlisa and keep holding her hand through her ridiculous obsession with Michael. Paula shrugged her shoulders as she listened to Marlisa fantasizing about Michael choosing her over Callie and how Callie will eventually understand it was meant to be. Somewhere in that pea brain of hers, Marlisa really thought she was going to have her happy ending.

Of all the men in the world, and Paula has known many of them intimately, Marlisa was ready to give up everything for her sister's husband. Although Michael, who is still head over heels in love with his wife, is certainly a good catch, Marlisa didn't seem to understand that he had already been caught.

Besides that, he is not the least bit interested in Marlisa or in reliving the mistake he made with her during a tumultuous time in his marriage. He cheated one time with Marlisa and rather than make excuses or pass blame, he shouldered all the responsibility. He's still paying for it with his separation from Callie as they try to rebuild their marriage. As far as Paula knew, Michael had never chased Marlisa or even led her on, but that hasn't stopped her infatuated little sister. It's like Marlisa's possessed and won't take no for an answer. So far, her fixation on Michael and the fantasy that goes with it has served Paula well. It's allowed her to gain more control of the business and more of Marlisa's inheritance money. Paula had been siphoning Marlisa's company shares since before they even had their first company meeting. And all she had to do in return was to plan a few simple schemes that sent Marlisa chasing after her dream man and out of Paula's hair for awhile. Paula knew in no uncertain terms that between the two of them, she was definitely getting the best end of their deal.

However, everything that she had worked for could all be snatched unfairly from her if she didn't keep Marlisa happy. Their latest plan called for patience and she had warned Marlisa that she would have to endure the painstaking hours it would take to listen to all of the recordings made from bugging Callie's office. Paula was sure something was going on with Callie and Stephen Russell, the investor in Alise's restaurant. Sooner or later, they would have real evidence to give to Michael to prove Callie was stringing him along. Paula had no doubt that Callie loved her husband, but she also had some type of connection with Stephen. Paula could almost smell it in the air when the two of them were near each other. She had witnessed it first hand and she was sure Michael had no idea. Last year when he thought Callie might be putting him off for Stephen, it had caused a lot of trouble between them. There's no way he would put up with Callie secretly messing around with Stephen while treating him like they were always on a first date.

Paula frankly didn't care if Callie was playing around with Stephen or Michael or both of them. She thought about the two men vying for Callie's attention. Stephen was hot. He was rich, sexy, with beautiful hazel eyes and blonde hair. His southern accent made him charming and seductive. He was definitely fantasy material, but then again, so was Michael. Although Paula tried not to think about her brother-in-law that way, there was nothing wrong with her eyes. He was definitely a good looking man. Not to mention smart, ambitious and CEO of his own successful advertising company. He was one of the nice guys, but not a pushover. He had just the right balance of passion and respect for women. He was the type of man that was comfortable protectively embracing a woman in the light of day and then throwing her over his shoulders to take her to the bedroom at night.

Women looking for male companionship know that men like Stephen and Michael are rare. Paula assumed that both of them have women throwing themselves at them on a daily basis. But for whatever God only knows reason, Callie had not one, but both of these prime, flawless, male specimens wanting her. Not to take anything away from her sister, but as pretty and smart and rich as she was in her own right, she had no idea how to work all of that. It pained Paula to see her naively wasting her attributes.

Paula had learned the hard way that life is short. You're born, you don't even get all the stuff you want and then you're dead. Callie should be enjoying every pleasure that comes her way, but instead she seems to be toying with both men just a little. It's like she has no idea how good she has it or could have it living it up with two very rich, very charming and very good looking men. Hell, if Callie worked it right, she could have the best of both worlds– the safety of a secure, happy, sexy marriage and the excitement of a hot, sexy affair. If Callie had that kind of vision, Paula couldn't do anything but respect and envy her. She might even feel bad for helping Marlisa interfere with her marriage. Probably not, but she might at least give Callie a heads up so that she could see Marlisa coming. Callie had no idea of the depths Marlisa was willing to go to for Michael. Paula sighed heavily.

"Callie, you just don't get it," she said aloud.

"*I know*," Marlisa agreed. "Now you understand why Michael would be better off without her."

"I wasn't talking… oh, never mind."

"But you understand, right?"

"No, Marlisa, I don't," Paula said a little more sharply than she had intended. She had let Marlisa jabber on for as long as her nerves could take it. "Michael is in love with his *wife… your sister* and even if it doesn't work out between them, you shouldn't be in the picture. Can't you work some other neighborhood for your man stealing needs? It's not like he's the last man on earth!"

"But it has to be Michael," Marlisa said weakly.

Paula sighed again. It was no use. Love sick Marlisa was so needy for a man that she made herself an easy target. So Paula decided once again that taking Marlisa's money, lying, cheating and manipulating her was actually serving a purpose for a greater good. Paula acknowledged that "greater good" also happened to be her own personal happiness, but still, why fight it? It is what it is.

Besides, Paula had no intention of policing Marlisa's backstabbing. If she wanted to fight for her sister's husband, so be it. And if by chance Marlisa landed Michael or managed to break up Callie and Michael for good, then so be it for that, too. After all, Paula knew she wasn't the bad guy in all of this. And who knows? Michael just might lose his mind and choose Marlisa over Callie. Of course, Paula was convinced there would have to be heavy drugs and hallucinations involved for that to happen, but in the end, it didn't really matter to her.

She had made her position clear from the beginning and Marlisa understood that everything was done at the risk of complete failure. The only thing Marlisa had going for her was her limitless acceptance of deception and Paula could work with that. So while Marlisa was blathering on and on about Michael, Paula had come up with a new and improved plan that would kick things up a notch or two. What's more, the quicker she got Marlisa off the phone, the quicker she could concentrate on Alise.

"Ok, you've gone through every recording from the bug in Callie's office, right?"

"Yeah, there's nothing there."

"Well, I guess I have to take your word for it since you won't let me hear the tapes for myself."

"There's a lot of business stuff on them that I don't think you need to know."

"So you realize you're making me work with one hand tied behind my back, right? I mean, I can't get any inspiration from those recording since you're keeping me in the dark."

"Oh, please, being in the dark is right where you belong, Evilene. I just don't trust that you won't use what you hear on those recordings to do some underhanded stuff with our company. And by *our company*, I mean Callie's and mine."

*Oh, you got me there,* Paula thought snickering to herself. She had wanted to launch a takeover, but couldn't get enough access. Unfortunately, Callie had completely shut her out. Those secret recordings would have been a perfect way to get a foothold in the company. So she had turned to Marlisa, but her youngest sister had shut her out, too. Marlisa could act like an imbecile sometimes, but she still had her moments of clarity. So, since Paula couldn't use the tapes, she opted to keep Marlisa occupied with the tedious job of listening to hours of recordings for as long as possible. Now it looked like "as long as possible" had just ended.

"Here's the new plan, but it still involves listening in on Callie's conversations. This time we–"

"I've already listened to enough! Callie is not talking to Stephen about anything except business! New plan Paula! We need a new plan!"

"Hear me out, Marlisa! This time we have to bug her personal phone! Why would she talk lovey-dovey in her office? She wouldn't! But on her personal cell phone, now that's a different story. There's an app that you can download on her cell phone which will allow you to listen to her every conversation, even when she's not on the phone."

"What do you mean?"

"I mean that as long as she has the phone with her and turned on, it will pick up her conversations. So if she's having dinner or something with Stephen and puts the cell phone on the table, you can still hear her conversation."

"I don't know, Paula. That's getting a little too personal. It's stooping really low."

"Are you serious? You slept with her husband and you lie to her face every day! So now, while you're right in the middle of plotting her final demise, conferring with "Evilene" herself to bring your own sister to her knees, you decide to grow a conscience? Gimme a break!"

"I'm not trying to "bring her to her knees" or "plot her demise," Paula! It's not even about all of that drama! It's just that Michael was meant to be with *me!* All I'm doing is trying to set things right and Callie will eventually understand!"

"Oh, yeah, right, I'm sure she will. It's a shame she's so selfish and won't just hand her husband over to you right now."

"Well, smart comments coming from somebody who doesn't even have a man, doesn't bother me."

"Well, dumb comments coming from somebody *who doesn't have a man either*, irritate the hell out of me! You say you want my help with this Michael thing, but then you act like you just want to argue with me. Girl, believe me, I do not have time for your nonsense!"

"It's not nonsense! It's just that…," Marlisa took a deep breath before continuing, "I'm not feeling too good about spying on Callie like that. It's one thing to bug her office, but her personal cell phone? I mean, I'll probably hear every private conversation she'll have, since she takes the phone with her everywhere she goes. I don't know if I'm comfortable with that."

"Right. Every private conversation she has with Stephen …*and* Michael."

*And Alise.* Paula added silently.

Marlisa grew quiet and Paula smiled. This really was lowdown, dirty, backstabbing stuff, but it could work and that was the only thing that mattered. Even if they didn't get anything too damaging, with technology being what it is, all Paula really needed was good clean recordings of Callie and Stephen voices. She could splice a whole conversation together if she needed to. It didn't have to be perfect, it just had to fool Michael into thinking what they wanted him to think.

"So Marlisa, what will it be?"

"How am I supposed to get a hold of her phone to do this?"

"We'll figure that out. I mean, we can easily set something up. I'll let you know how to do everything. But if you don't feel good about this plan, then it's best to just forget about it."

Marlisa remained quiet for so long Paula had to check to see if she had hung up.

"Hello?"

"Call me with the details." And with that, Marlisa hung up the phone.

Paula smiled in the darkness of her car as she drove in silence down the interstate. She still had Marlisa on her side which meant a tepid loyalty for now. Of course, Paula would ask for a little something extra out of Marlisa's financial portfolio before handing over the doctored tape. She just had to decide what she wanted. It would probably be more owner shares in the production company, which was more successful than Paula had dared to believe. Even if she never took over the company like she planned, she would always have enough money to do all the little things that made rich people happy. Paula licked her lips realizing just how much money motivated her. With renewed focus she now turned her attention to Alise, who was intent on bringing her down.

*I'm not going anywhere anytime soon, dear sister.*

Paula was finally a very rich woman and she was ready to go to all out war with Alise to keep it that way.

*Chapter 4*

Callie stood in the dark of her office staring out of the large window that overlooked the city. From her vantage point, the lights glowing from the buildings below mixed with the bright stars twinkling in the night sky made the city sparkle. It looked as if everything had been sprinkled with fairy dust. Sometimes, like tonight, Callie could stand at the windows, which were glass from floor to ceiling, and imagine she was drifting into the clouds of the night sky. It was always calming for her to just be still and quietly take in the view.

Now, as she stood in her bare feet looking up to the stars, feeling vulnerable and insignificant, she asked God "why?" Why did He allow Anthony to be taken from them? Why make it doubly painful to get the news at his welcome home party? Alise was so heartbroken, and Callie knew there was nothing she could do or say to make things better. She also knew that trying to force herself to say and do something to make Alise feel better would only serve to make things worse.

Callie knew this from firsthand experience. When their father died, people who thought they were saying comforting words were only saying things that made her cry. Callie knew they only wanted to help, but they didn't realize that the best way to help was to be there for her later. It would be later, after the funeral and after she was no longer the center of attention, when all the well wishers who stared at her sadly and with pity in their eyes were gone that she would need someone. Well wishers didn't seem to understand that grieving was a process that took time. The overwhelming support people give you when tragedy first hits can be smothering, especially when the only thing you really want is to be alone with your thoughts. It's always later, when everyone leaves and when it gets quiet that you realize how much you don't want to be alone anymore. Callie would make sure she was there for Alise, when she knew Alise would need her the most…later.

Michael had known when Callie had needed him most. He understood her so well. Callie smiled remembering that quiet afternoon months after her father's death when he found her in her home office and put a mug of hot chocolate with extra marshmallows on the table in front of her. He had made it just like her father used to make it for her when he made his coffee. She would hold her mug like her father and pretend she was drinking coffee, too. Then they would just talk –always about her. Callie's father would listen and smile and make jokes to make her laugh.

On that afternoon, Michael sat beside her with his mug and began to talk about her father. He held her hand and told her how much she reminded him of her father. He told her all the good things about Philip Elliot that he saw in her. This time it was Callie who just listened and smiled at the memories and repeated her father's jokes.

Callie felt like she needed Michael now. She needed someone to support her and help her wrap her head around the pain Alise must be feeling over losing her child. She needed guidance with her feelings of helplessness and the feelings of guilt she had because she was relieved it wasn't her own child who had died. She needed him, but Michael wasn't there and she didn't think she could go to him. Now, she didn't know what to do with all of her own pain.

Callie sighed heavily and let her forehead rest up against the glass. How could the night look so beautiful when there was so much ugliness happening within their family? Callie wanted to go home to Michael like she used to, but he had moved out and now had his own home. "Home" meant different locations for the two of them now. She shrugged her shoulders. That's what happens when a couple separates. They start to live separate lives, which seems silly when you think about how little time you really have with the people you love. It was that thought that almost made Callie follow Michael and the girls to his home. Instead she went to her office to watch the city sleep and where she knew she would find no memories of Anthony.

Callie was lost in her thoughts when she heard his footsteps behind her. Suddenly she felt his strong arms embrace her around the waist. Callie sighed and relaxed allowing the weight of the day's events to drift away. She leaned back against him and they stood in silence looking into the night. His chin rested momentarily on the top of her head before he buried his face in her hair, taking a deep breath of her honeysuckle scented shampoo. His eyes met hers in the reflection of the window and she smiled.

"Why'd you come?" she asked quietly.

"After everything that happened tonight, I had to be with you. I came as soon as I could."

"How did you know I would be here?"

"Because your office is where you feel safe," he answered keeping eye contact with her in their reflections.

"Hmmm, I have a home office."

"I know." He smiled. "But you wouldn't go there. You don't think I pay attention, do you?" He leaned down and whispered in her ear, "I know you, Callie Armstrong."

Blushing Callie turned to face him and looked directly into his eyes. He gently traced the outline of her lips with the tip of his finger and added, "I knew you wouldn't go home…too many memories."

Leaning down, he gently kissed her lips once, twice and then suddenly they were lost in their own passions. Callie felt as she had the first time she had met him - electrified. There was something about Stephen Russell that excited her. Over the months they had flirted and then suddenly it was more that flirting. It was more than an attraction, but Callie wasn't sure what and she wasn't sure if she wanted to find out. Would opening herself up to Stephen make her love Michael less?

Sometimes she thought that a part of her wanted to punish Michael because he had forever ruined "her innocence." She had trusted him completely, more than life itself and she could never get that back. She would never be fully his again, not like she used to be. His betrayal, with her own sister, had broken something inside of her. Callie had been thinking lately that maybe her growing need to be with Stephen was proof that she wasn't supposed to be fully Michael's again anyway.

Maybe she should be living for her own happiness and that meant finally giving in to Stephen. Right here, right now. It was time. Callie had always wanted him, but she had never been completely sure, until now. She grabbed the belt loops of his jeans, one in each hand and forcefully pulled him to her. He held her tightly, kissing her deeply before pulling away. He took a small step backwards and shook his head.

"Not like this. You know how I feel about emotional, rebound sex."

"Emotionally …sex ….what?" Callie said breathlessly. "Are you saying you don't want to?"

Stephen smiled and embraced her again. He nibbled her ear and then whispered, "I want you but …I don't want the regrets that might come with it if we did something now."

"So *you* want to, but you think *I'll* regret it in the morning?" Callie asked incredulously. She was ready. Stephen was wrong. "I won't regret it. I won't."

"Yes, you will. I know you will."

"Oh, so you really think you know me."

"Yeah, I think I do," he gave her a hint of a smile before continuing, "I know you always get the worse case of buyer's remorse that I've ever seen."

"Wh…What?" Callie sputtered. "I like to be careful that's all."

"Callie, you get buyer's remorse over a candy bar. You agonize over whether you should have chosen a Reese's Cup over a Snickers bar. And then, if you actually eat it, you then agonize over that decision because you're worried that the calories are going to show up on your hips."

"I do not," said half heartedly. She knew he was right, but she wasn't ready to concede the point.

"Yeah, you do. And by the way, your hips have not suffered one bit. Believe me, 'cause I keep a close eye on them."

"Don't try to charm me with flattery after insulting me."

"How did I insult you?" Stephen asked as he flashed that smile, the one that made Callie feel a little tingly. He was one of the sexiest, most charming men she had even known. His hint of a southern accent didn't hurt either. Callie already knew he could use his rugged good looks for good or evil. She folded her arms in front of her now in an effort to resist the famous Stephen Russell charm.

"You act like I don't know what I want. And to be honest, you're starting to make me sound a little flaky. Is that why it's so easy for you to turn me down?"

"No, whoa, let me just set the record straight. I'm not turning you down at all."

"It sure seems that way."

"Well, as a matter of fact, it's just the opposite. What I'm trying to say is that I don't want you to regret us getting together so much that you'll look back on it and call it a mistake. Because then… I'm afraid that you won't want to be with me at all after that. You might not even want me around anymore." Stephen averted his eyes momentarily before meeting Callie's gaze again. "And the truth is I don't know if I can take your rejection. I don't think you really have any idea how much you mean to me, Callie. This is not just about sex."

Callie stared openly at Stephen as she absorbed the meaning of his words. His confession had both surprised and deeply touched her. All this time Callie, in her uncertainty, had dodged intimacy with him. She had been pushing him away, but she didn't realize until now that maybe he wanted to be pushed away.

"You've never said anything like that before," she said barely above a whisper.

"I know. And keeping this relationship at a standstill in that department has been tough for me. But I know that in the long run, it's the right thing to do for us."

Callie looked away a little ashamed of what she was thinking. Somehow she didn't think it was as tough for him as it was for her. She didn't think he was completely holding out against sex– just sex with her. She wasn't sure how she felt about that. Was he being intimate with other women? Who were they? Callie wanted to ask him about it, but swallowed the questions once again. It really wasn't any of her business. It's not like they were really together, and besides, she was the married one. Separated, but still married.

If she really wanted to have sex, her husband was a ready and willing participant, but Callie knew that would just complicate things for her and Michael. She didn't want to fully commit to their marriage again until she could figure out the trust issues she still had with him. She knew her relationship with Michael could never be exactly like it was before, yet she was having a hard time with what it actually was now.

Callie looked at Stephen. He was brand new – no bad memories, no hurt feeling and no betrayal. She still loved Michael, even after he protected Marlisa from the fallout as best he could. Some might think that was noble, but Callie knew it was just classic Michael. It was one of the things she loved about him the most. He was always so honorable and that's why Callie was so surprised by his cheating in the first place. She also didn't like that Marlisa was the beneficiary of him trying to be so principled in the face of what the two of them did *together*. Marlisa, *her sister*, should have been held more accountable than him in some ways, and yet he shielded her as best he could. He should have been thinking about his wife's pain and not about Marlisa being ostracized from the family. Callie still held that against him, too.

However, even standing back and looking at all of her issues with her husband, Callie knew that he still loved her and that their relationship wasn't dead. When they were alone or just with the kids, it still felt right and she wanted to get what they had back. Callie also knew that eventually, she could make peace with Marlisa, too. They used to be close as sisters and there were still moments when the two of them felt like sisters, rather than adversaries.

The problem wasn't dealing with the many issues she had with Michael and Marlisa one at a time. The problem was that Callie was having a hard time trying to forgive both of them at the same time. She still had to see and talk to both of them almost every day–Michael about the kids and Marlisa about the company. She couldn't seem to separate them in her mind, which made it nearly impossible to do what she needed to do to heal both relationships. She needed to focus on her husband without her sister waiting in the wings and vise versa. Having to deal with both of them on a daily basis was like an open wound that never really had time to heal.

Callie had thought about selling her part of CM Music Productions, but she didn't have the strength to walk away from her livelihood. It was the one thing she had built from the ground up, and she wasn't ready to turn it over to Paula and Marlisa. Callie didn't know if she was being stubborn or practical or selfish, but she wanted to keep running her company. She had no doubt that Marlisa wasn't going anywhere. So, until one of them gave it all up, the sisters were stuck with each other.

Callie looked at Stephen who was studying her and seemed to be lost in his own thoughts. She realized just at that moment how much she needed him in her life…just like she needed Michael. She was afraid to completely let go of Michael and unfortunately, she didn't know how to completely let go of Stephen. Callie was confused and she was very tired of being confused. She had to choose.

"Come sit with me," he said reaching out his hand to her. Without hesitating she grabbed it and he led her to the couch where they sat down.

"I've been thinking about something for awhile now."

"Ok."

"You see, I think part of my hesitation is because I know that on some level our relationship is part fantasy."

Callie frowned. "What does that mean?"

"It means that we flirt and joke, but we've never had a chance to go beyond the surface of our relationship. It's been pretty safe and taking it to another level means the fantasy part is over." Stephen thought for a moment and then added contritely, "I know that there will be times when I might disappoint you and…"

"You mean like not being able to …uh, you know…"

Now it was Stephen's turn to frown in confusion.

"You know…*perform,*" Callie whispered the word. Stephen's eyes stretched wide as he realized what Callie meant by "perform."

"I've heard it happens to a lot of men and–"

"It doesn't happen to me!"

"I hear it's nothing to be ashamed of."

"Callie, believe me, this pep talk is not necessary! I'm just…I don't…you, you, you can't believe…"

"Why are stuttering?"

"I'm not stuttering! If you knew how ridiculous…how…you… Hell, woman, I'm good in bed!"

Callie couldn't help but laugh at his theatrics.

"Laugh now, but one day you'll see!" Stephen shuddered. "My goodness, saying that out loud is like blasphemy!"

"Blasphemy? Think a little highly of yourself much?"

"In that department? *Yes!* Absolutely! Hey, don't laugh."

"I'm sorry," Callie said attempting to look serious. "I mean I knew it was a touchy subject, I just didn't know it was a holy one."

"Yeah, it is – to a man, it is. So you need to ask for forgiveness."

"Forgive me."

"In church."

"Ok."

"And say a few thousand Hail Marys."

"I'm not Catholic."

"I don't care."

"Fine."

"And sprinkle a little holy water on your tongue."

"What?"

"It's just that you can't say something like that and leave it hanging out there like a curse."

Callie giggled. "You said 'leave it hanging out.'"

Stephen looked at Callie for a moment and then grinned. He leaned all the way back against the sofa, pulling Callie to him as he stretched his body along the length of it. Callie situated herself so the she could lie against his chest and still see out of the window. As she watched the stars and listened to his breathing, Callie knew at that moment there was nowhere else on the planet she would rather be. She was sure she would drift off to sleep when Stephen began speaking again.

"Now, after shaking that awful thought out of my head and clarifying that I am King Make Her Scream. No, wait, you can call me King What's My Name, Girl. Yeah, yeah...I like that better."

Callie laughed. "Corny, but ok, King What's My Name, what did you-"

"Girl."

"Girl?"

"You're supposed to call me King What's My Name, *Girl.*"

"Oh, I'm not calling you that."

53

"Don't worry, you will."

Stephen said it with such a thick southern accent that Callie couldn't help but chuckle. Whenever he spoke sincerely, she could barely detect the rhythmic drawl born of a Texan upbringing. But when necessary, he could cash in on his sex appeal and pour on that southern charm. Right now, she could almost picture him on a horse, squinting under his cowboy hat and coming dangerously close to flashing that smile that made Callie go weak in the knees. He had his "southern game face" on and she had to admit it worked – at least on her.

Still grinning broadly in the dark, Callie reached out and took hold of his hand, intertwining her fingers with his. Although he used his fingers, which were interlocked with hers to gently massage the back of her hand, Callie didn't realize just how deep in thought he was at the moment. He had grown very quiet as he used his other hand to tenderly caress her arm. When he spoke again, he did so with a serious but gentle tone.

"Like I was saying, I've been thinking about this for awhile. I wanted to find a way where we could just concentrate on each other. Discovering ourselves together and finding out what's real. I think, like me, you want us to be more than what we are, but it's hard to do that under these conditions."

"Yeah, it's not ideal with you always flying off for your other business ventures and me, stuck in an emotional triangle."

"So, why don't we…Will you go away with me?"

Callie stilled as she stared out the window thinking. She could tell that Stephen was holding his breath as his heart began beating faster.

"Where would we go?" she whispered.

"So, that's not a 'no'?"

"That's not a 'no.'" She could feel him relax and suddenly she was smiling, enjoying the idea of going away with him.

"Where would we go?" she asked again.

"I was thinking Paris. I thought we could go right after the holidays for a few weeks." He hesitated again, as if he was waiting for a negative reaction from Callie that didn't come. "I have a house there. Paris can be very nice."

"I found myself in Paris," Callie said pensively.

"Huh?"

"It's from a movie. *Sabrina*, the one with Julia Ormond and Harrison Ford."

"Well, since we're quoting movies do you know this one 'Have a good time, bring me back something French'?"

"*Home Alone*," Callie said chuckling."I know that one pretty well since my kids say that whenever anyone announces that they're going to the bathroom."

Stephen thought about it for a moment and then they both laughed, but before long they had quieted down. They lay together for a while in a comfortable silence, sometimes whispering and a few times Callie felt herself doze off. As dawn broke and they could see the beauty of the night give way to the beauty of the sunrise, Stephen decided it was time to go. Nudging Callie gently to shift her weight off on him, Stephen stood up.

"I think I should go. I don't want people to come into the office and see me here."

"It's Sunday."

"And we both know that somebody records in the studio every day, even on Sundays. It's always booked, so there'll be people around."

Callie nodded and yawned as she sat up. "I should be going home too. I need to get some sleep."

Stephen bent down and kissed her on the top of her head. "I just want you to know, you have nothing to be ashamed of."

"Ashamed? *Now* what are you talking about?" Callie asked looking at Stephen. He seemed absolutely serious, except for his eyes. He could never hide his mischief completely because his eyes always gave him away. He knew her, but she knew him, too.

"I'm talking about your obsession with sex."

"I am not obsessed."

"Oh, no? As soon as I came in here you were all over this." Stephen made circular hand motions around his chest.

"So that's how you saw it?"

"That's how it was. You wanted all of this." He demonstrated again with his circular hand movements. "I'm telling you this because I know as soon as I turn my back and walk away your eyes are going to be glued to my butt. So I'm letting you know it's nothing to be ashamed of. Looking isn't touching."

"Oh, good, 'cause I was concerned," Callie said sarcastically, decidedly turning her head as Stephen began walking away. She was willing herself not look at him. However, before he reached the door she turned at the same moment that Stephen turned.

"Like I said, looking–"

"Goodbye, Stephen!"

"–isn't touching."

Callie threw one of the accent pillows from the couch at him. Ducking, he quickly let himself out of the office. The pillow bounced against the door seconds after Stephen closed it firmly behind him. Callie hugged the other accent pillow as she sat grinning to herself thinking about Stephen. He could always make her smile.

Miles away Marlisa smiled too as she took off her headphones and dropped them on her nightstand. She would play back the entire recording from the beginning, but what she had just heard live was already enough. Leaning back against her pillows she thought about Callie and Stephen. Paula had been right about what was going on right under Michael's nose and Marlisa marveled at her oldest sister's intuition. It was good having Paula on her side.

Marlisa breathed a sigh of relief. Now she was sure everything was going to work out for the best. At least Callie wouldn't be alone when Michael left her. With Stephen in her life, Callie was sure to come around to welcoming Marlisa back as a sister again. Callie might even agree to be in the wedding.

"Mr. and Mrs. Michael and Marlisa Armstrong," Marlisa whispered in the dark. It was going to happen. There were only a few more pieces to put in place.

*Chapter 5*


Callie frowned when she pulled up into her driveway in the affluent neighborhood near Potomac, Maryland. Michael's SUV had been haphazardly parked, blocking part of the entrance to her three car garage. Walking briskly past the tinted side windows of the black Escalade, Callie quickly peeped through the front windshield. She half expected to see Michael sitting behind the wheel waiting for her, but the vehicle was empty. Vanessa's car was not in the driveway and was probably in the garage, but Callie was still a little confused. Weren't they supposed to be at the house in Bethesda that Michael had rented after they separated, instead of here, at the family home they all used to share? Maybe she had gotten things mixed up.

Callie hurriedly opened the front door to her home, not sure what to expect. She hoped nothing had happened to the kids or anybody else in the family because she didn't know how much more she could take. Callie could feel her heart thumping in her chest as she let her imagination take over. She just couldn't figure out why he would be there so early on a Sunday morning.

As soon as Callie opened the door she could smell bacon. Walking the length of the hallway leading to the kitchen, she paused momentarily at its closed door and listened. Relief flooded through her at the sound of Michael's voice. He was singing a song that made Callie giggle. She quietly pushed open the door and watched him cooking, singing and dancing to the beat in his head before she interrupted his performance.

"Are you seriously singing that song?"

"What? That song's a classic."

"Classic?" Callie repeated. "That's what I'm going to tell your employees at the next Christmas party."

"Oh, you wouldn't dare."

"Oh, yes I would. They need to know how the boss they think is so cool is nothing but a big corn ball."

Michael laughed as he carefully removed the heavy skillet filled with eggs from the heated eye of the stove.

"They'll never believe you."

"Maybe not, but they'll believe the video I took with my phone."

Michael looked up at Callie with such surprise that Callie burst out laughing.

"You didn't really…"

Callie shook her head no and Michael grinned and went back to preparing breakfast. He spooned the scrambled eggs onto a platter and turned his attention to the bacon frying in the other pan.

"You scared me there for a second. Threatening to mess with my rep." He laughed, still busying himself at the stove while Callie slid into one of the high back kitchen chairs at the breakfast bar to watch him.

"You know, if you ever bring it up, I'll pretend I don't even remember that old Captain and Tennille song. But you, on the other hand, can't make such a claim." Michael eyed her with a sly smile as he handed her a glass of orange juice. "You have *Love Will Keep Us Together* on your iPod. I saw it."

"What were you doing looking through my iPod?" Callie asked

sipping from the glass.

"I was just curious. I wanted to know if you had your own CD on it. Some singers listen to themselves *all* the time. I saw an article about narcissism in entertainers."

"Narcissism?" Callie sputtered, spraying orange juice from her mouth onto the kitchen breakfast counter. The remains now dribbled down her chin. "Are you calling me…"

"No, no, no," Michael said quickly. "No need to get so excited," he added, laughing as he handed her a napkin.

"But you–"

"I know you better than that Callie Armstrong. But I *was* wondering how often *do* you watch your own videos or listen to yourself?"

Callie tried to look serious, but that was made difficult by Michael watching her squirm. He had a big grin on his face and that made Callie smile, too. She had had a successful jazz CD that had worked out so well, she was doing a follow up. And yes, she did listen to herself. She knew Michael was having fun at her expense as he waited for her response, so she decided it was her turn to have a little fun with him.

"So what?" Callie said finally. "I'm not ashamed that I like listening to my own songs or any song, for that matter. I like what I like." She shrugged her shoulders. "I know it might be hard for you to believe, but everybody's not a phony baloney like you."

"Phony baloney, huh?"

"Yep. I don't pretend like I don't remember songs to save face."

"So you won't mind if I tell everybody on your staff you have a playlist called "sex songs" on your iPod or that you're an undercover rap fan?"

"Oh, so somebody's been a busy bee and a nosy bee, huh?" Callie asked watching as Michael picked up her iPod from the counter that led to the butler's pantry. "Now while I should take offense to that rap remark, baloney man, I'll just tell you again, I like what I like."

"I'll let them know you lead off with "Do Me Baby" by Prince," Michael said as he scrolled through the mp3.

"Oh, please. I sing raunchier Prince songs at our staff meetings." To emphasize, Callie did her best Prince imitation by stretching her eyes, flicking her tongue and singing a high pitched "Oooohhhhh!"

"Uh huh," Michael said not looking up as he continued to scroll down her playlist. "And how about Pony by Ginuwine?"

"There's nothing embarrassing there. It's just an old school beat."

"Oh, so you don't realize all that singing about riding on his pony has nothing to do with an actual horse, right?"

"Well, a girl's gotta ride something." Callie giggled as she relaxed back in her seat and crossed her legs. "Again, not embarrassed."

"And your undercover rap songs include–"

"I object to that classification!"

"–songs like *Pop that Cooch*–"

"Hey, hey, hey!" Callie said cutting him off. Alert now she stood up and looked behind her towards the kitchen door. "Keep it down, the kids might hear you," she added in a whisper still watching the door and listening for footsteps. When she turned back around, Michael was standing next to her grinning with a breakfast plate in his hand.

"Eggs?"

"It's just that I don't want the kids to know…"

"…that their mother 'likes what she likes?'"

Michael lifted the plate higher and closer to Callie. She hesitated and tried not to smile. Then she politely took the plate, nodded her thanks and sat back down with as much dignity as she could muster.

"Sorry, there wasn't any "phony baloney" to cook, so will bacon do?" They both laughed as Michael bent down and kissed her on the forehead.

"Anyway, the point is, no matter what's on my iPod, your secret is *not* safe with me. And it's not just the song, it's all the wiggling that you like to call dancing. After all these years you still haven't found the beat."

"Oh, please."

"And I've told you before that you don't need to find every beat on a song. Just pick one and stick with it. But I saw today that you're a hard man to teach because nothing I said stuck." Callie shook her head in pity. "It's like water rolling off a duck's back."

"Ok, well I see you're pretty confident, so I guess you can handle the whole truth about that now."

"What truth?" Callie asked smiling in anticipation.

Michael put the breakfast plates he had just fixed for Ashley and Maya on the kitchen table in the breakfast nook. Then he walked to Callie at the breakfast counter and took her hand. With his other hand he gently touched her cheek. He looked so serious that Callie became serious too. She held her breath as she looked into his eyes.

"The truth is, ever since we first met..." Michael looked down. "This is harder to say than I thought."

"Ever since we first met what, Michael?" Callie asked concerned now. Michael sighed deeply and looked back up at Callie.

"I've had to dumb down my dance moves just so you could keep up. *But*," he said gently, "I did it all for love." Michael walked over to the stove again and took another deep breath.

"Whew, I feel better now that I've gotten that off my chest," he said turning around to face Callie just in time for a spoonful of eggs to land on his nose.

"See? This is why I didn't break the news to you before," he responded laughing. This time it was his turn to wipe his face with a napkin. "I thought we were beyond food throwing?"

"We're never beyond food throwing."

"So I see."

"Not too well 'cause you missed a spot."

"Why don't you come wipe it off for me?"

"Wipe it off yourself, funny man."

"I've been doing a lot of that lately."

Callie and Michael both laughed as he dabbed at his moustache.

He was still so sexy to her, but he was more than that and Callie was feeling herself getting confused again. She wouldn't allow her doubts and mixed feelings to ruin their moment now.

"You know, I wish I had recorded you just so that I could show you the playback. If you saw what I saw, you wouldn't want to ever talk about anybody's dancing again."

"Now that's just the jealousy talking."

"Oh, really? If you want another opinion, just ask Alise because she…" Callie trailed off. Michael leaned dejectedly against the kitchen counter. The mood in the room was immediately somber as they were both brought back to the reality of the tragedy.

"How is she?" Michael asked quietly.

"Not good. When I left she was going to try to get some sleep."

"When you left? So she was up all night?"

"Huh?"

"That's where you were all night, with Alise, right?"

Callie let her mind drift briefly to Stephen before forcing herself to concentrate on the moment at hand.

"Uh, no… she wanted to be alone. And I didn't want to come home to an empty house."

"Yeah, the girls didn't want you here alone, either. Neither did I. I would have called you to let you know we were here, but I wanted to give you time with your sister." Michael folded his arms across his chest. "So where were you?"

"I went to my office."

"Oh, yeah…I didn't think of that."

*Stephen did.*

"No, that's not fair," Callie mumbled, scolding herself for raising that thought against Michael.

"What did you say?"

Callie suddenly felt emotionally drained. It had been a tough twenty-four hours and now she was talking to herself. She pushed the plate of food away and got up from the table. "I'm not hungry," she said quietly. She took a deep breath and then added, "I'm going to take a shower and then lie down for awhile."

"No church?"

"Not today," Callie said shaking her head." I don't know what I would say to God."

"Maya wants to go. So does Ashley. I think they just feel…helpless."

Michael and Callie stood looking at each as sadness seemed to envelop them both. Michael walked over to Callie and embraced her tightly. Slowly and gently, they rocked back and forth in each other's arms. Callie closed her eyes and let the tears fall. The quiet was interrupted when Michael's cell phone on the counter began to vibrate. Callie startled, but Michael hugged her tighter and rubbed her back.

"It's ok," he whispered, gently caressing her back.

"Aren't you going to see who that is? It might be a business call."

"There is nothing or no one more important than the people in this house right now. Whatever or whoever it is can wait."

Callie pulled back from Michael and looked into his eyes. He was right. Family first and she needed him just as much as the kids. Standing on her tippy toes she kissed him gently on his lips.

"I'm going to take that shower now."

"Ok. I'll go check on Maya and Ashley. They have to hurry if we're going to make the early service on time."

Arm in arm they slowly walked up the stairs together. As Michael stopped to knock on the door of each of his daughter's rooms to call them to breakfast, Callie continued alone to the master bedroom at the end of the hall. She grabbed the doorknob and paused, well aware that it used to be Michael's bedroom, his doorknob, his loyal wife. None of that was true anymore.


Coming out of the shower, Callie wrapped herself in her plush lavender bath towel and began to dry off. She decided to forgo the lotion and walked naked to her dresser. Grabbing undergarments out of the drawers she caught a glimpse of herself in the mirror and froze.

*What are you doing Callie?*

She thought she had things all figured out, at least temporarily when she was with Stephen. She would give herself some distance from the emotional chaos of her life. But wasn't that just running away?

Callie studied her face and body. She had aged and things had moved around a bit, but she still looked good. And not just for her age. Callie stared at herself and nodded. No, she looked good because she took care of herself, and of course having money helped. She didn't have to worry about the cost of using the best beauty products or getting her hair done at the best salons. She could afford a dietician to plan her meals and a trainer to come to her home for workout sessions. She had a successful business, employing a full staff at work and help at home. She had the luxury of pampering herself, the blessing of three healthy, beautiful kids and two good men that cared about her. So why wasn't she happy? Was she going through a midlife crisis?

Callie grimaced. Maybe she should go out and buy herself a fancy red sports car. Isn't that what you're supposed to do in the middle of a midlife crisis? She thought about Stephen and sighed. Maybe she had already gotten that "sports car." She just didn't expect to care so much about it or know that it would have such an impact on her life. And she certainly didn't expect her "sports car" to care so much about her, either.

Callie put on her underclothes and grabbed her favorite bathrobe out of her closet. Pulling on the robe she realized Stephen offered her a chance to start over. With him she was nobody's wife or mother or sister. She was just a woman. It had been a long time, back even before Michael, since she felt so free. With Stephen she only had to make herself happy. Callie knew this was selfish, but having a chance to reinvent herself was tempting. A part of her, a big part of her, wanted to see where this all led. She didn't want to always wonder about the excitement she missed out on because she decided to go back to her old, familiar, predictable life before exploring her options.

On the other hand, being with Michael was really good for her *because* it was familiar. Plus she really was happy being responsible for the people she loved. More importantly, she couldn't explain why, but being with Michael just always felt right. What if things never felt that right with Stephen or any other man? She would have lost the best thing that ever happened to her because she wanted an adventure, a detour in her life. Callie didn't dare let herself think about it for long, but the question crept up in her once again. What if she could have them both?

Tying her robe belt tightly around her waist, Callie walked quickly out of the bedroom. She wanted to give her girls a hug before they left for church. However, when she peeped into Maya's room what she saw made stopped her in her tracks. She was mesmerized watching Michael combing their youngest daughter's hair. Maya had always cried when Michael had been forced to do her hair. Callie received more than one phone call after the separation with a tearful Maya complaining that her daddy gave her "clown hair." Callie was never sure what that meant except that Michael could never fasten the hair clips securely. Maya's other descriptions of her messy hair was always lost between her tearful hiccups. After the separation, hair combing time used to always be a source of stress and arguing for Michael and Maya. Apparently that had changed while Callie wasn't paying attention.

As Callie watched now she knew, without hearing the conversation that they chatted easily with each other. Maya had a content look of trust on her face and Michael had a serious look on his as he concentrated on her ponytail. Maya didn't need reassurances that her father was doing the best he could. She didn't need to hear that Michael would get better at doing her hair and at doing a lot of other things that Callie had always done. She didn't need to be told all of those things that Callie used to say to calm her down because those things were happening now. A lot of time had passed and a lot had changed since their family had lived together under the same roof. If she hadn't thought of it before, Callie couldn't ignore what was right in front of her face. Relationships drift, for better or worse, they drift and the people involved get used to living with the changes. Watching Maya and Michael was living proof of that.

Callie suddenly realized more than ever that this holding pattern she had with Michael and Stephen couldn't last much longer. These relationships were drifting, too. Soon Callie would have to choose. She couldn't have them both and deep down Callie knew it wasn't really an option. She would lose one of them and, if she didn't hurry up, she just might lose them both.

Callie smiled as she studied Michael with his daughter from a distance. They looked so much alike. Both of their complexions could be described as "lightly toasted." As a matter of fact, all three of their kids had Michael's complexion and hair texture. It was Callie with her caramel colored skin that stood out amongst them, much to the chagrin of Ursula, Michael's mother. Callie sometimes wondered if Ursula would have embraced her only son's children if they had come out with Callie's browner skin color.

Callie shook that silly thought out of her head. It didn't matter what her dreaded mother-in-law wanted, Michael never let his mother rule his life. If he did, the two of them never would have been married. Ursula faked a heart attack when he told her they were engaged. She never liked Callie, but she liked Marlisa even less. For the first time, Ursula took her side over Michael's during their break- up. However, as ashamed as she was with Michael's behavior, she was in no hurry to see him reconcile with his wife. Unfortunately, that was a position she and Callie also shared.

Callie watched a moment longer and then backed up to go down the back staircase. She didn't want to disturb their father-daughter moment by walking past the open door. Once downstairs, Callie drifted towards the kitchen sink lost in thought. Absentmindedly she began to do the breakfast dishes. One of her old habits was to clean whenever she had something serious on her mind. She was deep in her thoughts and almost didn't hear Michael's phone vibrating on the kitchen table.

She hurriedly walked over to it thinking it might be the same person who had called earlier. It might be a business call and she certainly didn't want to be the cause of him missing something important. Callie grabbed the phone intent on rushing it to Michael, but after looking at the number she stopped in her tracks. Marlisa. Callie stared at the phone until it stopped buzzing. Moments later the phone showed a voice mail notification. Tentatively looking around her, Callie then stood absolutely still as she carefully listened for footsteps. Hearing no movement and feeling sure she was alone, she looked back at the phone in her hand. Slowly, Callie hit the voice mail retrieval button and gingerly put the phone to her ear. Marlisa's voice came on.

*"Hi Michael, it's me."* Marlisa spoke seductively and Callie felt herself tensing up. *"I just wanted to see how you were doing and if you needed any help with the girls. I figured Callie would be caught up with Alise's needs and leave you and the girls to fend for yourselves. Not that I blame Callie for helping Alise. I don't. Not in the slightest. But I think we all need each other as a family right now. Callie and I left Alise's house right before midnight. You know you might want to check on her since I don't think she went straight home for some reason. Maybe you can check with Stephen, the business partner. We should make sure she's ok. Anyway that's it. Call me when you get this. Bye Michael."*

"That heifer," Callie whispered.

It was almost as if she knew that Callie had been with Stephen and wanted to clue Michael in on it. But how would she know? Callie wondered if Marlisa had followed her. Although it wasn't above Marlisa to spy on her, Callie couldn't figure out why she would do it last night after they all got the tragic news. Callie closed her eyes to help her concentrate. Try as she might, she didn't remember seeing any headlights following her on the road last night. Callie's mind was racing. She was wondering if Marlisa knew anything, but then abandoned that thought. Marlisa was probably taking a calculated risk like she did last year when she took a bunch of pills, hoping Michael and Callie would be there for her "Save me Michael" show. Maybe Marlisa was just hoping to use doubt to put a wedge between Callie and Michael again. If it worked last year, it was possible that it could work again.

Furious with her sister's old tricks, Callie deleted the voice mail and the record of her incoming call. Suddenly she had a sickening thought. Marlisa had seemed so comfortable calling Michael that Callie couldn't help but wonder if they had been in close contact again. After cautiously looking towards the back staircase and the other kitchen entrances again, Callie quickly scrolled through Michael's recently dialed call list looking for Marlisa's name and number. Nothing. Michael wasn't calling Marlisa unless he was deleting the call record like she just did.

Remembering the call that had come in a little earlier, Callie scrolled to his missed calls. The name she saw was familiar, but it wasn't Marlisa's. She scrolled a little more and saw that Michael had added the number and other information to his contact list. Callie slowly put the phone down on the kitchen counter and stared at the name glowing from the screen. She knew it well, but hadn't uttered it in years. Sighing, she turned her back to the cell phone and let herself fall against the counter's edge. He was in contact with Raylene again. Callie blinked and looked up the back stairs where she had last seen Michael. *Raylene.*

*Chapter 6*

Alise sat in her car now parked in her garage. She had just come from Anthony's gravesite again. It had only been two weeks since his funeral and she had stopped at his gravesite every day since then. She knew it wasn't logical, but each time she left the cemetery, she felt like she was abandoning him all over again. She didn't want to leave him all alone in that dark, cold place. She didn't want him to think she had forsaken him after being responsible for his death. Alise didn't know if this was a normal part of the grieving process or how long she would feel this way. She just knew she couldn't help herself. Her child still needed her and for once he would be her priority.

"Mom?" It was Jackson. "What are you doing?"

"I'm just thinking."

"In the dark? In the closed in car of a closed garage?"

Alise smiled sadly in the dark. She knew what her son was thinking and the truth was that Alise had thought about it for a moment, but only a moment. When she had gotten the news about Anthony she was devastated. When she had to plan the funeral, she felt mentally unbalanced. However, when she saw him in the coffin, she felt "it." She wanted to crawl in the casket with him and stay there.

Because that was when she realized she would never look upon his face again and in that moment of realization, she had truly wanted to die.

Alise now looked up at her youngest son standing in the doorway of the garage. Light from the kitchen streamed in from behind him and she could see he had his hand on the garage light switch. He just stood there like a statue, not sure if he should turn the light on or not. Alise could tell he was worried and she felt selfish for only thinking about herself. Jackson hurt too, and she was hurting him more by scaring him so badly. He had gotten into the private school, just as Alise thought he would. It was part of her plan. Even though her plan didn't matter anymore, Jackson still needed to leave soon to get settled in and start the new school year miles from home. She wouldn't let him go worrying about her. Refusing to let another son down, Alise got out of the car.

"Are you all packed?" she asked closing her car door and walking towards him.

"Well, I've been thinking about that. Maybe I shouldn't go right away. I mean, if I wait a couple of weeks, I won't really be behind. They're probably going to be doing a lot of orientation and review stuff that I don't really need. Plus I can just catch up anyway. You know I'm smart, right?"

"Oh, well, I guess I know now."

"Yep, I just got it like that," he said smiling.

Alise smiled back and hugged her son. "You know your mom is strong. right?"

"I know, but this is different from anything we ever faced before."

Alise knew she would never be the same, but that didn't mean she had to be completely different, either. She had never been a quitter and Jackson needed to be reminded of that.

"You're right. This *is* different and that makes it harder, but we will get through this and we will be stronger for it, ok?" Jackson reluctantly nodded his head. "I love you Jackson."

71

He nodded his head again.

"Now let's get the take out menus and figure out what kind of food we're going to chomp on tonight!"

Alise put her arm around her son and turned him towards the kitchen. Once they were inside, she closed the garage door behind them. She decided at that moment she would keep her deepest sorrows from spilling over on him. He didn't deserve to have to deal with her emotional drama. She couldn't allow herself to wallow at his expense; she would have to do that in private. Even if she had to pretend to the world that everything was all right, and she knew she might have to pretend forever, Alise would do so for the sake of her other two kids. They still needed their mother. She would just have to put her energy into other things to take her every thought off of Anthony. She had Jackson and Jamal's futures to think about as well as running her restaurant and picking up the pieces of her life. Without meaning to, Alise's focus suddenly jumped to Paula.

For almost a year all Alise could do was to think about Paula. Yet after learning about Anthony's death, Paula had barely crossed her mind. Alise hadn't seen or heard from Paula since the night they argued in the very kitchen she was standing in now. She wondered what kind of underhanded things Paula had been up to during the last few weeks. Distracted by her new thoughts, Alise opened the drawer and took out a handful of take out menus without looking at them.

"Your choice," she said handing them to Jackson.

"Chinese?"

"Yeah, fine with me. Go ahead and order and just get me my usual."

Jackson took the Ming Gardens menu and handed the rest of the stack back to Alise. She smiled and took them from her son, still thinking about Paula. She furrowed her brow trying to remember if Paula had even come to the funeral. She knew she hadn't seen her and nobody mentioned Paula being there, not that she could remember. Of course, not talking to her about Paula would have been with good reason. Her sisters probably thought it would set her off. Then again nobody mentioned Paula *not* being there either. With their extended family, somebody would have made a snide remark about Paula missing her own nephew's military funeral. That would have been mentioned loudly whether they thought it would set Alise off or not. It would have been a good piece of family gossip and to spread it, family members would have whispered about it right in front of her son's casket if necessary.

Alise watched Jackson animatedly giving their takeout order over the phone. He looked relieved compared to the way he looked only moments before. Alise needed to assure him that she was okay, otherwise he would have a hard time being away from her. She would have to pretend and change her focus for a while. Again, Alise's thoughts drifted to Paula and their unfinished business. She could concentrate on that because there was no way Paula was walking away unscathed.

Alise allowed the beginnings of a plan to take shape. She drummed her fingers on the kitchen counter, trying to corral her thoughts. She allowed herself to think briefly about Anthony again and flinched at the sorrow she felt. To play the part that she needed in this family drama, grief would have to wait in the wings. Sadly she knew that no matter how long she averted her attention, grief would patiently wait in the wings for her forever.


Alise cleaned up the kitchen, throwing away the empty Chinese food cartons and wiping down all the counters with a bleach disinfectant spray. After taking out the trash she came back into the kitchen and took a big sniff.

"Febreze," she said as she was still able to smell the lingering spices from their dinner. Alise loved food. She loved cooking it, eating it and sharing it, but some dinners liked to stay well past their welcome. She had learned a hard lesson during her time experimenting with West Indies dishes. She loved the taste, but she swore the curry was turning her curtains yellow. Still, it was the love of all food that drew Alise to the restaurant business and she knew the importance of a thorough clean-up. Alise stood with her hands on her hips and nodded as she surveyed the spotless kitchen. Satisfied, she turned off the kitchen lights and started up stairs.

Jackson had gone up a while ago and he seemed a lot more at ease than he was when he had found his mother in the garage. They had spent a nice evening talking about what he wanted to do with his life. As Alise talked with her youngest son, she was happy that he was looking forward to his new journey, but she was also sad that he would be leaving her. He was a smart kid and he seemed to have grown up overnight.

Talking to Jackson about his new school reminded Alise that soon she would be living all alone in her big, three bedroom home. During their dinner, there were times when Alise had wanted to push her food away, scream, cry and let all the anguish that had built up over the last few hours out, but she didn't. She had controlled herself for Jackson's sake. Then she had realized that handling her emotions better was also for her own sake –mentally. For the first time since the tragedy felt like it had torn her heart out, she was able to completely focus on something other than her own grief.

Although she had tried to give Jackson her full attention, it wasn't concentrating on him that kept her mind busy. It was trying *not* to concentrate on Paula. She thought that it would have been a little more difficult to keep her mind from drifting into that black hole of grief that had swallowed her up for the last few weeks. However, her mind had been overwhelmed with thoughts of Paula. She believed that the only thing that would keep her from teetering off an emotional cliff would be finishing what she had started with her older sister.

Her first plan was designed to expose Paula's deceit and force her out of Callie and Marlisa's company. Alise had thought revealing Paula's misrepresentation of the will would be enough to do that and, at the very least, it would give Callie and Marlisa their father back. Alise had also hoped it would turn Marlisa away from Paula so that the three of them could run Paula out of town. Alise relished the thought of doing battle with Paula, personally, legally and publicly to ensure Paula would not profit from her lies. At the same time, their open fighting would serve to uncover the real Paula for all to see. For Alise, shining a light on Paula's true character was going to be the best part. Paula would have never been able to recover from her fall from the top of the pedestal so many of their family members still put her on. Most of their aunts, uncles and cousins only saw Paula from afar and she had them fooled. They had no idea what type of things Paula was capable of doing. Even Callie and Marlisa were still a little in the dark, although Alise was sure Marlisa knew more about Paula's dirty deeds than she let on.

Alise had been so distracted with getting out from under Paula's blackmail that she had nearly forgotten about the weird exchange she saw between Paula and Marlisa. It was on the day that Paula received her company shares of CM Music Productions. Alise closed her eyes to help her remember more as she thought back to that day. She couldn't hear what they were saying, but because of the look on Paula's face, she believed Marlisa was in control. The only thing Alise knew is that it had something to do with …what was it? Alise frowned while thinking. North Carolina, maybe?

There was no rush to investigate at the time since any move Alise made against Paula would have put her sons in jeopardy. However, whatever was going on between those two seemed pretty big back then. She didn't know if their private dealings would help her cause, but she didn't think it would hurt. Alise made a mental note to talk to Marlisa as soon as possible. The more she had to use against Paula, the better. Things had definitely changed, and while her original plan had been good enough at the time, it wasn't anymore.

Standing at the top of the stairs holding on to the banister, Alise looked out over her family room. She knew Paula was waiting for her to make a move. She also knew that Paula would be ready and see her coming. As Alise stood alone contemplating what to do she realized that to surprise Paula, she would have to use her older sister's Achilles heel. But to do that meant she would have to do something very difficult and unfortunately, she would have to do it at Callie's expense. Alise closed her eyes to gather resolve. Callie had already been through too much. Their whole family had been through too much and under ordinary circumstance she would never make such a move. But these weren't ordinary circumstances, so an ordinary response…well, that wasn't good enough anymore, either.

*Chapter 7*

Alise opened the door for Callie who, after giving her older sister a big hug, rushed into the living room to take her place on the window seat. Alise couldn't help but smile. Ever since Callie was a little girl she loved window seats. It seemed like she had a fascination with beautiful glass enclosures because she also loved French doors, floor to ceiling windows, sliding glass doors and big, glass revolving doors. Alise giggled remembering a family trip to New York when Callie was about eight years old. While hurrying to get inside a compartment of a revolving door at the United Nations building, Callie missed her timing and got her head stuck. No one could go in or out of the U.N. for a moment, but that didn't deter Callie from rushing into the same revolving door on the way out of the building.

Callie seemed to love looking out at the world and had a great appreciation for nature. Unfortunately, that's the part that really stumped Alise. When given the choice, Callie chose to stay indoors. For someone who needed so desperately to *see* outside, you would think she would rush to *be* outside. Not Callie. Alise couldn't think of a time when Callie showed any real interest in participating in the world she so closely watched. When they were kids, Callie would forgo a fun, family outing unless conditions were just right. She loved the beach, but if it was too humid she would ask to stay with their grandmother. She loved watching snow, but it was usually too cold for her to play in the snow with the other kids. She loved the flowers in their mother's gardens, but the bugs made her too itchy to help their mother care for them. So she just watched from behind the glass - watched and waited.

Sometimes Alise thought she was so afraid to make a mistake that she seemed to avoid taking risks, choosing to remain overly careful and thoughtful. Callie's personality made her a bit of a loner and maybe that's why Alise thought it was her duty to protect her sister. Callie always seemed more fragile than the other sisters. Not weak, just...fragile.

As Alise watched Callie sitting and staring out the big bay window it occurred to her that maybe she had it backwards. Maybe Callie wasn't timidly keeping watch, waiting for the right conditions to go out into the world. Maybe she was keeping watch to make sure nothing or no one unwelcome came into *her* world. Maybe, for the whole of her life she had been standing guard and keeping out all of the chaos and destruction in exchange for quiet order. The other sisters thrived on drama and competition, but most of the time Callie just wanted to be left alone.

Alise smiled. Callie didn't know it, but this careful, thoughtful person was Alise's rock. When she went through all the cheating Terrance did in their marriage, Callie held her hand. When she went through her messy divorce, Callie was there by her side. Alise wished she had gone to Callie with the truth when Paula first started manipulating everyone with her lies, but Alise didn't want any help. She wanted Paula all to herself and now that she had started down that road alone, she would have to finish it alone. Callie was going to hurt a little more for a little while longer, but Alise swore she would fix it for her. She just needed a little more time and then Paula would be out of their lives again.

Alise walked across the room towards her sister. Sitting, Callie had slipped off her shoes, put both feet in front of her on the seat cushion and sat hugging her bended knees. She was quiet and sat very still. Looking at her, Alise knew whatever was bothering her sister was serious. Sitting on the other end of the window seat, Alise took off her slippers, propped her legs up on the cushions and leaned back.

"So what's up?"

"Huh?"

"Don't 'huh' me. You're here for a reason."

"I can't come by just to be with my sister?"

"Sure you can. You do all the time. But something's up and don't try to deny it. You are as transparent as this glass," Alise said pointing at the window, "I can see right through you."

Callie looked at the glass. "Nobody can see through this glass. It's filthy."

"It is not filthy."

"I can write my name in the dirt on it."

"No, you can't!" Alise said indignantly. She rubbed the glass with her palm and created a noticeable dirt smudge. "Ok, it's just slightly dusty, but you can't write your name in it."

Callie looked at Alise and put her finger tip to the glass.

"C," she said writing the clearly visible letter in a big sweeping movement.

"You're just proving my point, nothing's there," Alise lied.

"A"

"I don't see anything, so you're wasting your time."

"L"

Alise slapped Callie's hand off the glass.

"All right, just stop it! You are such a butt!"

Callie burst out laughing and Alise chuckled in spite of herself.

"I don't know why you don't just hire somebody to clean. With the restaurant, you certainly make enough money to do that now."

"It's not the money. It's just that I don't want anybody in here nosing around."

"Well, besides the fact that every cleaning lady doesn't go through your underwear drawer and besides the fact that you have them sign a confidentiality agreement, what do you have to hide? As far as expensive stuff, I mean, as long as they clean it before they put it back, so what?"

"I'm not talking about stealing or putting a muzzle on them. I was thinking about exposing very personal stuff that I don't want anybody to know- period."

"Stuff like what?"

"Well...I don't know. I'm just on guard because I know Terrance is out to try something."

"Still?"

"He wants to find something to use to get me out of the house." Alise thought again about her ex-husband who had teamed up with Paula to blackmail her. "I can just avoid everything by taking care of *my* house *my*self. After all, I can clean with the best of them."

Callie stared at Alise for moment and then raised her finger to the window.

"L"

Alise grinned broadly at Callie. "Ok, you've made your point. You really are a little butt, you know that?"

"Hmm, no, I didn't know that," Callie replied frowning, pretending to take the question seriously. "No one has ever said that to me before."

"*Anyway*, while I'm still speaking to you, I'll go back to my original question because I know something is bothering you. So, what's up?"

Callie looked at Alise and then sighed deeply. "No the real question is how are you doing, Alise?" she asked gently.

"I'm ok," Alise said quickly and turned her head to look out the window. The leaves on the trees were turning. She would have to do a lot of heavy duty raking very soon.

"Do you want to talk?"

Alise responded with a slow shake of her head. They just sat together quietly until Alise had calmed her emotions. She didn't want to talk about Anthony. As a matter of fact, she didn't want to talk at all, but she owed Callie this visit. For one more day she wanted to be at peace with her sister. What was coming was going to be hard, but necessary in order to deal with Paula. For one more day she needed to be with the sister she loved before she turned her back on her. So Alise turned to face Callie and readied herself to give her complete attention to whatever it was that Callie needed from her now.

"I'm fine Callie-fornie," Alise said knowing using Callie's childhood nickname would make her sister smile.

Like always, Callie grinned at the mention of her nickname. Then she hugged her knees tighter and looked contritely at Alise. "It's just that what I have to say is … ridiculous. Especially compared to what you're going through. You have a heavy heart, and I want to offer my shoulder for you to lean on, not talk about a bunch of …oh, I don't know…high school stuff."

"Well as luck would have it, high school stuff is right up my alley. Ah, that was a great time in my life, too," Alise said smiling broadly. "There was always somebody to talk about, a party to sneak out the house for, and a boy to steal from somebody! Yep, those were the good old days."

"For rule breakers."

"I wasn't a rule breaker, I was a rule maker! I ran the school, you know."

"So I've heard–again and again."

"I made girls pay for my advice 'cause they knew my ideas were worth it."

"And you're proud of that."

"Well, you know, it's my legacy. I remember that time when I had to put Sharon Jackson in her place."

"Oh no, not the Sharon Jackson story."

"She had just transferred to the school and thought she was not only going to sit at my lunch table, but sit *in my seat*. So I walked up to her and everybody was watching and I said 'Excuse me, that's my seat.' And she said 'No, excuse you 'cause I don't see your name on it.' And you remember she had long hair–"

"I don't remember anything. I wasn't there."

"–so she flicked her hair over her shoulder."

"Are you really going to tell this story again?"

"So I flicked my hair, too. It's not like she was the only one who could grow hair. Then I told her–"

"We can do this the easy way or the hard way, your choice," Callie and Alise said simultaneously.

"I don't mind you helping the story along with color commentary, but dialog's my department. Is that ok with you, my little ray of sunshine?" Alise asked. She raised her eyebrows and stared at Callie as she waited for Callie's response.

"Oh, for heaven's sake Alise, you're like those middle-aged men always telling the story about how they caught the touchdown pass that won their high school homecoming game."

"Well, Callie, we can talk about what you want to talk about *or* we can talk about what I want to talk about. And unless you have something to say right now, I want to tell my Sharon Jackson story."

"I don't know, Alise. I might be jumping to conclusions about something, so maybe I'll just stay quiet for now." Callie put her head down on her knees, which were still bent up to her chest, and repositioned her arms tighter around her legs.

"Ok, well, anyway, where was I? Oh, yeah, so Sharon decides to stand up and everybody's watching because–"

"Ok, Alise."

"–they knew I didn't take no stuff, right. And here some new girl was trying–"

"Ok, Alise I'll talk."

"–to challenge me in front of my–"

"Ok Alise! I'll talk! I'll talk! Just stop telling the Sharon Jackson story!"

Alise abruptly stopped talking. "Well, first of all, you don't have to be rude, but in spite of that," she said folding her arms across her chest and smiling sweetly at Callie, "I'm all ears."

"Alright, there is a little something on my mind," Callie said and then paused.

"What?" Alise asked, concern softening her voice.

"It's Raylene. She's been calling Michael."

"Raylene? *That* Raylene?"

*"Yeah, *that* Raylene."

"Not some other Raylene, right?"

"How many Raylenes do you think he knows?"

"He could know another Raylene," Alise said, shrugging her shoulders.

"Yeah, he could, just like another Callie could start calling, too. But that's not likely."

"Oh, so what are you, a professor at the Name Percentage Institute now?"

"Yeah, and I also chair the Clean Windows, Clean Mind Society."

Alise chuckled. "You are so lucky I'm a better person than you are, otherwise I would not be putting up with your behind today."

"I know. I'm sorry. I'm just in a mood right now. I've been thinking about this too much. Alise, he already had her number in his phone, so she had to have called him more than once!"

Alise sat motionless for a moment as she looked at Callie. She could see Callie was really bothered. Reaching out, she put her hand on her younger sister's knee.

"Callie, just because she *might* have called him before doesn't mean you should be worried. It probably doesn't mean anything."

"Do you think it means something if he's calling her back?"

"Is he?"

"I don't know for sure. I can't check his cell phone bill since we don't have a joint account anymore. But he put her information in his cell phone address book. Work number, home number and full address. Why would he do that if he wasn't contacting her, too?"

"I suppose he wouldn't." Alise mused as she sat back again, "but that still doesn't really mean anything more than old friends getting in touch with each other."

"She was more than an old friend."

"I know. She was his old girlfriend."

"No, she was an old girlfriend that he was in love with right before me."

"But he chose you, Callie."

"But he didn't "unchoose" her. She dumped him and it always bothered him that he didn't really know why. And it always bothered me that he seemed like he got over being in love with her so quickly. Like falling out of love was so easy for him."

Alise nodded remembering things differently than Callie. She knew Michael before Callie did. As a matter of fact she introduced the two of them. Alise had been a waitress at a restaurant near the college Michael went to and he came in almost every day and sat in her station. She was able to learn quite a bit about the handsome, heavily sought after Michael Armstrong. She knew he was a really good guy and Alise also knew that deep down, he was absolutely miserable without Raylene. Michael seemed lost after they broke up and Raylene dropped out of college. Then she just disappeared and Michael had no idea what had happened to her.

Alise had thought Callie would be a good match for Michael and she turned out to be right. Callie was the best thing that ever happened to him. He seemed to instantly fall for Callie and as they became good friends, he fell deeply in love with her. However, Michael hadn't gotten over Raylene as easily as Callie believed. He only pretended to for Callie's sake. He had talked to Alise about his breakup with Raylene months before he met Callie and months after they were introduced. He always wanted to know if Alise had seen or talked to

Raylene. He would ask Alise in a very casual manner, but he was heartbroken, and he was also scared that something bad had happened to her. Although his love for Callie was real, Alise knew his love and heartbreak over Raylene was real, too.

Callie knew Raylene as the only woman besides herself that Michael had loved and wanted to marry. She knew how much Ursula, Michael's mother, adored Raylene. Ursula still had pictures of her almost daughter-in-law on her fireplace mantel. For Callie, Raylene was a ghost that she competed with, but could never really declare victory against. She had once told Alise that if Michael was the prize, he was hers by default. Callie had no doubts about the genuineness of her relationship with Michael and neither did Alise. But Alise never told Callie the whole truth – Michael knew why they broke up. Although he never discussed any details with Alise, she knew he only pretended he didn't know anything for Callie's sake.

Alise pretended a few things for Callie's sake too. She knew Callie wanted assurances that Michael would choose her if Raylene was still in the picture, and Alise just wasn't completely sure. Callie and Michael had, until recently, built a happy family together and their relationship read like a road map. It showed every twist and turn and most times they knew where they were going because they had agreed to go together – dating, marriage, house, kids, and careers.

By comparison, Michael and Raylene's relationship was not at any particular destination when it ended. It had just suddenly stopped in the middle of the road. They had a loving relationship that didn't come to a conclusion and Alise had a fleeting thought as she looked at her sister —maybe Callie should be worried. Raylene was no longer just a ghost, and Michael might feel as if he had some unfinished business with her. She also reminded herself that, sadly, Michael was capable of infidelity since it was the cause of his current separation with his wife.

The other thing that was bothering Alise was how difficult it was to process this news because she had genuinely liked Raylene. No matter how tired or irritated Alise had been with customers, when Raylene came into the restaurant, just a quick conversation with her had Alise feeling positive and looking on the bright side of things. Raylene had been great to be around because she seemed to radiant happiness. Before Callie, Alise had rooted for Raylene and Michael, but she didn't think Callie would understand. As a matter of fact, Callie might think it was a betrayal. Alise looked at her sister realizing it didn't matter what either of them thought. It didn't matter what Raylene wanted. The questions were what did Michael think and what did Michael want?

"Did you ask Michael about her?"

"No way. He would know I went through his phone."

"So what? You want to know, don't you?"

"I do, but I would rather he didn't know I knew anything yet. I need more intel first. Besides, I might be jumping the gun."

"You're not jumping the gun," Alise said a little too quickly.

Callie didn't know what Raylene and Michael's relationship was like. Women were always challenging her standing as Michael's girlfriend, but Michael never wavered. He only wanted Raylene just like he had only wanted Callie when she came into the picture. From what Alise could see, Michael had never had a shortage of women, but he wasn't a "dog" either. He was actually a romantic. Perhaps when there is an endless supply of flowers to pick out of the garden, at some point you don't want to bother with just any bloom. It has to be the perfect rose. Apparently in Michael's garden there had been two such roses and he had found and chosen them both.

"You're not jumping the gun," Alise said again more steadily, "But you are right to find out more before talking to Michael. Maybe Michael is just curious. I mean, he never ended it on his terms, so maybe he just needs to find out what happened to her so that he can put a period at the end of their relationship."

"So, it really could be nothing," Callie asked watching her sister closely.

"Yeah," Alise said distractedly. She was thinking about how Raylene had first convinced her that she could own and operate her own restaurant. Callie had put up the money for Alise to make it a reality, but it was Raylene that had originally planted the idea and made Alise believe she could really do it someday. The simple fact was that Raylene was the type of person you couldn't help but wish her well, and Alise appreciated the level of friendship she had created with her. Alise was coming to terms that if not for Callie, she would have been happy to hear from Raylene. Could it be the same for Michael? Alise thought hard about her sister's question and then answered it again.

"It's something, Callie."

"You think something's going on between them?"

"I didn't say that. I said it's something. Do you believe it's possible to be in love with two people at the same time?" Alise asked. She was half expecting Callie to get a little upset at the implications of the question, but instead Callie's eyes drifted to look out the window again. Nervously fidgeting on the cushion, Callie seemed to be trying to get comfortably situated, but she didn't answer.

"I've heard people say that you can," Alise mumbled, responding to her own question before focusing on Callie again, "but do you believe you can?"

"I suppose it's possible," Callie said quietly. "You might have to go away with them to find out for sure if…it's real or just a nice fantasy."

"What? You want Michael to go away with her?"

"No! I wasn't talking about Michael, I was talking about me…*eeting* …meeting a person that I don't…we don't even know."

Alise watched Callie fidgeting on the seat cushion again.

"You're not making sense, Callie. Do you believe you can be in love with two people or not?"

Callie swallowed hard as she looked at Alise. "Yes," she said barely above a whisper.

"So how do you think a person chooses one over the other, if they want to be with both?"

Callie shook her head and shrugged her shoulders.

"Well in Michael's case, the question is, do you stick with the one you've already committed your life to or try a new direction with the one that can take you down an undiscovered path? I'm thinking Michael would stay with his family and make things work out for the two of you. When you think about it, it's really an easy choice."

"Unless you want an adventure. Unless you want to feel young and free and happy in a different way. I think it's selfish, but it is understandable."

"And avoidable if you stake your claim on Michael now. He won't risk losing you again for an adventure. Just go back to him, Callie. It's just that easy. Reconcile. Have him move back in as you guys still work on things."

Callie turned from Alise to look out the window. She raised her finger and added the "I" and "E" to her name in the dirt film on the glass. This time Alise didn't react and Callie didn't smile. This time they sat in silence.

"How concerned should I be?"

"You shouldn't be concerned at all if you take him back. Right now. Today."

"And if I don't?"

Alise frowned as she studied her sister. "What do you mean if you don't? Why wouldn't you?"

"I'm not sure if I'm ready right now. I have to figure some things out."

"Ok, *well*," Alise said slowly. This time it was her turn to fidget uncomfortably on the seat cushion. "You have to keep in mind you're dealing with the Ex-Trifecta."

Callie nodded her head at the familiar phrase. She watched as Alise used her fingers to emphasize the three scenarios involving an ex-lover that, when all three are present, causes the greatest problem in current relationships.

"Point number one: your man was in love with his ex. Point number two: she ended it with him, so it may not feel final. And that brings us to point number three: since he was in love with her and she broke it off, your man might have "what if" fantasies about her – especially when he sees her. What if she's forgiven me? What if she still loves me? What if we can pick up where we left off? What if I had never messed up?

"Even if it doesn't lead to anything permanent, when people have been in love, you can't let them start wandering down memory lane together and talking about all the good times and the way they felt about each other. The next thing you know, they'll get all caught up in some kind of love time warp that you can't get in with them." Alise leaned over and put her hand on Callie's knee again. "Are you willing to take that chance with Michael and his ex?"

"I don't know, Alise," Callie replied uneasily. "I have to think about some things."

"*Okay*," Alise said a little confused as she leaned back again. "Here's some free high school – no, *grownup* advice for you. I know you said forgiving someone takes time and that you can't put a clock on it. And that makes sense because you would want everything to happen naturally and honestly. After all, you're going through a healing process and it's hard to rush that. But on the other hand, it's been many months and I think you should at least be leaning one way or the other by now. So my best advice to you, Callie, is," Alise paused, remembering Michael and Raylene as a couple, "you need to hurry things along."

"You mean my decision?"

Alise nodded her head slowly. "Yeah, your decision," she said as she and Callie looked at each other. "Put a clock on it."

*Chapter 8*

Paula drummed her perfectly manicured fingernails on the restaurant table. She was running out of patience with Marlisa. It was like training a monkey. All she had to do was pickup Callie's phone, add the app, download and activate. The catch was that she had to do it quickly before Callie noticed her phone missing. Unfortunately, Marlisa couldn't type in the web links and passwords on the install fast enough. Plus she kept forgetting what to do next. She was nervously fumbling her way through the process, making one mistake after another and Paula was getting more irritated by the second. Paula knew that if Marlisa couldn't get it done, then she would expect it to be done for her. However that is exactly what Paula *didn't* want to do. This was Marlisa's job if she wanted to get the goods on Callie. There was no benefit for Paula, especially since Marlisa was going to block her access to all the information again. Paula was always clear about her job which was to be the brains behind the operation and not to do the heavy lifting. She wasn't budging on that point no matter what Marlisa threatened.

That brought her to another issue that she had to fix in a hurry. She was growing weary of Marlisa's threats. Paula had already decided that after she makes the damaging recording for Marlisa, she was done with project "Get Michael." She could handle her little sister in the fallout over her decision, but Marlisa was not a major concern for her now. As a matter of fact, Marlisa was only a distraction, greedily consuming Paula's valuable time and brain power. Marlisa's obsession with their brother-in-law weakened her and as far as Paula could see, it was all for nothing anyway.

Paula needed to set about the task of neutralizing Alise, but first she had to get "butt thumbs" here out of the way. Marlisa had been working on the first step in the process for fifteen minutes and still hadn't uploaded the app. It looked like all the practice in the world was not going to help her remember what to do and not fumble her way through it. Paula looked at the time on her own phone and got even more irritated. If she waited too much longer she would be late for her massage. She snatched the phone from Marlisa. They had purchased the exact same model as Callie's phone in order to make sure Marlisa didn't get hung up on where everything was located. Clearly, it was a waste of money, especially now that Marlisa was flustered. Paula would go over it one more time, slower. But then she had to leave.

"Ok, pay attention this time," Paula said tersely.

She showed Marlisa the steps to add the spyware again and gave the phone back to her. Now she gestured for Marlisa to start the process. It had only taken Paula a few minutes from start to finish, but in that same amount of time, Marlisa hadn't even managed to find the app online.

*Maybe they could find some spyware apps for idiots*, Paula thought as she watched Marlisa. She was sure something like that was on the market. After all, how stupid are you if you keep people in your life that you need to spy on anyway? If you don't trust them, you need to grow up and learn how to handle the situation correctly. You suspect your employees are doing something they're not supposed to be doing? Handle it. Fire them even if you have to use trumped up charges after setting them up. You suspect your man's cheating on you? Handle it. Cheat on him back. Put down the wine glass and tissues and then put on your high heels, your low cut blouse and your tight skirt. What goes around comes around and by the time you suspect it, it had probably been happening for a while. Why waste time collecting evidence? The only thing all that evidence collecting is going to do is prove you're a victim, and Paula hated the thought of being a victim.

She watched Marlisa getting frustrated with her own inability to type accurately on the phone display. Her nails were getting in the way and she couldn't figure out the exact amount of pressure to put on the touch screen. Marlisa looked up helplessly at Paula, whose eyes lingered on Marlisa's before she slowly averted her gaze to the man at the next table. Paula had been watching him watching her and she liked what they were both thinking.

"Paula, I need more help!"

"Well, then cut your fingernails."

"I'm not cutting my nails!" Marlisa said as she held out her hands to admire her beautifully French manicured nails. "My nails are real you know."

"Yes, I know, which means they'll grow back. But in the meantime you can just get acrylics."

"Acrylics! Like yours! I don't want to do that! I don't like the idea of putting on fake stuff. It's like lying about yourself."

"Really? So what's with all the Chinese hair you have going down your back? You don't look Chinese."

"Hair is different, Paula," Marlisa said, rolling her eyes.

"Yeah, it is different. It's a bigger lie if you're not into faking it. Don't worry. It looks nice Marlisa, but extending your hair or extending your nails—still fake stuff."

Marlisa shook her head and gave out an exasperated sigh. "No, Paula, you just don't get it. It *is* different, at least to me."

"You know that's my problem with you, Marlisa!" Paula snapped, releasing her frustration. "You always want to find a loophole for yourself so that you can feel better."

"What are you talking about?"

"I'm talking about the fact that when a person plays dirty, they win dirty. But you want to play dirty and think that somehow you can walk away with a clean win. You can't do that, Marlisa! *You're spying on your sister and trying to steal her husband.* That's dirty! Then you actually expect Callie to somehow be happy for you if you succeed with your dirt. You can't have it both ways! But as long as I'm in the picture, I get to be your loophole because you tie all the underhanded stuff to me. Then you think you get to walk away from this mess as pure as the Virgin Mary.

"But the fact is, Marlisa, you're no better than I am. Everything you've done and continue to do means you're willing to play to win by any means necessary! I get that. I respect that. But when you pretend you're above me somehow, that your morals are intact, well, that's when I lose all respect for you!"

"So you don't respect me? So what? If you haven't figured it out Paula, I don't care what you think."

"That sounds like something I would have said. We're like two peas in a pod."

Marlisa put the phone down and leaned in towards Paula. "You only see how we are the same because of our methods, but you don't understand how we're different, so let me enlighten you. I'm not like you because I have my reasons for doing what I do, and they don't start off with trying to hurt people. To hurt family! So, while my ways of getting things done may seem familiar to you my motives are pure and my heart is pure."

Paula laughed a big throaty laugh, getting the attention of the other lunch patrons in the restaurant. "You are delusional."

"But at least I'm not a criminal."

Paula sat up straight in her chair.

"Oh, I see that got your attention," Marlisa said with tiny smile.

"Not really," Paula replied. Narrowing her eyes, she relaxed back in the chair and returned her sister's smile. "That threat is getting really old. It's a little played out if you ask me."

"Maybe. But somebody like you has a lot of dirty secrets buried in her backyard. So I guess it's time we move on to another one of your little graves. Like, hmm, let's see, how about what's really going on between you and Alise? Callie said she's going to find out and, you know, I just might help her if you're too busy to help me."

Paula looked around the room eyeing the other patrons as they tried not to make eye contact with her. She was seething and she was more upset that Marlisa, of all people, could get to her like she had. It was weird that when Marlisa dug down deep she could really pack a punch. Paula liked that about her little sister. So while she was angry, she was also strangely invigorated. Even so, Marlisa would not get away with challenging her so openly. Paula now stared at her little sister. Marlisa had another hand to play using Callie, and the anger of the situation made Paula want to turn the table over right then and there.

She had the nerve to push Marlisa and Marlisa had the nerve to push her back—all the way into a corner. The truth was that all the sisters had that feistiness in them—the thing that made them bite back when threatened. They probably all got that trait from their mother. The problem was their fathers. Callie and Marlisa both had Philip Elliot in them, which left them both lacking that "killer instinct" in different ways. Callie had great focus, but she thought too much about the consequences. She was far too careful for her own good, and it caused hesitation. On the other hand, Marlisa had the patience to wait for the opportunity to strike no matter the consequences, but she could be distracted by shiny objects. Paula smiled wryly knowing that with Callie's focus and Marlisa's moral ambiguity, they would make quite a team.

Calming herself down as she continued to stare at Marlisa, Paula carefully contemplated her position. She realized that the smart play was to keep Marlisa at odds with Callie, at least for the time being. In order to concentrate on handling Alise, Paula had to make sure she kept Marlisa occupied and vulnerable and kept Callie out of the picture completely. Helping Marlisa would be the most expedient way to do both. She couldn't take the chance of Marlisa and Callie working together and figuring out the paternity scam. Right now, she had her hands full enough with Alise alone. Paula continued to stare at Marlisa as she tried to think of all the angles. No, there was no way around it. The best alternative was to keep Callie and Marlisa at each other's throats and not give them a reason to put their heads together. As far as Callie knew, Paula was just a nuisance, and it wouldn't do Paula any good to have another sister gnawing at her ankles. Not now. Not when she hadn't figured out how to handle Alise or control Marlisa, who now seemed to be drunk with power.

Paula sneered at Marlisa and then snatched the phone from the table. "I'll do it," she said as she stood up. Then in an afterthought, she threw the phone back down on the table.

"Don't you need the phone to practice?" Marlisa asked. She genuinely looked as if she was trying to be helpful. She was happy again, acting as if their vicious exchange never took place.

"No, because I'm not stupid."

"Then again," Marlisa said as she smiled and handed the phone back to Paula, "you're not as smart as you think you are, either."

*Chapter 9*

Paula sat at the bar of the hotel nursing a scotch and soda. She needed to ease some of the tension she was feeling after her lunch date with Marlisa. Paula had decided to skip the massage because she was so on edge that she was afraid she might take things out on her masseuse. If Kameko rubbed her too hard or touched her wrong, Paula didn't trust herself not to punch that little Asian woman in the eye. She didn't want to risk losing that kind of self-control because of Marlisa, especially since that kind of unfortunate behavior would cost her dearly.

She had worked hard on her image with all the hotel employees, and it was important that she be considered a great guest for a number of reasons. One reason was that the more the staff liked her, the more protective they would become of her. If anyone were to come nosing around and asking questions about her at this hotel, Paula was confident the service staff would send them packing and alert her of every encounter. She knew it would only be to her detriment to have the hotel personnel "fall out of love" with her. So she was always extra considerate. She remembered the employee's names, asked about their family and, above all, gave great tips for everything.

Paula took another sip of her drink and, still wishing for that massage, she rolled her shoulders in an attempt to rid her body of its stiffness. Eddie, the bartender, brought her another drink. He knew her pattern of drinking and seemed to instinctively sense her mood to be a two drink minimum this afternoon. Paula gave him one of her rare sincere smiles. She had a good thing going here and felt more at home with this group of ready to please strangers than her own blood. She genuinely liked much of the service staff, although she certainly didn't consider them as her equal. However, many of them, like Kameko and Eddie, still rated very highly with her. She had rescheduled her appointment for the morning and left Kameko, who had been her masseuse since she began living at the hotel, a generous tip with an apology note. If she had to endure a little stiffness until the morning, then so be it.

When Paula first came to town, she had stayed with Marlisa until her little sister had one of her famous tantrums and kicked her out of the condo. Paula had originally stayed at the hotel just because it was a roof over her head. However, it wasn't long after checking in that she just decided to stay. She was bringing in enough money to pay for living accommodations and the amenities were hard to beat. She had maid service, room service, laundry service, a luxury spa, restaurants and entertainment lounges right at her finger tips. Paula had even begun taking tennis lessons, although tennis was never actually played at her "lessons" with the twenty-five year old instructor.

Paula knew she could get most of the same amenities at a luxury condo, but she wasn't ready to do anything that would tie her down to this city, including buying real estate. She had no idea when, or if, it would be in her best interest to leave town in a hurry. Experience had taught her to keep her life as portable as possible.

Paula checked for the time on her cell phone. She would go upstairs to her suite and take a nap soon. She had already ordered her dinner to be brought to her promptly at 7:00 p.m. and then she would see what the night would bring. There was always some type of function or entertainment at the hotel that would engage her whether she was an invited guest or had to crash the party. That's another one of the things Paula loved about living there; she could pretend she was anyone and blend in. It was one of her games and she was good at playing it, especially with the married men on business trips. She would be their fantasy for the night, which didn't necessarily mean they would end up between the sheets. That was her call entirely and only if she thought the man to be worthy. However, Paula would always give them something to dream about with the chase. Men loved the chase.

Paula looked around the bar and spotted a candidate for her "Almost" game. It was something she liked to play with men who would never be able to get a woman like her in bed unless money exchanged hands. The man, who now sat at a corner table, was middle aged, balding, thick black rimmed eyeglasses and was not quite tall enough to look her directly in the eyes. Paula was sure he was at the hotel at the expense of some company, because by the looks of him, he couldn't afford the rates on his own. Although, he looked stylish enough in his off the rack suit, shirt and tie, it was his shoes that gave him away. He was wearing his comfortable "suit shoes," that he probably wore to every church service, wedding and funeral. So while the suit was fairly decent, the shoes were rundown at the heels, lackluster and at least fifteen years out of date. It was funny how some people dressed to impress only from the ankles up. Then they would try to pass themselves off to others by pretending to be more than what they really were, while being completely unaware that their shoes were giving them away.

By contrast, Paula's look shouted rich, classy and sexy. She was confident that as soon as she walked up to the "I have to pay my dates" guy, he would start imagining the story he would tell his friends about their encounter.

*So there I was sitting at the bar and this really rich, sexy woman walked up to me…*

Paula smiled thinking how she would cozy up to him, steer their conversation to sex and get him to buy her a few more drinks. Then, when she'd given him the impression she was ready to go for anything, he'd get the nerve to ask her to his room. That's when she'd give him the creative brush off. Sometimes it's in the elevator where, after sufficiently rubbing against his "happy spots," she'd pretend she got an emergency text message and leave in a hurry. Sometimes she'd pretend he insulted her by assuming she was that easy to get in bed and do something dramatic like throw a drink in his face. Sometimes she'd start talking about getting her sexual thrills with knives and cutting. That tactic never failed to scare the guy so much that he'd make an excuse to leave *her*. Every man she toyed with was made to believe, he "almost" sealed the sexual deal with her. It was all very amusing to Paula and there was never a shortage of "contestants" to target whenever the mood struck her to play. She couldn't wait to get started with the pitiful guy sitting alone in the corner.

Grabbing her drink and napkin off the bar, Paula quickly swiveled her bar stool and found herself face to face with another reason, actually the main reason, that she still lived at the hotel. Stephen Russell.

"Well, well, well, fancy meeting you here," Stephen said flashing the sexy smile Paula had come to expect.

"Yeah, it's really weird for two people who love the bottle to meet in the bar of the hotel where they both live."

Stephen chuckled and sat on the bar stool next her. Paula quickly swiveled back around in her chair, completely forgetting about her game and the balding contestant.

"Hey, I resent the 'love the bottle' comment. You need to speak for yourself."

"I happen to have it on pretty good authority that it's not an overstatement of your character."

"Oh, yeah? Whose authority?"

"Mine, as a matter of fact," Paula answered playfully. Her reply was quickly followed by the old "hair toss, bat the eyes and pull the skirt up to cross your legs" flirtation combo move. She did it more out of habit than anything else since unfortunately, she already knew it wielded no power over Stephen. Paula had pulled out all the stops for the first few months after she moved in, but it was to no avail. Her power over Stephen did not lie within the sexual realm. It was her connection to Callie that had him eating out of her hands.

"Now Stephen, you remember what happened two weeks ago, don't you?"

"Please tell me you're not going to hold that against me," Stephen replied groaning. "I can't say that was my best moment. But then again, it was far from my worst."

Paula laughed and this time out of habit she used the classic "lean forward to show more cleavage and try to brush a boob against his arm" move, but he promptly ignored it.

"But in my defense," Stephen continued unfazed by Paula's sexual overtures, "I had had a hard day."

"Not because of one of my sisters, a.k.a. your business partners, I hope? I know Callie can be a handful when she has something on her mind."

"What does she have on her mind?" Stephen asked. He had stopped smiling and now looked at Paula with great concern. "Everything's ok, isn't it?"

Paula smiled coyly. Now she had his attention. Just the mention of Callie and he was as attentive as a poodle waiting for a treat. She knew he would hang on her every word as usual, so she took a sip of her drink and savored her moment of control.

"Well, I'm not exactly sure, but it seems like something new is going on with her."

"But you don't know what it is."

"No, I don't… not really, anyway. But I think she's about to make a big decision."

"A big business decision?"

"No, there's nothing like that coming up for us, so it must be something personal."

"Hmm," Stephen said quietly as he motioned to Eddie the bartender.

"The usual?" Eddie asked. Stephen nodded his head and turned back to Paula.

"You can't even make a guess as to what's going on with her?"

"No. Well… maybe. I think it has something to do with Michael, but you know how that story goes. It's been the same for a year now— she wants him and then she doesn't. There's got to be some reason that she's dragging her feet on reconciling. Do you have any idea why?" Paula eyed Stephen carefully. Stephen shook his head "no" and took a long gulp of his drink.

Paula had figured out a long time ago that Callie and Stephen had a strong connection, and she was amazed at the restraint they both showed. As far as she could tell, they hadn't had sex—yet. However, Paula knew something was bound to happen sooner or later, and when it did, she needed to know about it before anybody else. She wanted to be able to sell the information to Marlisa for more of her little sister's company stock. Hopefully the emotional upheaval would send Callie into such a tizzy that she'll loosen her reign on the company, leaving Paula to fill the void. Callie had practically disappeared from CM Music Productions when she found out about Michael and Marlisa. What on earth would the fallout be if Michael found out about Callie and Stephen, from Marlisa of all people? Paula licked her lips just imagining all the chaos.

However, Paula knew she had to be careful while spying on her sister with Stephen. Paula had seen Callie visit many times, but Paula made sure to stay clear of her. She didn't want Callie or Alise knowing how close she was to Stephen because then she was sure they would warn him about her. Fortunately, if her sisters didn't know about their friendship, then they had no incentive to discuss private family matters with an outsider. Their mother had taught them that family privacy was paramount and all the sisters had it instilled in them practically from birth. Fight as much as you want inside the house, but the neighbors only get to see the united family front. Right now, Callie and Alise had no idea about Stephen's friendship with her, so there was no reason for Stephen to be an exception to their family rule.

Paula desperately needed all parties to stay ignorant of her interactions with them. The left hand could not know anything about the right hand. Her sisters didn't know about her friendship with Stephen and by the same token, so far, Stephen only knew what he was told by Paula. Her sisters weren't there to fill in the blanks for him. He already knew she was the oldest sister and that there was an issue with the will which gave her some ownership of CM Music Productions. She then told him how much she felt like an outsider in her own family, and that she had no real experience running a company. Since she wanted to be considered a worthy business partner, she had asked for his help, along with his discretion, as her business tutor. She told him it was important that she prove herself to be an important member of the family who could carry her own weight, and he seemed to immediately sympathize with her plight. It didn't take much convincing on her part for him to agree to quietly help her behind the scenes and keep their relationship secret.

Over time, they became friendly, but no matter what the topic of their conversation, business or pleasure, the talk always turned to Callie. That's when Paula realized he was extremely willing to help her help Callie. Paula, as a close relative of the object of his obsession, was someone he always seemed eager to see. They always had a fun conversation and Paula had to admit she really liked Stephen.

"Another hard day at the office?" Paula asked after watching him down the rest of his drink and signal for another. "'Cause the way you're tossing them down is putting me to shame."

"Like you could ever keep up with me anyway." Stephen grinned at Paula as he reached for his refilled glass.

"Maybe I could. You don't know." Paula smiled back and then

picked up her own drink.

"Sounds like a challenge. And if it is, I'll have to take it up with you later. I was just thirsty when I came in."

"Chicken."

"Just because I *can* drink everyone in here under the table, doesn't mean I want to. Especially in the middle of the afternoon."

To emphasize his point, Stephen took an exaggeratedly tiny sip from his glass. The liquid barely touched his lips.

"Ok, you're off the hook for now, but how about a rain check?"

Stephen chuckled and shook his head. "Mrs. Robinson, you're trying to get me drunk."

"First of all, the line from the movie is 'Mrs. Robinson, you're trying to seduce me.' And although I am older than you Stephen, we are nowhere near the age difference of the Dustin Hoffman-Anne Bancroft *characters.* You know," Paula said getting a little worked up, "I'm extremely insulted that you have the nerve to imply something like that! Because she was really only a few years older than him in real life and a few years older is entirely appropriate!"

"Now hold on a minute! I'm not trying to insult you. It's nothing like that!" Stephen replied with a mix of excitement and amusement. "It's just that the movie, *The Graduate,* is on TV now. See for yourself." He pointed towards the flat screen television behind the bar. They watched the famous scene play out on the screen without the sound.

"I don't have to tell you that you're a beautiful woman, Paula, and you don't ever have to concern yourself with age."

"I may have overreacted," Paula conceded after taking a deep breath. "It's just that I'm around my sisters all the time, and in a room with them I will always be the oldest. By the way, nice save with the 'beautiful' comment because I was about to tear your head off your shoulders."

Stephen threw his head back and laughed. "Oh, now where have I heard that before?"

"From one of my sisters, I'm sure."

"You sisters," Stephen said shaking his head and chuckling, "You all seem to play for keeps."

"Only when we have to. Clearly you've stepped on one of the Elliot sister's toes before. Let me guess, Callie?"

Stephen smiled and looked down at his drink, but he didn't answer. Paula hadn't quite figured him out yet. While he was always eager to hear about Callie, he never really talked about her himself. He listened and asked questions, but he never shared any details. Never. Paula wasn't sure if Stephen's tight lips were a sign that her new idea to control Alise would work on him or a clear indication that it wouldn't. At any rate, Paula knew the best way to keep him there while she tried to figure it out was to talk about Callie. Her little sister seemed to be the only topic that would ensure Paula kept Stephen's full attention.

"You know, Callie was always the quiet one, but really tough. When she had it out for you, you never even saw her coming."

"I can imagine that," Stephen said smiling.

"Have I ever told you my favorite story about Callie?"

"You mean the birthday one?"

"Oh, no, not that one," Paula said laughing. "But that is a good one."

Stephen now joined Paula as they laughed remembering the story about little Callie dressing up because she erroneously thought that she was having a surprise birthday party. Although it was a funny story, the problem was that the story, and almost all the other young Callie stories, weren't true. However, Paula hadn't made them up, either. She was an experienced liar and knew if she just made everything up as she went along, she would eventually forget the details. If Stephen asked questions later or, God forbid, wanted her to retell it, she needed to be able to recite it exactly like she had the first time. Someone like Stephen, who was hanging on her every word, would notice her inconsistencies and Paula couldn't have him asking Alise or Callie for clarification.

So she told him family stories alright—from old television shows. Although Paula mostly used stories from *Good Times*, a hit comedy series in the seventies, she had also used quite a few episodes from the Brady Bunch. She wasn't sure of Stephen's viewing schedule as a kid, but it was quite possible that he might have watched the Brady Bunch in re-runs and might recognize a story line or two. So to keep him on his toes, Paula also mixed in *227,* another family show from the past that she doubted Stephen even knew existed.

The birthday story Stephen was referring to was actually a Brady Bunch episode and Paula had simply substituted Peter Brady's plight for Callie's. Stephen had loved imaging Callie as a little girl running around the house dressed up for the surprise party that she thought she was having. He had laughed long and hard, enjoying what he thought was a young Callie's mishap turned into a funny, family anecdote. Paula smiled now thinking about it. It was a good episode.

Being an only child, Stephen was always ready to hear more about the sisters. Unfortunately, even if she wanted to, Paula couldn't have told him much about growing up with her sisters, especially Callie and Marlisa. The reason for that is simple—she didn't remember much about them. They were as invisible to her as two little ghosts running around the house. There was an age difference and Paula was a teenager doing teenager things when her sisters were still young kids, but that was not why she didn't know anything about her sisters. Paula knew nothing about her youngest sisters because she didn't want to know anything about Philip Elliot's daughters.

Sure, Philip Elliot took care of Paula and raised her as his own child while her real father, who lived only a few blocks away, did nothing. However, Paula knew she would never have the status of Callie and Marlisa because their father loved them and wanted them just because they were his. Paula never had that and never would. Her biological father died without so much as a good-bye, and no matter what Philip Elliot did for her, she would never be his blood.

Paula never admitted it to anyone and sometimes she even denied it to herself, but she wished that her real father had asked her to come to his hospital bed before he died. She wished that he had told her that he loved her and then had asked for her forgiveness for being an absentee father. Paula knew without a doubt she would have forgiven him right there on the spot, if only he had asked. But he hadn't, and all the love and kindness from Philip Elliot would never make up for the abandonment she felt whenever she thought about family. Callie and Marlisa wouldn't understand how she could never let herself love them unconditionally like sisters should. They would never understand it because there was a condition. For Paula to accept her younger half sisters, Philip Elliot couldn't be their real father either and that was technically impossible. As consolation for the truth, Paula did delight in making each of them *think* they weren't his child through her paternity scam. While her main intention was to get her hands on the inheritance, which could only be claimed by the biological daughters of Philip Elliot, deceiving Callie and Marlisa about their father was a satisfying bonus.

On the other hand, Paula did have a lot in common with her one true sister, Alise. They had the same father, although Alise didn't find that out until she was eighteen. Against their mother's wishes, Paula made sure she told Alise the truth about being the product of their mother's indecision on which man she wanted. For a while their mother chose both—Philip Elliot who became her new husband and Paula and Alise's father who became her ex-husband. Alise wore the pain from the truth like a true warrior and Paula had hoped that Alise's new knowledge would make them closer. It didn't. Even though Alise wasn't a blood Elliot, she still stayed loyal to them; Philip, Callie and even Marlisa. Sometimes the very thought of that made Paula want to scream.

If Alise wanted to try to be something that she wasn't, that wasn't Paula's problem and as far as she was concerned Alise had chosen sides. Callie and Marlisa were absolutely the biological daughters of the one man who raised them all. The DNA test they took last year proved it beyond a reasonable doubt. Too bad nobody but Alise knew she had tampered with the results and too bad for Alise that she had chosen the wrong side. Paula liked the good life her "inheritance" had given her and she was not ready to give it up. She had to protect herself and it was possible Stephen could help her do just that.

Although Stephen's cooperation was needed, Paula thought she had found a way to leverage her association with Stephen that might help her neutralize Alise. She knew she had to pick a tactic and one such tactic was to preempt Alise and go to Callie and Marlisa with all the awful details of her deceit herself. She could try to appeal to their sympathies with her story of feeling like the family outcast and try to make them feel her pain at being left out of the will. She would also have to tell them about blackmailing Alise, but then let them know it was just to get enough time to prove herself as a good business partner. She could then openly accuse Alise of being selfish by allowing the lie to stand at the cost of her sisters' pain. What could Alise do to counteract the truth? Nothing except tell her version of the truth, which would include the fact that Paula had tried the plan before, but Alise had refused to go along with it.

Paula thought a little bit more about what else the truth could bring out. Alise could give the kind of details about Paula's character that she had kept to herself all these years, like the heartless way Paula delivered the news about Alise's true paternity. Although that was a very long time ago, Alise's story would resonate with Callie and Marlisa. It would also be hard for Paula to explain using Alise's children in her blackmail scheme. Paula cringed a little when she realized what would happen when everyone found out how far Alise went to protect her kids so that she could finally reveal the truth to the younger sisters. She lied to her son and told him she wanted him to go into the military just to keep him out of Paula's grasp. Everybody knew Alise feared for her son in the military, but this would show that she feared Paula's actions more. As a result, Anthony was dead. Paula didn't think there would be any coming back for her from that. Callie and Marlisa would hate her right along with Alise. Stephen would probably hate her too and she certainly didn't want to make an enemy out of him. No, the truth would not be the way to go. What was she thinking? Telling the truth was never a solution. It was just an easy way out for those people who had no imagination.

Besides, Paula didn't need a truthful, family cleansing to wash away the emotional cobwebs, she needed something to surprise Alise with and then use it like a bat to beat her with. When all is said and done, there are only a few things that are of great importance to Alise: her children, her sister and her business. Since Paula had already used the first two as much as she could, it was time to move on to the last item on the short list - Alise's restaurant. It was a very successful business venture and Stephen, the man standing before her, was part owner.

Paula realized early on that Stephen was a very clever businessman, but she had since realized that he was very taken with Callie – no *in love* with Callie. Was it possible that a man in love would want to become more intertwined in business affairs with the object of his affection? Was it possible to get Stephen to trade stock with her? He would get shares of Callie's company and in exchange, Paula would become part owner of Alise's restaurant. Paula thought about the possibilities if she got her hands on a piece of Alise's dream. She just needed to throw enough grenades to distract all interested parties while manipulating emotions. She was sure she could make it happen. Paula knew no matter what Alise threatened, she would think carefully before taking a chance of damaging her restaurant and her primary source of income. Alise would also think twice before hurting Callie, another part owner, once again because of a vendetta. All Paula really needed was something to hold over Alise's head to stop her like when she threatened Alise's boys and like now, when Alise is concerned about Callie's reaction. Threatening Alise's livelihood, reputation, and dream is the next logical step.

Paula didn't realistically think she could permanently stop Alise.

However, since all she was really looking for was time, distracting Alise would suffice. Whatever Alise had planned for her, Paula knew it would be like a train—slow moving, but very damaging. Paula figured she could side-step whatever was coming her way and come out unscathed as long as she had the right preparations. With more time she could get one last big payday from Marlisa, sell all her stock in both businesses to some unsuspecting investor and take off. She really didn't need her sisters. She was living proof that family was overrated.

However, she didn't want money to be an issue when she left this time. She didn't want to move from place to place trying to figure out a way to make the kind of money she deserved. Paula just wanted to live out the rest of her days as a very rich woman. If the numbers swirling in her head were correct, when she was done, she would have more than enough money to do anything she wanted without working another day in her life. Unfortunately, if she sold now, she would have a finite number in her bank account, which was not to her liking, and no new income coming from dividends. Her funds would be depleted sooner rather than later, unless she took a step down to living in the upper middle class. Paula had no intentions of living comfortably on a budget. *Absolutely not.* She deserved more.

She looked over at Stephen who apparently was expecting another Callie family story. Paula had been prepared to use the *Good Times* episode that she had recently seen on TVLand, the cable channel that only showed old sitcoms. However, time was really running short for her so Stephen would have to get his "Callie fix" at another time. Instead, Paula decided to test the waters on her new idea.

"You know Stephen, I've been thinking. You have helped me so much in so many different ways. You've always made me feel like I had a friend in this town and you've gone above and beyond for me from a business perspective. Don't you want to get credit for that?"

"I'm not sure what you mean."

"I mean that thanks to your business expertise, I didn't fall flat on my face. And not only that, your ideas actually helped Callie. Callie is always interested in my viewpoint now," Paula lied, "but we both know that I'm getting credit for simply repeating your advice. I don't think that's fair."

"I don't need any credit. I get plenty of pats of the back already. When you have money and a little power, people, even people that you don't know, line up to tell you how great you are. They don't even bother to find out if it's true or not."

"Well, in this case it's true and in this case it's not "people" it's me and Alise and especially Callie. I feel like a fraud when she gets all enthusiastic about what are really your ideas."

Paula gave him her sincere, modest look. She had practiced it for years and had it down to a science. The tilt of the head, emotional look in her eyes, tiny smile right before she looks away embarrassed. She knew it would work on Stephen just like it worked on everyone else that didn't know the real Paula. If he had known anything about her and her situation, he would know that Callie was never enthusiastic about Paula's ideas. Not because they were so terrible, but because Callie made it a point not to listen. Paula was not allowed to ever discuss new directions or ideas for the company directly with Callie. All business communication from Paula was to be put in writing and emailed to Callie's assistant or else Callie would automatically disregard it. As far as Paula knew, none of her direct requests have made it past Callie's email spam folder.

"Hey, I have a thought," Paula said brightening, "why don't you come into business with us? I could sell you some of my shares!"

"Oh no, I couldn't do that. That company is part of your inheritance and you've done a lot of work to prove you belong there."

Paula smiled broadly at Stephen. That was just what she hoped he would say. While Stephen didn't know her complete story, Paula didn't really know his complete story, either. Although, from the things he said, she believed he had some real issues surrounding the money and business he had inherited from his father. Paula tried to get him to talk about it once, but he shut up so fast that she just left it alone. Of course, she didn't mind his not talking since she wasn't interested in hearing him ramble on about his feelings. Everybody has problems and Paula didn't need another invite to a pity party if he was going to take it there. Besides, that night she needed to concentrate on other things, like how to get his pants off. Paula now looked at Stephen pretending to contemplate the situation.

"I know!" she said suddenly, "how about we trade owner stock? I'll give you some of Callie's company and you give me some of Alise's! That way we keep everything in the family. The inheritance stays intact and you get to go into business with Callie and help her directly. How about that?"

"I don't think so."

"Why not?"

"Because we can't just trade stock like Christmas cards."

"How come?"

"Because there are details to consider, Paula. Details that I don't want to have to deal with. Besides I would have to discuss it with Callie and Alise and I don't see any reason to make drastic changes in either one of their lives right now."

"They don't have to know now. It could be our surprise."

Stephen laughed. "You are persistent, I'll give you that. Thanks, but no thanks. I was already a surprise business partner once with Callie and I certainly don't want to do it again."

"What if I ran it by Callie first? I can confess to getting your help and see how she wants to handle it, ok? It that fair?"

Stephen didn't answer. Instead he waved Eddie over and paid both their tabs.

"Are you thinking about it?" Paula asked quietly.

Stephen gave a tiny smile, drained his drink and then sat the empty glass on the bar. "Bye, Paula," he said and without looking up, he began walking towards the exit.

"Stephen!" He stopped, but he didn't turn around.

"Will you at least think about it? Please?" Paula pleaded to his back. Stephen turned his head to the side showing Paula his beautiful profile. He hesitated so long, that the anticipation made her hold her breath.

"Thanks, but no thanks, Mrs. Robinson."

Paula watched as he exited the bar and made an immediate left towards the lobby elevators. As she let herself breathe again, she realized how panicked she now was about her situation. She had no game plan and she was feeling squeezed by both Marlisa and Alise. She motioned for Eddie to refill her glass and then looked up at the movie on the screen behind him. *The Graduate* was still on.

"Mrs. Robinson, my ass," Paula snapped, feeling angry about Stephen turning her down. But then she suddenly realized that she was more irritated with herself than with Stephen. She looked down at her drink and frowned. Sometime while living in the lap of luxury, she had let herself get soft. Marlisa was manhandling her, and Alise could already be working on how to make her life difficult. How did she lose control?

Her only plan of action now or until she thought of something better was to avoid Alise completely. After all, months have gone by in the last year when she didn't see or hear from Alise at all. Grief could do powerful things to a person. It changes people in unexpected ways, and Alise may just want to be left alone for a while. She could be in such a state of anguish that she won't even want to leave the house, let alone worry about sister problems.

Paula rolled her tense shoulder as she again thought about her missed spa appointment. She just needed to relax a little. Maybe she was just worrying too much too soon. Paula decided that a simple but effective way for her to live to fight another day was to quickly get the goods for Marlisa, cash in on it and then just walk, no *run* away. In the meantime, she would have to stay out of Alise's way—at all cost. She could do that, and in the long run, it would still be a victory for her. Paula nodded her head feeling better and let herself smile a little.

Sometimes simple plans are the best plans.

Downing her drink in one gulp she slammed the empty glass on the bar, threw a fifty dollar bill next to it and got up. She started walking towards the exit to follow Stephen to the elevators when she felt the familiar vibration of her cell phone. Taking it out of her purse to check the text message she stopped immediately in her tracks. The message was simple:

*Come now.*
*Alise*

## Chapter 10

Marlisa bit her lip as she stood just inside her office door watching for movement from Callie's office. It had taken six of those expensive bars of Callie's favorite soaps wrapped in toilet paper to effectively stop up her private bathroom's toilet. Marlisa had first thought of using one of Callie's hand towels, but when the plumber got to the root of the problem Callie would know without a doubt it was sabotage. At least with the biodegradable soap and toilet paper, willful interference might be harder to prove. Marlisa needed something to force Callie out of her office so that Paula, who was waiting in the stairwell, could quickly slip in and download the spyware to Callie's cell phone. Of course, that's presuming that Callie doesn't take her phone to the rest room with her. Marlisa didn't think so, but she might take her purse, and if the phone was still in the purse, then they were screwed. Callie usually set her phone out on the desk to keep it handy, but nothing had seemed normal around the office for the last few days. For some reason, everybody was acting like they were under the curse of the full moon.

Marlisa could excuse Alise, who came in a couple of days ago looking for Franklin, the lawyer. She was demanding to see a copy of their partnership agreement and raised holy hell with the poor receptionist in legal when the agreement couldn't be located. The only thing that calmed Alise down was finding out Franklin was out of town because of a death in the family. Then she had left as suddenly as she came. Marlisa had calling her later and she knew that Callie had called as well, but all phone calls had gone to her voicemail.

Then as Callie was about to leave to check on her, Stephen had made one of his rare appearances to the office. Marlisa had expected they would talk in Callie's office where she hoped to get another recording of a personal conversation, but Callie refused to even see him. Marlisa shook her head now remembering Stephen banging on the door asking for Callie to give him a few minutes. She never opened the door, he left angry and Callie has practically lived in her office since then. Now it seemed like it was going to take a stick of dynamite to get her out, but the office is the only place Paula can get to Callie's phone. So while food has been delivered to her, meetings have been moved to her office or done by conference call, a trip to the bathroom was the only thing Marlisa could think of that would force Callie out of her sanctuary. However, first she had to disable the toilet in Callie's personal bathroom and then get her assistant away from her desk.

Marlisa had come in before dawn to get to Callie's bathroom without being seen, but it was only sheer luck that she wasn't caught in the act of stuffing the toilet. Although she knew Callie was always in the office early, Marlisa had no idea that Callie started her day even before the sun did. As Marlisa was finishing her task, she heard the elevator and had to run and hide in her own office. Everyone knew she never sauntered in before ten in the morning and being seen by anyone, especially Callie would have been a red flag that something was going on. So as not to raise anyone's suspicion, Marlisa couldn't be seen coming or going until late morning. She ended up lying quietly in the dark of her own office for hours on the most uncomfortable couch ever made. She rubbed her back now and looked at the Swedish designer sofa that she had tried to nap on earlier. It looked great, but Marlisa only realized now that she had never actually sat on it. As a matter of fact, no one has probably ever sat on it and certainly no one has ever slept on it. It was for show like everything else in their office. All the real work occurred at the end of the hall at Callie's desk.

Marlisa sighed loudly and peeked out of her door again. If they couldn't get Callie the Camel out of the office or if she takes the phone with her when she goes, they would have a large plumbing bill for nothing. The plumber was working on things right now. Marlisa gasped at a sudden thought—suppose the plumber finishes before Callie needs to go? Then Callie would have a working toilet and no reason to leave the privacy of her office. Marlisa walked back to her desk and wearily plopped down in her chair. If the timing isn't right, they would have to make a new plan and she was not up to having to deal with Paula any more than she had to at this point.

Paula had been in a fouler than normal mood for the last two days and it didn't help matters that the two of them shared an office. All Paula had done under her full moon spell was mumble about how she was now forced to deal with some "undesirable pain in the ass" who had summoned her like she was a queen. She had told Marlisa she had put off talking with that crazy "client" for as long as possible, but unfortunately, she had to attend a meeting this afternoon. Marlisa didn't ask questions because she really didn't care. If Paula was doing any business, it wasn't on behalf of the company. Callie would never have allowed that to happen. So it was probably some underhanded stuff that finally caught up with her and she now has to face the music. It was probably the wife of a man she had slept with or something along those lines. It didn't matter to Marlisa as long as Paula's "business" problems stayed Paula's problems. Marlisa didn't even want to know about it unless it interfered with her own agenda.

Besides, she had enough to deal with coming into the office just to be pushed around by Callie. Marlisa had to admit that putting up with

Callie and putting up with Paula were two different things. Callie was important to the business and had always been in Marlisa's life. Paula had no real value to Marlisa for business or personal reasons, so Paula's happiness or complaining held no value either. As if on cue Marlisa's cell phone buzzed. It was Paula.

"Good holy hell! What is the problem?"

"She hasn't come out yet. I told you I would text you when she did."

"I can't believe you have me waiting in this dark, dingy stairwell afraid that a rat will come out at any moment and challenge me for a cracker!"

"First of all, there are no rats in this building. As a matter of fact, there are no rats even on this street. And –"

"You don't know that!"

"– *and* the stairwell –"

"You cannot possibly know the rat count in this city!"

"– is clean and well lit. I do know that so just have a little patience, please."

"Easy for you to say in a nice, cushy, expensive office while I stand here having to deal with the dirty underground of the inner city!"

Paula hung up and Marlisa smiled at her sister's hysteria. Paula's real problem was that she hated being in a position where she had to take orders. Marlisa had no doubt that forcing Paula to do this at all was at the root of her ridiculous complaints. She seemed to be cracking under the pressure and Marlisa wasn't foolish enough to think Paula wouldn't give it all back to her seven fold when the time came. At this point, all she needed was Paula's cooperation for a little while longer. Once Paula helped her get Callie and Michael where she needed them, Marlisa would take care of the rest. Then she planned on ducking for cover.

Marlisa was the youngest, but she knew without a doubt that Paula was a street fighter. However, most of her information on Paula's character wasn't from firsthand experience as her sister. She was too young when Paula left for the first time to have that kind of insight. All she knew from a sister's perspective is that Paula was mean and never shared her snacks with the rest of them. Most of what Marlisa learned about her oldest sister came from the summaries her private investigator wrote for her.

Marlisa had hired him last year to do a little digging into Paula's past after she had accidently come across Paula's North Carolina church scam. It was information about that church scam that gave Marlisa leverage to blackmail Paula now. Although, from her P.I summaries, Marlisa didn't think the "blackmail well" would ever run completely dry. Thankfully, Marlisa wasn't foolish enough to think Paula would allow herself to be blackmailed forever, either. Paula was sure to strike back before then and unlike Alise, Marlisa didn't want to stand and fight her on principle. The whole "duck and cover" thing would work just fine once she and Michael were together.

Right now though, she still needed help to bug Callie's phone and get a good recording so that she could reveal proof of Callie's infidelity, real or engineered, to Michael. Even though she may not even need any additional recordings, Marlisa was more interested in hearing private conversations between Michael and Callie. She might get some insight into how close they were to reconciling or splitting up for good. If they were close to getting back together, Marlisa would need to hurry her plan along. However, if they were close to a break up, Marlisa could toy with the timing of her delivery for the best possible effect. At any rate, the first step was still to get Paula access to Callie's phone. Marlisa's cell phone buzzed again.

"What now, Paula?"

"*What now?* I know you are not trying to talk to me like that! I am tired of being banished! Where is Callie?"

"She's still in her office."

"How do you know? Did you see her go in there? As far as I know I could be waiting here in this God forsaken tunnel for her to come out of her office and she's at the salon getting her toenails polished."

"Paula, I saw her go in myself."

"Go check!"

"She's there."

"Go check! And if you don't go check, I will!"

"Ok, ok. Hold on."

"Marlisa put the cell phone on mute and rolled her eyes. Then she leaned back in her chair thinking more about her sisters. Except for her relationship with Stephen, Callie was basically an open book. However, Paula and Alise and their interactions were a different story. While Marlisa couldn't wait to be done with Paula in the short term, she thought it was different for Alise. Whatever was going on between those two probably involved some sort of scam that's come back to haunt them both. Did something happen while they were all growing up? Marlisa knew just because she or Callie didn't remember, doesn't mean a young Alise wasn't party to something she now regrets.

Marlisa didn't think Alise would purposely work with Paula on some back alley deal, but it was evident that neither one of them wanted to rock the boat too much now. If it was big enough, Paula wasn't above blackmailing Alise and Marlisa didn't think Alise would be above blackmailing Paula if she had leverage. Marlisa giggled as she listened to Paula's exasperated sighing. Apparently, the ability to blackmail ran in the family. She took the phone off mute to give Paula an "update."

"It won't be long now. She's had two coffees and her fridge is full of bottled water, which she goes through pretty quickly."

"It better not be too much longer or this is over!"

Marlisa wanted to say something rude to her impatient sister, but thought better of it. No need to get Paula more worked up. However her rude comment would have been lost anyway since just before Paula hung up, she held down a button on her cell phone to get a loud piercing tone. Marlisa jumped at the earsplitting sound in her ear and cursed Paula under her breath. Then she got up to take another peek down the hall.

Even though she remained calm and confident with Paula, Marlisa was extremely anxious. She knew that getting Callie out of the office was relatively easy compared to what she had to do next. By far, Marlisa's bigger challenge was getting the attention of Kellog, Callie's assistant, so that Paula could get in and out of the office unseen. This task of cooperation would prove to be difficult because Kellog didn't like Marlisa and unfortunately, Marlisa antagonized Kellog by never calling her Kelly like everybody else. It was just that Marlisa could not believe that a mother could actually name her child after the company that made her favorite childhood cereal. So, Marlisa never failed to let anyone forget it. And then there was the other thing that happened after Kellog's interview with Marvin, Callie's right hand man.

*"Marlisa," Marvin said stepping into her office wearing a fake smile. He was Callie's personal assistant and Marlisa knew he couldn't stand her because of her role in Michael and Callie's break up. However, Marlisa suspected he never liked her to begin with, which was fine by her.*

*"Yes, Marvin," Marlisa responded without looking up from the documents on her desk.*

*"I have an applicant that I want to hire as Callie's new assistant. Since I got promoted and Callie is...well, not here, I need help around here. Callie's already approved it, but she's not here to sign the official paperwork for HR."*

*"Well, if Callie's not here, why does she need an assistant?"*

*"To help me out and—"*

*"So it's your assistant then."*

*"No, it's for when Callie comes back. She'll have someone already up to speed, plus we could use the extra help on the executive level right now."*

*"Marvin," Marlisa said leaning back in her leather office chair and finally making eye contact, "you are not an executive."*

*"Callie promoted me."*

"Because she felt sorry for you, and now you want to pay it forward by hiring somebody that has no business working here."

"She already works here, Marlisa."

"Oh, she does?"

"Yeah, usually with the local underground artists, booking them in the studio, helping with their marketing materials and things like that."

"Hmm, so that's why she's dressed all ghetto looking?"

Marvin sighed loudly. "Can you just sign this approval please?"

Marlisa got up from her desk and took the document out of Marvin's hand. She looked from the job application to Marvin, who watched her tightlipped with his arms folded across his chest.

"Her name is Kellog? Like the cereal, but misspelled? That's some hood stuff, right there. What's her middle name, Pepsi?"

"We call her Kelly, Marlisa," he replied, barely parting his lips to speak.

Marlisa stood in her open doorway and stared at Kelly sitting in the reception area across from Marlisa's secretary. Then after a moment or two, she walked back to her desk for a pen.

"I guess, I can sign it, but I'm not thrilled. Does she speak English well?"

Marvin frowned. "What? Is this a joke?"

"No and I'm not trying to be funny, Marvin. But anybody with four and a half inch heels, extra long fingernails painted with zebra stripes, wearing black lip liner and what looks like a petrified ostrich coat on a job interview, needs her English speaking skills questioned. We deal with professional people up here, not underground artists. So, tell me, Marvin, just how ghetto is Rice Krispies out there? Do we need subtitles when she speaks?"

Marvin moved quickly to shut the office door. "You don't have to insult her, Marlisa!" he yelled. "I wouldn't be trying to hire her for a job that she couldn't do or place somebody here that would not be in Callie's best interest!"

*"But Callie's not here is she!" Marlisa yelled back.*

*She pushed all the documents off of her desk in one quick maneuver. Callie had left her to take care of everything and that only magnified how little she knew. She wanted to cry most of the time because she was so far in over her head. She didn't know anything, and if it wasn't for Marvin, everything would have fallen apart the moment Callie stopped coming into the office. No one had any idea when Callie would come back, either. She was heartbroken over discovering her husband in bed with her sister. Being that she was the sister, Marlisa knew she had no right to complain and would not get any sympathy from anyone, least of all Marvin.*

*She stood breathing heavily after her outburst and looking at Marvin who appeared angry enough to spit nails. She couldn't afford to alienate him any more than she already had. She needed him too much and she had no idea what she would do if he walked out on her, too.*

*Calmly she looked around and found the human resource document in the pile of papers that she had strewn across her office. Without another word, she signed it and handed it to Marvin, who had then snatched the document and strode powerfully out of the room. He had flung the door open so hard that when it banged against the door stop, the force of it knocked down a picture from her wall. As Marlisa stood watching him stomp down the hallway, suddenly Kelly came into her line of vision in the open doorway. She stared at Marlisa just long enough to make Marlisa wonder if she had heard the conversation and knew what Marlisa had said about her. Marlisa didn't have to wonder for long. Kelly had definitely heard.*

Until the new partnership agreement, Marlisa had never thought too much about the staff. Unfortunately, with the new directives Callie had given out to all the employees, Marlisa now understood the price she had to pay for her dismissive treatment of them. After Callie gained complete control of the company, she told their employees that unless it was an emergency, Marlisa or Paula held no authority over them. They were owners in name only and Marlisa had no problem with that since she never made business decisions even when it was just her and Callie. However, the employees had always respected her position, but Callie had snatched that away from her. Now the employees could "go over her head" by going to Kellog, because as Callie's assistant, she was given more power than both Marlisa and Paula. It was a simple and effective way to make Marlisa's life miserable in the office and Kellog, who despised her, took special pleasure in complying with Callie's official policy.

Marlisa could only hope that after everything was settled with Michael, things would go back to normal. Callie would then come to her senses and welcome Marlisa back into her life again. She would reinstate Marlisa's authority in the office and they would heal as a family. Marlisa loved her sister. She hated hurting her, and she remained hopeful that the two of them would become close again. Callie just needed to understand that what happened between them was necessary in order to put things right for everyone.

Marlisa firmly believed that Callie knew Michael married the wrong sister, but again it all came down to timing. Michael didn't read the letter she wrote confessing her love for him before he ran off to meet Callie on the night that he proposed. If he had known how much she loved him then he would have never chosen Callie as his wife over her. Marlisa knew if she had delivered her letter even an hour earlier, it would have changed his mind. But she hadn't delivered it earlier and by the time he got it, if he got it at all, it was already too late. It all came down to timing. Precision timing. Narrowing her eyes, Marlisa watched Callie's office door with renewed concentration. She couldn't afford to get the timing wrong again. Her future with Michael and her renewed relationship with her sister may very well depend on it. As if she willed it to happen, Callie's door suddenly opened. Marlisa ran to her desk and buzzed Kellog.

"Uh, holla at me up in dis bitch," Kellog answered. She made it a habit of speaking to Marlisa in what she called "Eng-ghetto-lish." Marlisa had expected her to be ghetto, so Kellog made sure Marlisa wasn't disappointed.

"I don't have time for this. Listen –"

"I ain't gots to listen or do nuffin for you."

Marlisa was normally irritated with Kellog's performances, mostly because she liked to milk all of their conversations way too long. It was clear that she enjoyed messing with Marlisa, and while Marlisa could dish it out as well as she could take it, she had no time for all of that today. She made sure to get right to the point by getting Kellog's attention.

"Listen, Apple Jacks, I don't have time for your games today," Marlisa said speaking quickly and firmly. "I have a package for Callie marked "urgent and confidential." It's already been sitting in my office for a whole day. You can either come and get it or explain to Callie why you left it here to rot after being told about it. Be down here in fifteen seconds or it goes down the trash chute."

"You wouldn't dare," Kellog snapped.

She now spoke with her normal diction that was so perfect she could have taught English at an English boarding school. Marlisa had been wrong about her. She had a BA in communications and had received a study abroad scholarship that allowed her to spend a year in France. Kellog championed a freedom of expression attitude which caused Marlisa to misjudge "a book by its cover."

However, Callie did have to alert Kellog to the fact that as her assistant, she would be dealing with people who were not all connected to the music industry or shared her expressive spirit. She explained that Kellog was sitting with her at the very tip of a large financial umbrella and even though some business holdings were separated for legal reasons, at some point everything came through her office door. So while Callie believed Kellog to be quite capable, she also told her new assistant that her appearance needed to lean more upscale and conservative. She even sent Kellog out for a very expensive beauty and shopping day as a bonus for her accepting the job. Marlisa knew Kellog, who loved and respected Callie, would never want to disappoint her by losing an important package.

"Just bring the package down here, Marlisa," Kellog said nervously.

"Your fifteen seconds are up. I'm dropping it down the big trash chute."

Marlisa hung up and grabbed the "important" package from her desk. In order to lure Kellog from her desk located right outside of Callie's office, Marlisa had created a very effective prop. She had filled a large document box with blank copy paper, marked it "Urgent and Confidential" and then express mailed it overnight to herself. The fake package had all the post marks and delivery stamps required to make sure Kellog didn't question its authenticity, even close up.

Standing at her office door, Marlisa saw Kellog rushing down the hallway towards her. She quickly pressed "send" on her cell phone to launch her pre-typed text message to Paula and then she tossed her phone onto the torturous couch. By that time Marlisa saw that Kellog had almost closed the gap between them. Hurriedly turning right from her office door down another hallway, Marlisa could feel the nearness of Kellog, who was now jogging. She looked over her shoulder just as Kellog reached for her arm. Squealing in surprise, Marlisa start running into a full out sprint with Kellog matching her speed.

The trash chute was at the very end of the hallway and even though she was running fast, Marlisa knew Kellog might catch her before she had a chance to actually open the door of the chute wide enough to shove the package in. She wished she had had the forethought of kicking off her high heel shoes first, but even as her toes scrunched down in pain she pushed herself to go faster. With only moments to spare, Marlisa reached the trash chute and had managed to open its door when Kellog grabbed her arm and knock the package loose. They both immediately dove for the box that had slid quite a distance back down the hallway. Kellog reached it first and grabbed it, but after

Marlisa used one of her heels to jab Kellog's hand, she released it.

Happy to have kept her shoes on now, Marlisa managed to wrestle the package completely away from Kellog.

As Marlisa struggled to run back to the chute, Kellog, who had fallen to her knees, held on to the hem of Marlisa skirt effectively stopping her progress. In an attempt to wrench herself free, Marlisa was simultaneously leaning forward trying to drag Kellog and reaching behind her to hit Kellog over her head with the cardboard box. Letting go of her skirt, Kellog used both hands to grab the package that had just been slapped across her face, but Marlisa quickly snatched it away. Now in a full out run, she reached the chute and was able to stuff the package down its open door. Marlisa turned back to Kellog and the two women, now disheveled and breathing heavily, looked at each other for only a moment before they both reacted.

Kellog suddenly turned to run into the stairwell just as Marlisa cupped her hands around her mouth and gleefully shouted, "Run, Frosted Flakes, *ruuun!*"

"It's burning now!" she added just as the exit door leading to the stairs closed.

However, Marlisa actually had no idea if they even had an incinerator in the building or if it was operational. Maybe not, but if the package did burn, Kellog would be in agony trying to explain what happened to Callie. If it didn't, at the very least, Kellog would be dumpster diving for a fake important package. Either way, Marlisa counted it as a happy ending. She couldn't wait to see the look on Kellog's face when she realized she had been tricked.

Marlisa smiled now just thinking about it. Then suddenly remembering the task at hand, she ran back down the hallway just in time to see Callie going back into her office. Marlisa gasped and waited holding her breath. If Paula was still in there, they were probably having it out right now. Marlisa backed into her office still watching Callie's door expecting fireworks, but none came. Paula was an accomplished liar, so it is entirely possible that she was calmly

126

lying her way out of everything. Of course, Paula always employed a "save myself first" tactic, so she could also be selling Marlisa out in the process. Marlisa took a deep breath and, turning wearily towards her desk, she made eye contact with Paula.

"So…"

"You can now monitor Callie live, listen to her calls and read all texts to and from her cell phone," Paula responded calmly from Marlisa's desk where she was sitting with her legs crossed. Then she got up and walked up so close to Marlisa that if felt like the hairs on their arms were touching. "It's done, and so are we."

"We're done when I say we're done," Marlisa replied with as much steely resolve as she could muster. Paula leaned closer, taking up space that Marlisa didn't even know existed, before whispering in her ear.

"We… are…done," Paula spat, enunciating each word carefully.

Marlisa felt a chill go up her spine, but she refused to balk. It was important to stand her ground with Paula until she got the recording she needed. She met Paula's gaze and then watched as Paula walked slowly out of the office. As soon as Paula made it to the elevators, Marlisa dropped the act and rushed over to close the door. Then she ran to the other side of her desk, collapsed in the chair and placed her hand on her chest hoping to calm the rapid thumping of her heart.

It had been a very long and stressful day so far and for some reason all of her sisters seemed a little out of sorts. It was like they were all masquerading as someone else. Marlisa wondered for a moment about the validity of astrological movements being responsible for strange and inexplicable human behavior. Does a full moon really affect people? If it did, Paula's full moon curse had turned her into Hannibal Lector, the horror character known for eating the internal organs of his victims. Marlisa still had to deal with Paula, so she didn't like the change. She closed her eyes and focused on calming her heartbeat. She didn't like it -not one little bit.

*Chapter 11*

Callie paced her office, unable to think about anything but her disagreement with Stephen. She had never seen him so angry with her. At a certain point it seemed like every word coming out of her mouth scorched him like fire. He had looked at her in a way that she would never forget. That's one reason she couldn't speak to him when he followed her back to her office. She didn't want to look into his eyes again because it hurt her to see how much she had hurt him. Although she thought that he deserved to have a conversation with her in order to have his say, she had refused to open her office door. She first needed to prepare herself to face him again.

Unfortunately, now that she was ready, Stephen was nowhere to be found. He just got on his private jet and left without a word to anyone except those who needed to know his flight plan. Even his secretary wasn't sure where he was and the board members of his company were giving her fits. Apparently he had left in the middle of some negotiations and was desperately needed, but he wasn't answering any of his phones. Now, after two days, the voicemail boxes were full. Callie could no longer leave him a message, but she doubted that she would be high up on his list of calls to return anyway. Besides, the other messages she left him, numbering in the double digits should let him know that she desperately wanted to speak with him. She needed to get the last things they said to each other out of her head.

"All done, Mrs. Armstrong."

Callie startled and turned quickly to face the plumber.

"Sorry, didn't mean to scare you."

"That's alright. Doesn't take much nowadays. Did you find out what the problem was?"

"Uh, yeah, but....I snaked it out so I can't be completely sure, but it does look like it was purposely stopped up."

"But nobody uses that bathroom except me."

"Maybe the cleaning people? I've seen it happen before. They accidently drop something in there while cleaning and don't realize it until after they flush. Sometimes they even bring their kids in with them and, you know kids. They drop toys and stuff in, just playing, you know? But nothing gets reported 'cause the kids shouldn't be there in the first place. Like I said, I don't know for sure—-could be a few things."

"Hmmm," Callie said pensively. "I've never had a problem like this before, but I don't want to have it again. I'll check to see if there's any new cleaning staff or any other issues like this in the building. I own all the real estate on this block, so if there are issues, I want to get a jump on fixing it."

"Good idea, Mrs. Armstrong. If you need me for anything else, just let me know."

Callie smiled and nodded at the plumber as he waved and walked out of the office. She knew that he would leave the bill and pass along the information he had just given her to the office manager. However, Callie wanted to follow up on things herself. She didn't want to be surprised with any plumbing issues in the buildings. Whether it was human error or something actually going on within the pipes, the sooner she knew the better.

Walking briskly out of her office, Callie stood with her hands on her hips baffled. Where in the world was Kelly? She was extremely surprised not to know where she was because Kelly always kept her informed. Callie never had to guess where she was or what she was doing, but besides that, Kelly was always there when she needed her. She looked at her watch and shrugged her shoulders. Kelly was probably at lunch, which was where Callie just decided she should be, too. A girl's got to eat. She would just send Kelly a quick email to ask her to begin checking into the plumbing issue as soon as possible.

Callie sat down at her desk and yawned. Maybe she would take the rest of the day off. She had come in before dawn, got a lot of things done and wasn't sure if she would be able to concentrate for too much longer anyway.

Opening up her email, Callie quickly typed up an email to Kelly and pressed send. She was about to grab her cell phone off the desk, when it began to vibrate. Callie's hand froze over the phone as she contemplated answering it. It was Michael and she hadn't spoken with him for anything more than a "kid check" since she saw he was in contact with Raylene. She had been putting him off, but now she realized it was time.

"Hi, what's up?"

"Finally! Have you been hiding from me? Or shall I rephrase that to, why have you been hiding from me?"

"I haven't been hiding, Michael. Just busy."

"Too busy for lunch?"

"Um…no. Not too busy for lunch. When and where?"

"Now and my place."

"Your place?"

"Yeah, I think we need a little privacy, just in case you order my special dessert"

Callie couldn't help but chuckle.

"I love to hear you laugh," Michael said with such a sincere tone that Callie's smile froze on her face. She missed him.

"Well, I hope to laugh a lot more with you," Callie responded, smiling gently. "I hope lunch and dessert will be worth the trip. I'm hungry and…I had planned on taking the rest of the afternoon off."

"Oh, don't you tease me, girl."

"I'm not teasing. I miss you, but…"

"But?"

"I do have one thing I think we need to talk about. Just to clear the air."

"Ok, what?"

"Not over the phone. We can talk after lunch."

"Deal."

"But before dessert."

"Oh, it's one of *those* conversations," Michael said groaning.

Callie laughed. "What's one of *those* conversations?"

"It's the kind of conversation that may mean there is no dessert. It just depends on how mad you get. So now I'm redoing the menu so that we have dessert first."

"How mad *I* get?" Callie asked smiling. "What about you?"

"Doesn't matter how mad I get. Like most men, I always save room for dessert."

"I'm thinking this dessert for sex metaphor needs to be retired," Callie replied laughing. "So what time should I be there? Oh, wait a minute, are you cooking? I need to know if I should stop and eat something before I get there."

"Cooking jokes, really?"

Callie giggled as Michael gave her the speech about his training as a chef at a five star restaurant.

"Michael, you were ten years old on a field trip and you helped make scrambled eggs. Get over yourself, please."

"Hey, I still learned from the best, so you should feel honored."

"Ok, I'm honored. What time, Chef Michael?"

"As soon as you get here. I'm ordering take out."

They both laughed and said their good-byes. Callie hung up, grabbed her purse and opened her office door to what she could only describe as "a scene." Marlisa was standing in the middle of the hall directly in front of her office door. She was shoeless and breathing as if she had just run from her office. She had a large noticeable hole in her stockings and a button missing from the middle of her blouse, exposing part of her stomach. Her normally perfectly styled hair was wildly tousled and the distressed look on her face troubled Callie. Staring at Callie, Marlisa looked as if she was willing herself not to cry.

However, Marlisa was not alone in the hallway watching Callie. Just to Marlisa's left, Callie's assistant stood staring silently at Callie too. While Kelly was wearing both of her shoes, her left heel was broken and she compensated by tilting to her right. The pockets of her dress pants were ripped and she was wearing only one hoop earring. Her hair was decorated with round, white confetti that looked to be the remnants from a manual 3-hole punch and her blouse was only partially tucked into her pants. Callie was speechless as she looked from one to the other. Then finding her voice in the silence, she finally asked the two of them a question.

"Do you guys have something to tell me?" They both remained silent. "Well?" Callie said gently.

"Um," Marlisa began with a shaky voice, "Have a good lunch with…uh, whoever you're having lunch with, but don't be too long."

"Yeah, and uh," Kelly said limping forward, "I got your mail." She handed Callie a damaged document box marked "urgent and confidential." Callie took the box and looked at Kelly and then at Marlisa, whom she addressed first.

"Well, Marlisa," Callie began, "I don't know how you knew I was going to lunch since I normally eat at my desk, but…"

"Oh, I just guessed. It was…a good guess… I guess," Marlisa said nervously.

"Ok, well, thank you for the well wishes," Callie said, even more puzzled by her sister's behavior. Turning to Kelly, Callie looked at the box and added, "And thank you for the mail, but it's not mine. It's addressed to Marlisa."

She handed the beat up box to Marlisa and eyed the two disheveled ladies who now stood glaring at each other. Kelly was scowling, but Marlisa had a tiny smile. Callie shook her head as she walked past them both. Must be a full moon.

*Chapter 12*

Callie grinned broadly at Michael standing just inside his doorway, waving her inside. "You've got to be kidding me. I'm not going to ask why you even still have that."

"Every now and then I like to relive some good memories."

Michael had opened the door wearing the chef hat that was given to him on his school field trip when he was a kid. He had squeezed it on his less-than-kid sized head, and with the tight fit it looked as if his circulation was compromised.

"You know if you faint because you cut off the oxygen to your brain, I'm not going to the hospital with you," Callie said stepping into the foyer. "Even though riding in a speeding ambulance with the siren going is tempting, they're going to want me to fill out the paperwork and I'm just not in the mood for any of that today."

"So you would leave me alone with strangers?" Michael asked. He had closed the front door and was now walking towards his kitchen. Callie followed.

"Helpful strangers, yes. Like the EMT's, doctors, nurses. But I'm prepared to tell anyone who asks that I'm just a Good Samaritan who was out for a walk and helped a man I saw lying flat on his face in the yard …in his underwear."

Michael laughed and took off the hat. He raised and lowered his eyebrows in quick succession. Callie laughed realizing he was trying to stimulate his blood circulation, but he still looked silly to her.

"You look pretty goofy, you know."

"Thanks," he responded as he tossed the hat on to one of the kitchen chairs. "But why would you tell everyone you found me in my underwear outside, when they'll be able to see I'm fully clothed and indoors?" Michael looked down at himself as if to emphasize the point.

"Because if you pass out for ridiculous reasons, like drinking too much or purposely cutting off circulation to your brain, then you leave yourself at the mercy of the friends who find you. And I plan on pulling your pants down, dragging your behind to the door and rolling you outside. That's the "mercy of your friends rule" and I don't know when I'll have another chance to enforce it on you."

"Well, if that's the rule," Michael said shrugging his shoulders, "then there's nothing I can do about it. Wine?" He had grabbed a large mixing bowl and handed it to Callie. Then he took out a bottle of wine from his wine fridge. "You can drink straight from your bowl or directly from the bottle. Don't worry about passing out drunk, you're amongst friends."

"Oh, please," Callie said pushing the bowl away and grabbing the bottle. "It takes a lot more than one bottle of wine to do the trick. You better have a case in there. Plus I'm pretty sure, "Mr. I Hardly Drink," that you'll be down for the count way before me. During our initial break up, I practically turned into a professional."

"Oh, I forgot how you Elliot sisters are drinkers."

"We are not!" Callie said laughing, "but we do have our moments—especially when times are hard."

Callie sighed deeply thinking about Alise. As if reading her thoughts, Michael walked over to her and put his arms around her.

"How is Alise?"

"As well as could be expected. I think I'll go over there a little later to see if she needs anything."

"Good idea. What about you? What do you need?"

"Just you," Callie said smiling. She had made a decision about the two of them and she hoped nothing would happen to change her mind after their talk today. She could be happy without being so selfish. She still loved him and because of that, she believed he deserved her full attention. Leaning in she kissed Michael passionately as he brought her into his arms.

"Mmmm, maybe we *are* going to have dessert first," he whispered and smiled. Callie responded by kissing him again while rubbing his biceps. She closed her eyes and moaned softly as he nibbled her earlobe. Although she didn't want to do this before the talk, she was ready to give in to her passion, and kissing fervently she began to unbutton his shirt. She put aside every other thought and concentrated only on the man directly in front of her. She wanted her husband again and it excited her so much that it actually scared her a little. Suddenly Callie's phone buzzed from the kitchen table, signaling an incoming call.

"Ignore that," Michael whispered as he began to undo the buttons on Callie's blouse.

"Don't worry I plan to," Callie said breathlessly as she yanked Michael's shirt off of his shoulders. "Still in great shape I see," she added while rubbing and kissing his bare chest. Suddenly, Michael's phone began vibrating from the kitchen counter top.

"Ignore that."

"I plan to," he replied kissing her neck and removing her blouse.

Callie's phone buzzed again. This time she stopped and reached for it. "Maybe it's one of the kids. Hello?"

"Hello, Callie? Come quick, it's a fire!"

"A fire! Did you call 911?" Callie asked excitedly while putting her blouse back on.

"Where's the fire?"

136

"It's in the boiler room!"

"The *boiler* room?" Callie stopped getting dressed. "Marlisa, we don't have a boiler room."

"We don't? Then where is the incinerator?"

"We don't have an incinerator."

"We don't?"

"No."

"Oh, I must have dialed the wrong number."

"You think you dialed the wrong number? You dialed my phone to alert me to an imaginary fire in a boiler room we don't have? Well, please do not keep me in suspense and tell me who did you mean to dial?"

"Well, I thought—"

"Oh, never mind Marlisa!" Callie yelled and hung up.

"What was that about?" Michael asked slightly amused.

"Marlisa has been acting very strange today, and Paula has been in the foulest mood. Honestly, Michael they drive me up the wall!"

"Whoa, calm down." Michael walked over to Callie and opening her blouse again, he traced his fingers along the lace in the front of her bra. "You sound stressed."

"I am a little," Callie replied with a mischievous smile. "I would love to do something that would relax me. Any ideas?"

"Hmm, let me think," Michael said as he bent down to kiss her lips. Pushing Callie up against the wall, Michael continued to kiss her as he lifted her skirt. A small sigh escaped Callie's lips and her breathing became heavier as he caressed her hips.

"Yes," Callie whispered followed by another small sigh.

"Ignore that," she said quickly, referring to Michael's phone that had began vibrating again. However, before he had a chance to respond, Callie's cell phone began vibrating as well. Michael and Callie both looked at the phones puzzled. It was clear that their phones were being redialed since the vibrating would stop only momentarily before beginning again. Still staring at their cell phones, both Michael and Callie jumped when Michael's house phone rang. They looked at each other and Michael quickly left the kitchen to go pick up the home phone receiver in the living room.

Pulling down her skirt, Callie went to look at her caller ID. She had six missed calls from CM Music Productions.

"For you," Michael said entering the kitchen again with the cordless phone.

"Me?"

He could only shrug his shoulders as he handed Callie the receiver. It was clear that he was as confused as she was. Callie slowly took the phone and put it up to her ear.

"This is Callie," she said tentatively.

"Oh, thank God, Callie, you have to come quick, it's a robbery!"

"A robbery? Where?"

"It's …uh….it's scary…and uh, it's…across the street!" Marlisa let out a long wail and began to cry.

"Marlisa what is wrong with you!"

"You have to leave out of there now," she said between loud sobs. "Your lunch should be over now."

She was crying so hard that Callie could barely understand what she was saying. She began mumbling so incoherently that Callie removed the phone from her ear and just looked at it a moment before hanging up. Visibly shaken, she looked at Michael confused.

"Something is definitely wrong with her. I'm seriously thinking about drug testing."

"What?" Michael asked surprised and a little amused again.

"Yeah, you should have seen her today right before I came here. Drugs, Michael. I don't think I can explain it any other way."

"She's not on drugs, she's just being Marlisa. Besides, I cannot process the idea of Marlisa on something like crack. It gives me the shivers," Michael said making a face as he rapidly shook his head.

"Well," Callie said smiling at Michael's theatrics, "if I go in tomorrow and all the office furniture has disappeared, I guess I'll have the answer to the crack question."

"Not until she tries to sell it back to you."

They both laughed and Callie began getting dressed.

"Whoa, what are we doing? Aren't we supposed to pick up where we left off again?"

"Maybe later. Let's eat and talk or rather talk and then eat. I really want to clear the air about something. Marlisa's breakdown or whatever that was just reminded me of that."

"Ok," Michael said and sighed deeply.

"Well, Michael, you don't have to sound so excited about it," Callie said wryly as she sat at the kitchen table to put on her shoes. "We can get back to...you know, later."

"I'll tell you one thing," Michael said buttoning his shirt, "Marlisa has impeccable timing. Breakdown or not, she couldn't have planned her interruptions better. It was like she was right here in the room."

With no response from Callie, Michael looked up to see her pensively looking down at her hands. He gingerly sat down in one of the kitchen chairs and watched her in silence. Before long she looked up at him and made an attempt at a small smile. Michael frowned with worry.

"Ok, I can't take the suspense any longer. I know that whatever is going on is serious, so...what's causing you to look at me like that?"

"This is hard," Callie whispered. "I'm not sure how to start."

"Ok, don't worry about how," Michael said as he moved his chair from the other side of the table to be near Callie as he faced her. "Just talk to me."

Callie took a deep breath and closed her eyes. Opening them she looked at Michael who had gently covered her hand with his. He was very concerned now, but Callie feared what his reaction would be when she brought up the subject.

"It sounds petty, but I have to know about something."

"Ok, what?"

"Raylene."

Michael removed his hand from Callie's and sat back in his chair. "Raylene? Why would you be asking about Raylene?"

"Because I know you've been in contact with her again."

Michael just stared at Callie for moment. Then he got up from his seat and moved the chair back to the other side of the table.

"What difference does it make if I've been in contact with her, Callie?" he asked as he leaned against the island and folded his arms across his chest.

"Why are you so defensive?"

"Because this is so out of the blue! What are you asking me?"

"I'm asking if you are...trying to get close or...if you're seeing each other."

"Like you and the cowboy?"

"I am not seeing Stephen!"

"Well, I'm not seeing Raylene, in the same way that you're not seeing Stephen."

"I haven't slept with him if that's what you're wondering. Have you slept with her?"

"I think I'll answer you the way you answered me once. It's none of your business."

"Fine then!" Callie jumped up and grabbed her purse and phone. "You're right it's none of my business! So let me get out of your way so that I can give Raylene a clear path right into your arms!"

"Wait a minute, wait a minute!" Michael yelled, grabbing Callie before she could make it out of the kitchen.

"Let me go!"

"I'm sorry," Michael said calmly, "I'm sorry. Please stay."

"Why do you want me around? Clearly your secret lover Raylene is more important than me! Let go!" Callie screamed and tried to jerk her wrist out of Michael's hand, but he held on to her firmly.

"No," he said gently, "I need to tell you something first."

Callie glared at him as he released her arm and then held both of his hands in the air in surrender.

"Please sit down, Callie. I'm just a little sensitive about her, but as the woman I love now, more than anything, I can't have any secrets. Raylene or my past with Raylene is not more important than you. Can you sit down, please?"

Callie continued to glare at him, but she didn't move to either sit down or leave.

"Ok, then stand."

Callie immediately went and sat down in a chair. Michael released a small smile as he looked at his wife.

"Ok, and things like that," he said pointing to her sitting, "is why I love you."

Callie didn't respond as she put her purse and cell phone back on the kitchen table again. Adjusting herself in the chair she looked at him expectantly.

"Well?" she asked calmly.

Michael grabbed a chair and placed it directly in front of Callie again. This time he moved in extremely close and leaned towards her.

"I've never told you everything about my relationship with Raylene, like how it ended. That was mostly because of how ashamed I was of something that had happened. I was selfish and unfeeling, and even now I haven't learned how to forgive myself." Michael grabbed Callie's hand and squeezed it. Then, turning her hand palm side up, he began to gently trace the lines on it. Michael lifted his head and looked into Callie's eyes.

"I have always tried to be respectful of women, you know, I wanted to be a good man."

"I know that. And you are a good man."

"I was really in love with Raylene."

"I know that, too."

"I wanted to marry her."

"Well, I know that because Ursula never let me forget it."

Michael smiled and reached out to gently touch her cheek. "But I love you and I have no regrets…except one."

Callie stared into Michael's eyes afraid of what she saw there for the first time. She waited patiently as he delved back into his memories and seemed to gather the strength he needed to continue.

"One day in my fabulously planned life, the woman who I was in love with at the time and the woman who I wanted to marry, gave me the unplanned news that I was going to be a father."

Callie's jaw dropped in surprise and she stiffened waiting for Michael to continue, knowing this story would only get worse.

"Yeah," Michael said quietly, "my reaction was a lot like yours. I was surprised, but I can't say I was happy with the news, and I told her so." Michael dropped his head. "I am ashamed to say that I told her I wasn't ready to be a father. It was too soon and it wasn't in my plans…so I asked her to…terminate the pregnancy. I couldn't believe I didn't want my own child and…neither could she."

Michael took a deep breath and looked up at his wife before continuing. "So the man you married, the nice, good man that I thought I had grown up to be, told the woman I was in love with at the time that I needed space from her, the pregnancy and my baby until I could get used to the idea.

"And because of that, Raylene left. For about a week I didn't know where she was, but I did know by then that I was being a selfish coward. I wasn't treating her right or dealing with the situation like a man. I was just thinking about this messing up my plans for my career. I needed to graduate and I needed to make a mark in this world without my parent's money buying my way. But I didn't think I could do that and take care of a family at the same time. I thought it was too soon to have a family. But by the time I realized just how immature I was being and how terrible I was handling things, she had gone off and …gotten rid of the baby."

Michael bit his lip and looked away from Callie. She could see the shame and hurt on his face.

"So that's why you broke up?"

Michael nodded. "When she came back after that week, she didn't speak to me again and before long she had dropped out of school and just disappeared. I never heard from again…until recently."

"Why now? I mean, did she go off and actually have the baby and only wanted to let you know now?"

"No," Michael shook his head, "it's nothing like that. She wanted to make amends, I think. I'm not completely sure, but she told me how she had always hated leaving the way she did. She wondered how things would have been different for us if she had stayed or if she hadn't rushed off."

"So she has regrets for leaving you?"

"At least for leaving me the way she did. The last conversation we had was about her pregnancy and it wasn't very pleasant."

"I can imagine. That had to be difficult for both of you having something like that still hanging between you all these years."

"Yeah, and I think she had an added burden because she also had some regrets for blaming me. She said she did it because she was scared and wasn't sure she was ready or even wanted to be a mother. But since she had doubts afterwards, it was just easier to blame me. But the truth was she didn't want to have my baby and that bothered her…a lot."

"Oh," Callie whispered, "and now she wants to set the record straight and let you know that you didn't make her do it. She wanted to do it."

"Right."

"And how do you feel?"

"I have to say in one way I'm relived, but in another way I think I'm a little hurt. It's weird knowing that after all these years of believing she ran off upset because she wanted my baby so much, to now find out that she didn't want the baby at all. It's hard to believe, I mean, if you know the type of person Raylene was. She was so sweet and easy to be around and always thought of other people feelings and—"

"I got the picture." Callie said cutting him off. They looked at each other and both smiled. "Do you still care for her?"

"I do. But I think a lot of my attachment, even now, had to do with not being able to talk to her and tell her I was sorry for the way I had acted and that I had changed my mind. I mean, she just left. She dropped out of her own life because of me, the man that was supposed to love her. The man that was always supposed to be in her corner, you know. It hurt, the way it ended and no matter what she says, I'm still ashamed of myself. Anyway," Michael continued wearily, "guilt is a heavy burden to carry, especially when it's a secret."

"Nobody else knew this?"

"No, this isn't the type of information you talk about to just anybody. I think Alise knew something because she talked to Raylene a lot, but even she didn't know I had asked Raylene to ...you know, do *that.*"

"Only you and Raylene."

"And now you," Michael replied as he stared at Callie.

"What?"

"Do you...look at me differently now?"

"No, you made a mistake as a young kid, but the fact that you carried this type of guilt all these years proves that you're the man that I knew you always were."

"But that's not the only mistake I've made that hurt a woman I loved."

"I know," Callie said quietly.

"I will spend the rest of my life making it up to you, if you'll let me."

"I will," Callie answered in a small voice. "We'll have the rest of our lives to make it up to each other."

Michael stood up and grabbing Callie's hand he gently helped her up, too. Cupping her face between his hands he kissed her tenderly on the lips.

"We are going to take this to the bedroom and leave the cell phones in the kitchen."

Callie grinned and then added, "And take your house phone off the hook."

Michael chuckled and nodded his head before kissing her passionately. As they made their way into the bedroom, Callie had already taken off her blouse and shoes and was working on her skirt when she heard the front door open.

"Hello!"

Michael and Callie looked at each other. It was Ashley.

Michael, who also had his shirt off, grabbed a tee shirt and pulled it over his head. "I'm tired of buttons," he said before walking out the bedroom.

"Hi, Dad."

Callie heard their youngest daughter Maya greeting Michael. Hurriedly buttoning her blouse and fixing her hair, Callie rushed to follow Michael into the kitchen.

"I thought you were going to drop Maya off at your mother's?" Michael asked Ashley as she dropped her school gear on the nearest counter top.

"Change in plans, Dad. I'm on the senior activities committee and we have a meeting today. I don't want miss it. And since the housekeeper has the afternoon off and Maya is still officially too young to be home alone, here we are."

"Why didn't you tell me about this change in plans?"

"I did. I called you and left a message."

Michael picked up his cell phone and saw five missed calls from CM Music Productions and one from Ashley.

"I figured I could drop Maya off here and let Mom take her home."

"But we haven't even eaten yet," Michael said pointing to the food.

"Oh, sorry." Ashley looked at the take out spread out on the counter still untouched. "It's so late you're probably hungry, so don't let us interrupt. Maya can have a snack and start on her homework while you guys eat. No biggie." Ashley looked at her father who didn't respond. "Just relax, Dad. Gosh, go eat. Take your time. Have dessert."

"There's no dessert on the menu. There was, but not anymore."

"No," Callie added suppressing a smile, "we won't be having …any today."

"What are you talking about? There's cake right there." Ashley pointed towards the take out as she poured herself a glass of milk.

"I'll take dessert!" Maya yelled excitedly, dropping her book bag and running into the kitchen.

"Yeah, me too," Michael said and looked at Callie. They both laughed and Maya, who seemed excited about eating cake, joined in the laughter as well.

"You know what?" Callie said still smiling, "Let's not worry about lunch. I was just about to leave anyway."

"Good," Maya said taking a bite of the chocolate cake that she had picked up while laughing, "I don't …like... Dad's house," she said between chews.

"Don't chew with your mouth full," Ashley said turning her nose up. She handed a napkin to Maya who had taken a seat at the kitchen table. "Mom you need to teach your kid manners."

"Why don't you like my house, Maya?"

"'Cause it smells."

Callie and Ashley laughed while Michael pretended to be insulted.

"What? It does not smell!"

"Uh huh, it smells like old man perfume in the bathroom."

"It's called aftershave, smarty pants and maybe you wouldn't smell it if you used the guest bathroom like I told you."

"That bathroom mirror is too high."

"Or maybe it's just that you're too short, shrimp boat," Ashley stated factually while texting. Maya promptly ignored Ashley after dismissing her with a wave of her hand.

"She's childish. *Anyway* Dad, I don't want to be mean, but our house just smells better. It smells fresh, like flowers growing after a summer rain," Maya said very seriously.

"Really? 'Flowers growing after a summer rain?'" Michael asked leaning against the kitchen counter smiling.

"Yes, Dad, that's what my emotions led me to say," Maya replied in a somber tone while still looking at her father.

"They're learning poetry in school," Callie whispered under her breath to Michael.

"Well," he said sighing deeply and now looking quite solemn. He frowned and then slowly nodded, as if he were in deep thought. "That was very…um, poetic."

"Thanks," Maya replied and then went back to concentrating on her piece of cake.

"Well," Callie said taking the remains of the cake from Maya, "that's enough. You're going to ruin your dinner. Come on let's go."

"Yeah, I gotta cut out too, Dad. I have a lot of important teenagery stuff to do. No time for the young," Ashley looked pointedly at Maya, "or the old," she added as she shifted her gaze to land on Callie and Michael.

"Bye Dad, Mom," she said as she kissed them both and then quickly left the kitchen.

As Callie wiped chocolate from Maya's face, she looked up to see Michael staring at her. He had a silly smile on his face and then mouthed the words 'I love you.' Callie smiled sheepishly and focused on Maya's clean up again.

"Mom, I'm not a baby. I can do that myself," Maya said taking the napkin from Callie.

"Of course you can." Callie raised her daughter's chin and looked into her eyes. "Sometimes I forget how grown up you are. Now get your book bag and meet me at the car."

"Okay," Maya said and after picking up her belongings, she grabbed the rest of the cake and quickly left the kitchen.

Michael walked up to Callie and pulled her into his arms. He slowly bent his head and kissed her long and hard. Pulling his lips away, he then kissed her tenderly on the nose. Callie opened her eyes to see Ashley watching them.

"I forgot my IPod," she said as she grabbed it from the counter beside the refrigerator. "And guys?" Still entwined in each other's arms, the both turned to look at their middle daughter. "That was about the grossest thing I've ever seen in my life. And I've dissected things in biology." Turning quickly, Ashley left them alone in the kitchen again.

"I'm glad we talked today. I'm glad I told you everything," Michael said ignoring his daughter's insult.

"Me too. I'm glad you trusted me. I think I love you more for that."


Marlisa sat stone faced as she took in everything she had heard through Callie's phone. Michael and Callie were back together. He trusted her with his secret, but Michael didn't realize that secrets have a way of getting out.

*Chapter 13*

Alise sat calmly at her dining room table not allowing herself to think about what she was about to do. She was going even further down this same dark road and she had to commit. There was no turning back and no taking back anything she said or did until it was all over. Alise couldn't afford to allow herself to have any doubts about what was about to happen. Paula would take the bait. She had to, otherwise all the emotional pain everyone had gone through would all be for nothing. Alise hated to think about it, but today's meeting with her older sister was either the beginning or the end of her ability to repair the damage Paula had caused. She had let Paula be in the driver's seat while she worked to keep her children safe and what good did that do? It helped Paula profit from all her lies, that's all. Everyone else suffered and if Paula walked away from this now, they had all suffered for nothing.

Alise had a sudden thought. What if Paula decided not to come? What if she had already figured out that she could just walk away, even if her secret was divulged to the family? The only real harm done would be to her reputation in the family because she was right about the legality of their agreement. Alise had checked with the company's legal department to make sure. There was nothing in the agreement regarding the company being divided due to any stipulations relating to the will. As far as the law was concerned, Marlisa and Callie freely gave away their shares to family members. Alise knew they could try to sue Paula for misrepresentation and unethical behavior for using the bogus will to manipulate the sisters, but they would all be old and grey with very rich lawyers before this type of issue was settled in the courts. Besides, that was not the type of remedy that Alise wanted, and even if it was, she was way too impatient for that. Legally suing Paula or freezing her funds or anything along that line wouldn't stop her from just up and leaving. She'd done it before and she could do it again, but Alise couldn't let that happen. Paula needed to be stopped and, for the first time, be held accountable for the harm she has caused.

So that meant Alise would have to try a new tactic. She had to make it emotional and very personal for Paula. She had to use the "If you can't beat them, join them" strategy and give Paula what she's always wanted—a "real" sister. Alise would have to convince Paula that she has renounced Callie, Marlisa and even the Elliot name. She knew she would have to give the performance of her life. She also knew that some of her convincing behavior for Paula's sake was going to make her ashamed of herself. But if she could get Paula to trust her and believe that she saw things Paula's way, Alise could work to take her down from the inside. Alise the Trojan horse. Even the thought of cozying up to Paula made her want to get on her knees and pray. It just *felt* wrong.

Taking a deep breath, Alise put herself in check. Paula couldn't even get a whiff that something was off, so Alise needed to concentrate. Her goal as Paula's ally was to find Paula's dirt and find it quickly. A private detective might help, but that would most likely take the kind of time that Alise could not spare. She would need more than sleeping with married men or suspicions of wrong doings. She would need to find something concrete and powerful enough that she could move on it right away. She was counting on getting her clues on where to dig up dirt directly from Paula, while at the same time making Paula comfortable enough to stick around town as she did it. The good thing was that Alise wasn't completely flying blind because she already had an idea on where to start shoveling first. North Carolina.

Alise knew that Paula was hiding something that had to do with North Carolina and that Marlisa knew about it. At the meeting last year, she had figured out that Marlisa had given Paula some of her stock in exchange for Paula helping her plot to get Michael. Since then, Alise has discovered that more of Marlisa's stock had been transferred to Paula and that puzzled Alise. She couldn't figure out why Paula was showing so much restraint or why she wasn't putting the squeeze on Callie. Callie didn't think she had a legal right to the company because Paula had "proven" that Marlisa, as the biological child of Philip Elliot, was the sole heir. That's the reason Callie agreed to share the company with Paula in the first place. Callie loved the company she had built and she would have been a much more lucrative target than Marlisa.

Alise had originally thought that it was because of the stalemate she had with Paula. Paula was fearful that Alise would expose her lie and, Alise was fearful that Paula would hurt her boys with the release of the videos. Now, with her new legal knowledge, Alise saw things differently. Paula was just too greedy not to go for more. After all, who could really stop her? Yet, the only movements of assets were small percentages of the production company from Marlisa to Paula. Although Marlisa would probably want the same deal she had with Paula before Paula was given ownership in the company to continue, Alise knew Paula would not. Everyone had given in to Paula and she could have asked or even demanded more of the Elliot sisters' portfolio, but she hadn't. Alise wasn't foolish enough to believe Paula was satisfied with what she had. She also no longer believed Paula was that afraid to be found out to be a scam artist. It was taking something bigger to hold Paula back and Alise was sorry to know it really wasn't her. She believed it was Marlisa and whatever she knew about North Carolina that was keeping Paula subdued.

Alise would find out if her line of thinking was correct very soon when she met with Paula. She knew Paula wouldn't tell her directly, but she would be able to gauge from Paula's reaction if it was worth looking into or not. Plus the meeting served to lay the disgusting ground work needed to keep Paula comfortable, happy and most of all, in town.

Getting up from the table, Alise went into the living room to get her cell phone from her purse. She checked to see if she had gotten a text from Paula cancelling the meeting. She really was nervous and decided to channel her anxiety into her hands by cooking. It was about dinner time anyway.

On her way to the kitchen, Alise decided to make a fresh dish of seafood paella for dinner. She would also make chocolate torte with port-berry sauce for dessert. Between the two dishes she thought her hands would be busy enough to provide the kind of distraction that would keep her calm. She had also decided to invite Paula to stay for dinner as a show of good faith. Paula knew how sacred mealtime was for Alise, so being invited to break bread with her would really show Paula how serious Alise was with her newfound outlook.

As Alise began laying out all the ingredients for the main course, she thought that a red wine would go nicely with dinner and that gave her an idea. She picked out a nice red grape from her collection and uncorked it to let it breath. Then she went to her refrigerator and took out a bottle of red wine which was only half-full, poured its contents down the drain, and then filled it up with cranberry juice. This would be her bottle to drink from and as she sipped on juice, she would make sure Paula only drank from the fresh bottle of wine she had just uncorked. Alise didn't trust herself to drink around Paula. Just a little bit of wine might make her grab Paula by the throat and pull her across the table. However, their mother always said, "A drunk man speaks with a sober man's tongue." Maybe if Paula had a little alcohol she would loosen up a bit and let something slip to her "real" sister. Of course, that all depended on if she believed Alise or not. It all depended on if Alise was right about what she thought Paula really wanted, which was a close sisterly relationship, but only with her.

Alise had just put the cork back into the wine bottle she had filled with juice when she heard a knock on the front door. Quickly she put the bottle back in the refrigerator and walked briskly towards the door. For just a moment she stopped in front of Anthony's picture on the entrance table in the foyer. He was in dress uniform and Alise suddenly felt calm. No more nervous energy. This was for her sisters and for herself, but mostly for Anthony. She put her fingertips to her lips, kissed them and then placed her fingers on the cheek of her son in the picture. Taking a deep breath she sauntered over to the front door and flung it open.

"Why am I here?" Paula asked sourly as she pushed past Alise into the foyer. "I am not in the mood, Alise. You have no idea of the day I've had waiting around practically in the basement for Marlisa to text me."

"Why were you waiting for Marlisa's text?"

"That falls into the category of none of your business. Now back to what *is* your business; why am I here, oh "queen of the world" who summoned me?"

Alise burst out laughing which startled Paula. That was not the type of relationship they had, and Alise knew it would throw Paula off balance a little. She had to do the exact opposite of what her instincts told her.

"What…what are you doing?" Paula asked puzzled.

"I'm laughing."

"But that's not like you to laugh—at least not with me. I'm not Callie, you know."

"I know."

"That's not who we are, laughing and all buddy-buddy and stuff."

153

Paula looked around. "Am I on camera or something?"

"No, why would I waste film on you?"

"There she is. Alise, "the sharp rock in my shoe," is back."

Alise had closed the door and started back towards the kitchen. "Come on. We can talk in here. I'm cooking dinner."

"Don't you even think that I'm going to eat anything from your kitchen," Paula said while following Alise. "I'm not going down like that."

"Going down like what?"

"You know what. Poison!"

"Oh for heavens' sake, Paula. I wouldn't poison you in my own kitchen. If I was going to poison you, I would sneak something into one your room service orders. Something untraceable that wouldn't work immediately. I wouldn't want them to test the food you were eating when you dropped dead. No, you'd be found dead later somewhere, like uh…in the sauna of that fancy spa you go to, lying in a pool of your own vomit."

Alise looked over at Paula who stood just inside the kitchen doorway and was openly staring at her. "What?"

"Seems like you've given this a lot of thought."

"More than you will ever know," Alise answered with a smile.

"What do you want, Alise?" Paula snapped.

"I want to tell you something that is hard to say, but I think I owe you this. Again, it's very hard to say, but after Anthony… left me, I have a new perspective on things. On life."

Paula responded by crossing her arms. Alise was quiet while she sliced chorizo for the paella.

"This is hard for me, so don't think I'm going to take too kindly to gloating." Alise looked up at Paula, "So don't do it," she added firmly before continuing. "But for the first time I understand a few things about you and I think it's important for me to admit the truth."

Alise had pulled out a skillet and added olive oil to it before turning on an eye of the stove to heat the pan. Then she added the chorizo as Paula stood still waiting for her to continue. Alise continued moving about the kitchen in the silence. She knew that Paula always took the self-centered, easy way out of every conversation. If Paula was really interested in what Alise had to say, her impatience would give her away. However, if she wasn't that interested, boredom had already kicked in and she would simply give Alise a snippy response before leaving.

"Admit what Alise? You need to start talking because I'm not getting any younger standing here."

"Ain't that the truth," Alise replied and then was quiet again, waiting.

"Well?"

"Ok, Paula, the truth is that I'm thinking about leaving town."

"Really? Why?" Paula asked intrigued. "I can't believe you could even entertain the thought of leaving Callie."

Alise quickly looked up from her food preparation at Paula and frowned. "Callie's part of the problem," she snapped. "Here I am grieving for my son and Callie has barely bothered to show up. Where is my sister when I need her? Oh, but when she needs me, there I am front and center as expected. I am tired of being a nurse maid for the Elliot sisters!"

Paula perked up with that last comment. "What exactly are you saying, Alise."

"I'm saying that I have lost a son and all Callie can think about is which rich, handsome man she wants to be with! That's the extent of her problems, and I'm tired of being overlooked. I wanted to be a good sister. I know Mama would have wanted her youngest taken care of and God knows you weren't capable because you left us! You left me to take care of them and now I realize that with my mother gone and the only father I have ever known in the ground, that I am the odd person out! Marlisa and Callie are the biological Elliot sisters and they both have a great inheritance, but what about me?"

Paula silently nodded her head in agreement.

"Callie won't even sign over her part of the restaurant like she promised! She practically has me begging to control my livelihood, while she expects me to hold her hand through her man problems!"

Alise began to slam things around in the kitchen. She grabbed a knife to chop up an onion and Paula jumped.

"Whoa, calm down. I could have told you about being on the outside of that tight little family. As a matter of fact, I did tell you and you chose to stay as their lap dog."

"I didn't ask you over here to hear you going on and on about "I told you so." You *left* Paula and I had no choice but to take the lead with my half sisters."

Alise could see the surprise in Paula's eyes when she referred to Callie and Marlisa as half sisters. She also saw the beginning of a tiny smile before Paula quickly hid it.

"Well, Alise, I'm here now. If you want to leave town, maybe we could do it together, you know? Try to get to know each other without an Elliot around."

Alise nodded her head slightly as she scowled at Paula. She couldn't quite make sense of Paula's reaction. Although she expected Paula to eventually come around and reciprocate her attempt to form a truce, she had the feeling that Paula was a little too eager. Alise's frown deepened. Paula seemed...relieved?

"I don't know if I can believe or trust you. At least with Callie I knew where I stood. I ignored it, but I knew. You are not a person anybody should turn to. "Trustworthy" is not on your résumé."

"What do you have to lose by trying, Alise? We never had a decent relationship because you were under the influence of Callie and Marlisa, so if it doesn't work out between us, so what? You can't miss what you never had." Paula had taken a seat at the island to watch as Alise prepared the food.

"I guess with all your looking, you'll want to eat, too."

"Well, with a charming invitation like that, how can I resist? Do you need any help?"

"So that I have to worry about *you* poisoning *me*? No thank you."

Paula burst out laughing. "This is your kitchen, where would I get the poison from?"

"From your purse. I wouldn't flatter myself to think I was the first person you slipped cyanide to."

Paula laughed again and this time Alise joined her. Although Alise was finally feeling more relaxed, she knew that putting her guard down at any time with Paula would be a mistake. She would have to still play everything perfectly. She couldn't push back too hard or seem too eager.

"You said you were thinking about leaving town, where would you go?"

"I had been thinking about expanding and opening another restaurant further south. Stephen had always wanted *Josephine's* to be an upscale chain and he wanted to first branch out north to New York or out west to California. I honestly want to get away from the cities and just live the simple life."

"Yeah, I know what you mean."

"I want to buy some land and have a nice garden and room away from my neighbors. Just me and God."

"Yeah," Paula said pensively. She picked up a slice of the cooked chorizo, that had been removed from the skillet and set aside, and popped it in her mouth.

"I was thinking of going to North Carolina."

Right on cue, Paula began coughing to the point of choking.

"Oh, what's wrong? Too spicy?"

Paula, in her coughing fit, could only nod. Alise grabbed a glass from the cupboard and added only a small amount of water to it. Paula snatched it from her hands and downed it as Alise grabbed the uncorked bottle of wine off the counter and then refilled Paula's glass to the rim. Still in the mist of her coughing fit, Paula eagerly drank all the wine from the tall glass. Then, taking the napkin offered by Alise, Paula wiped her eyes, tearful from her traumatic coughing. As she tried to regain her composure, Paula dabbed at the wetness around her mouth. Calm now, she set the empty glass down and breathing heavily, she looked at Alise while seemingly gathering her thoughts.

"All this talk about poison and all I had to do was give you a piece of sausage for you to choke to death on. Who knew?" Alise raised the plate of meat towards Paula. "Would you like another?"

Paula ignored Alise's joke and asked in a shaky voice, "Why North Carolina?"

"I don't know," Alise said putting the plate down and shrugging her shoulder. "Then again, why not North Carolina?"

"Because I don't think there's anything there but cows and hicks."

"Well, I like cows and sometimes hicks can be the friendliest people in the world. And I've always thought it was the perfect balance of southern life and city life. At least parts of it seem to be."

Alise busied herself in the kitchen with the food again, but not before refilling Paula's glass and then handing her the open bottle of wine.

"The food smells really good."

"Yeah and it's really easy and quick to make. Now making dessert will take a lot more concentration," Alise replied. "I hope you're hungry. I always make too much because I forget that it's just me now."

"Actually I am a little hungry," Paula said cheerfully. "But um…as far as moving to North Carolina…have you decided where you would go? I mean which city?"

"I haven't even decided if I'm even going there. As a matter of fact, I haven't even decided if I'm leaving at all. I'm sort of at Callie's mercy since she has so much invested in my business. What if she drags her feet on my expansion idea?"

"But let's say she was ok with it, what city are you leaning towards?"

"I don't know. I guess it depends on market research for a restaurant location and the areas with the best prices for land."

"You know," Paula said nonchalantly, "I can help you with the research and give you an idea of what cities to take a closer look at. We could even visit them."

"Well, research is not for the faint of heart, and I run a tight ship when it comes to my business."

"It's not like I'm doing anything else all day. Her majesty won't let me make a decision about something as simple as copier paper, so why not use the resources there?"

"Naw, don't worry about it. I'll figure it out."

"You'll actually be doing me a favor. I'm so bored during the day."

"I don't want to go from needing one sister to needing another one. I can do it myself."

"But—"

"Don't worry about—"

"Alise!" Paula said anxiously before taking a deep breath and calming down. "Let this be the first act of my sincere hope that we can build a good relationship."

Alise put her hands on her hips ready to respond, but before she could say anything, the doorbell rang. Wiping her hands on a dish towel, she walked to her front window in the living room and peeped out. In that moment, Alise felt her heart sink. She could see Callie's car in the driveway. With Paula here, Alise had the opportunity to seal the deal, but knowing what was in store for Callie made Alise's heart hurt. She stood looking out the window contemplating her options. She could actually not answer. That could go a long way with Paula, but it wouldn't be the same as telling Callie off to her face. Alise looked down the hallway and made eye contact with Paula who was staring at her from the kitchen doorway. Alise rolled her eyes to make sure Paula could see her annoyance and then marched over to the front door and hastily opened it.

"What can I do for you now, Callie?"

"I just thought I would drop by and see how you were doing. I waited for Tess to come back for the evening, she had the afternoon off. And then I had to get Maya settled in for the night." Callie tried to come in, but Alise blocked her.

"I'm not up for any company right now."

"What do you mean, Alise? Is that Paula's car out there?" Callie tried to bypass Alise and once again Alise blocked her.

"Is there something wrong?" Callie asked with such a look of genuine concern that Alise almost broke character. However, she could hear Paula creeping up behind her and knew what she had to do.

"Look, Callie, I don't have the strength to hold your hand and wipe your nose like I always do. I lost a child—"

"I know that, Alise!"

"—and all you want to talk about is your love life! Well, I'm damn sick and tired of it! I finally realized that you Elliot sisters don't care anything about me!"

At that moment Alise knew that she would see the look on Callie's face in her dreams. She had never distinguished between their paternities or ever made an issue out of it. Their mother wouldn't let them and the three of them never felt it. Only Paula, who was now standing so close behind Alise that she could hear her breathing, saw a difference between the sisters.

"Alise, I'm sorry if I did anything to make you feel this way. You're right, I have been selfish and I should have been more attentive, even though you asked me to give you space, I should—"

"Oh, so now you're going to blame me? You're inconsiderate and it's my fault! And by the way, when are you going to sell me your share of the restaurant? It's not enough that you Elliot sisters got everything handed to you by your father, but now you want to take what I worked for too?"

"No, Alise! I'll sign it over to you tonight. Let me just call Franklin and we can meet right now! I know this must be important to you ...and ...and..." Callie stuttered as she searched through her purse. Finally she pulled out her cell phone and raised it to dial. However,

Paula quickly stepped around Alise and after snatching the bugged cell phone out of Callie's hand, she threw it in the grass.

"We have sisterly things to talk about," Paula said placing a hand on her hip.

"I'm a sister too," Callie responded firmly.

"Well, technically," Paula said with a sly smile, "that's only half true."

As Paula closed the door on a stunned Callie, Alise and Callie's eyes met. Alise turned away and had to hold on to the nearby banister so that she would not collapse. Closing her eyes, she silently asked for forgiveness from both Callie and God. Then, after gathering her strength once again, she turned to face Paula, who seemed buoyant.

"I guess we should eat now," she said to Paula.

"Good, because I am starving!"

"After you," Alise said. She motioned for Paula to go ahead of her and Paula happily obliged.

For just a moment Alise hesitated and looked at the front door, remembering the look on Callie's face. She fought the urge to run out the door and stop Callie before she reached her car. She wanted to hug her, explain everything and apologize for saying such hateful things. Alise had contemplated bringing Callie in on this part of the plan, but she needed to make sure Paula was fooled completely. Callie's honest reaction did the trick and now Alise the Trojan horse had been invited inside the gates. She slowly turned away from the door to follow Paula, who had already made her way back to the kitchen. Alise had known that this would be the hard part and that there was no turning back or taking back anything—yet. Not until it was over and the ugly truth was out. Unfortunately, it was really just beginning.

*Chapter 14*

Alise sat in the dark of her kitchen going over the night's events. She had actually had dinner with the woman she liked least in the world. Her older sister Paula, a person Alise could barely stand to look at, had sat at her table as an invited guest. She had eaten her food and drank her wine, nearly three bottles worth, and was now sleeping it off in Alise's guest room. In the morning, Alise knew she would offer her breakfast and continue the charade. Even though Alise's newly formed relationship with Paula was for a purpose, she had no idea her emotions would get the best of her. She had no idea that she would not be able to sleep because of all the lies and pretending she had done only a few hours ago. Just the simple fact of having Paula in her house made it difficult for Alise to find peace.

Another thing Alise had come to realize as she mentally went over her dinner conversation with Paula was that even with alcohol, Paula had not let one new thing slip that could be useful. Fortunately, Alise didn't really need anything new. She only wanted confirmation on the North Carolina theory and she had gotten that for sure. Once Alise agreed to let Paula help find a location, Paula had relaxed and became quite the chatterbox. She talked about the neighbors they had while growing up, her great times in high school and some of the most uninteresting stories about her "fun" college years that Alise had ever heard. It took all of her strength not to chase Paula out of the house. Alise barely had time to think clearly because she was in character the whole night. Now in the dark of her kitchen, all Alise could do was think and her thoughts were becoming clearer by the minute.

Because Paula thought only her life story was important enough to be the topic of dinner conversation, she had said something that touched off another memory. She had mentioned her brief engagement to Gregory Gray and that reminded Alise of the last time that name was brought up for discussion. She now remembered very clearly that it wasn't Paula who wanted to talk about him, it was Marlisa. But why? Alise had never thought about it too much before, but now all she could do was think about it. How deep was Marlisa in with Paula? Did she actually know about Paula's scam and was going along with it because of their deal to get Michael? Alise didn't think she had the patience to play this game with Paula long enough to get the details on Marlisa's involvement in all of this. So, she had decided she would get it straight from Marlisa.

Although Alise was anxious and wanted to leave immediately, she couldn't take the chance that Paula would wake up and find her missing. It didn't matter the reason she would give, Alise knew Paula well enough to know that something like a disappearing act in the middle of the night would give Paula a reason to doubt. It would get her imagination going and that would make her question their new and fragile relationship. Alise had to stay put until the right moment, so that even if Paula woke up as she was driving away, her excuse and the timing for the return would be plausible.

Alise had already taken her full carton of eggs and thrown them into the kitchen trash can. Then she had taken out the bag lining the trash can, sealed it and put it by the garage door. At precisely six thirty a.m. she would take the bag out into her garage, place it into the outdoor receptacle and wheel the large outdoor can to the street for the early morning trash pick-up. Once that was done, she would get into her car and drive over to Marlisa's condo for a face to face. This was far too delicate a matter for a phone call and she didn't want to give Marlisa the simple out of hanging up. Alise believed that if she moved quickly, she could get the information she needed, stop at the store and be back in a timely manner to resume her role playing with Paula.

She looked up at the note she had already written and taped to the refrigerator for Paula. It gave the excuse of an early morning grocery trip for more eggs. Alise smirked. A real cook was never caught without eggs. Then again a real sister would never have said those things to Callie and a real mother would never have put her son in harm's way to settle a score. The smirk was gone from Alise's face and she now sat emotionless looking at the time on the microwave glowing in the dark. Only thirty-nine more minutes to go.

*Chapter 15*

Marlisa heard the banging and immediately sat up in bed. She thought she was having a bad dream, but then realized the tremendous pounding was on her own front door. Groggily, Marlisa got up and staggered to the chair of her vanity to grab her robe. She was too tired to be alarmed, but as she hurriedly made her way to the door, she was aware that her neighbors might take issue with this early morning disturbance.

Marlisa couldn't imagine who would be at her door, making such a racket this early in the morning. Besides, she had a doorbell, so unless the building was on fire, they had better be prepared for a very unpleasant conversation with her. After making her way to the door, Marlisa looked out the peephole and then quickly opened the door.

"Alise, why are you banging on my door like the police!"

Alise pushed past Marlisa and was now standing in the living room with her hands on her hips.

"I don't have time, Marlisa, so I'll make it quick and you'd be wise to follow my lead."

"What?" Marlisa asked, closing the door. She followed Alise into the living room and now stood shivering as she faced her older sister.

She was wearing a short pink robe and had one big roller in the front of her hair. On the way to the door she had managed to put on her matching pink slippers, but standing in the cool of her home she was feeling chilly. She wrapped the robe tighter around her and glared at Alise.

"I would be happy to make it quick, Alise. Although, I think you-"

"North Carolina."

Marlisa immediately closed her mouth.

"I told you I don't have time. I still have to pick up some eggs, so give me the details right now, Marlisa. What did Paula do and where is the evidence?"

"What makes you think—"

"Stop it! I told you I don't have time! I know you have something on Paula. I know you're using it as leverage in some kind of twisted plot the two of you are cooking up to get Michael away from Callie. Let's just make this visit as easy as possible, because the more time I spend here, the more anxious I will become!"

"But Alise, I don't know what you're talking about!"

"Do you want me to leave?"

"Yes."

"Now?"

"Yes."

"Then give me what I came for."

Marlisa stood looking at Alise who did seem to be getting more on edge by the second. Slowly she made her way towards her formal dining room. Hesitating for only a moment, she kneeled down in front of the two long steps that separated the two rooms. Reaching along the edge of the top step near the wall, Marlisa pushed on the familiar latch and out popped a drawer from the bottom step. It was filled with documents, but Marlisa didn't reach for any of them. Instead, she reached on the underside of the drawer and released another latch that opened a small door at the opposite end of the same step.

"What the hell is all this James Bond stuff you got going on here?

Should I really be concerned about the stuff that you're into, Marlisa?"

"I'm just careful," Marlisa said closing the drawer and sliding over to the small door that opened like a safe.

"Yeah, well, feel free *not* to tell me all about it. Just give me what I came for."

Marlisa had reached inside the compartment and grabbed Paula's complete private investigator's file, but then hesitated. Thinking better of it, she released the large folder and grabbed a much thinner envelope. It was the original blackmail envelope that contained only the preliminary information she had collected herself when she had first approached Paula. She had never added it to Paula's official private investigation file, nor had she mingled any information from her private investigator's file to it. If the information was good enough to make Paula jump last year, then Marlisa didn't see why Alise couldn't just reuse it. There was no need to give Alise more that what she asked for or clue Paula in on the fact that she was still being investigated.

Besides, Paula's North Carolina scam had really run its course for Marlisa and she knew it the moment Alise and Paula had that big argument. If she needed Paula's help again, she would just surprise her with a new line of blackmail. Marlisa pulled out the envelope and closed the secret door. Standing up, she handed it to Alise and folded her arms across her chest. After snatching the package, Alise opened it and briefly looked at its contents.

"So," Alise said looking at a piece of paper, "she used Gregory Grey's information to help her in some type of scam. That's why you called me and asked who he was last year."

"When I saw it, I just thought his name seemed familiar."

"That's a shame." Alise mused as she shook her head from side to side. "Even a dead ex-fiancé's reputation is fair game for Paula."

Stuffing everything back into the envelope, Alise hurriedly left the condo. Marlisa looked at the time on the clock on her living room wall and rolled her eyes. Alise had some nerve disturbing her sleep like this! Walking slowly to her bedroom, she took off her robe and had just snuggled down under the comforter when, once again, she heard loud banging on the door. This time she jumped up startled and hurriedly ran to the door as she heard Alise screaming her name.

"Marlisa, open this door!"

"What is it, Alise!" Marlisa yelled, no longer concerned for the neighbors, "What do you want now?"

Alise held the package in her hand and shook it in Marlisa's face. "I took a closer look at this and I can't believe you!"

"What?"

"You had all of this the *entire time*! You had the power, and I had no idea how much power you had, to send Paula on her way. But you chose not to!" Alise now pointed her finger in Marlisa's face as she continued ranting. "You let her turn all of our lives upside down and walk away from what she did to those people in North Carolina! And for what? Just so that you could try to take Callie's husband! For a man? Really? A man who does not even *want* you!"

"He wants to be with me!"

"If he *wanted* to be with you, he *would* be with you! Nobody, not even Callie is stopping him!"

"You don't understand how it is between the two—"

"I understand this, Marlisa, and you better listen real close." Alise quieted down and stared at her baby sister for a moment. "After I'm done with Paula," she said calmly, "I'm coming back for *you*."

Alise turned and quickly walked away leaving Marlisa standing in her doorway in complete shock. She couldn't allow herself to think about Alise's words. She couldn't allow herself to think about Paula's anger or Callie's disdain towards her, either. She focused on Michael and all that she had gone through to fix their relationship. She would be with Michael sooner rather than later, and it was that thought that made her believe having her three sisters turn against her was all worth it. *He* was worth it. She closed the door slowly and thought about her next steps. She would make sure that by the day's end, Michael would know of Callie's deceit. He would know his wife wanted to be with another man, and then Marlisa knew he would turn to her again for comfort. However, this time he wouldn't leave her. She was sure of it.

*Chapter 16*

Paula was happy to have finally had a good night's rest. For the first time in weeks she felt like she could relax just a bit. Alise had finally seen the light and not a moment too soon. Paula didn't have another hand to play after Stephen turned her down. She was just going to hang around long enough to get more of the company from Marlisa to sell and then simply disappear. However, with Alise's change of heart, Paula was still going to get more of the company to sell, but now she would stick around for a while. If Alise was really going to move to North Carolina, Paula would steer her away from the towns near Charlotte and then pick a place to settle down, too. Maybe if things were going well, she would stay in close touch with Alise, but Paula wasn't going to hold her breath. Alise was upset– grieving. Who knows if what she says today, she'll still mean tomorrow? All Paula had wanted was time, and since Alise was not breathing down her back, she had it. Although Paula didn't believe for one second that she had all the time in the world.

Alise had made her a really good non-poisonous breakfast and had been a good hostess, but Alise had been a little too quiet and a little too annoyed about something during breakfast. Paula felt as if she had already overstayed her welcome and, not wanting to push, made a quick exit. They had broken some ice, but they hadn't really bonded. Paula was not sure if they ever would, but at the moment, it didn't matter. She didn't have to look over her shoulders for Alise. All she had to do was keep a sharp eye on Marlisa. And that was fine with Paula. Marlisa she could handle.

Paula opened the door to the office that she shared with Marlisa and wasn't surprised to be alone. Marlisa wouldn't be there for hours, and Paula was anxious to get started on researching relocation areas for Alise. However, she already knew the best place for Alise was anywhere but the outskirts of Charlotte, otherwise known as the "scene of the scam." Paula didn't think of what she did as a *crime,* it was more like a business deal. However, since it was technically dishonest, she would concede it was a scam and she didn't want Alise to get even a whiff of her wrongdoings. Although Paula would prefer another state completely, she would still give Alise options for North Carolina like she asked.

The bad news for Alise was that Paula was prepared to lie to make other cities, even those within the state, look a lot more appealing than "the red zone." Then, once she had Alise looking in another direction, her work would be done. Until then, she would be Alise's new BFF or BSF – Best *Sister* Forever or until one of them double-crossed the other. That is, unless Alise was really serious about her newfound views of the Elliot sisters. If that was the case, Paula's life would be perfect. After fleecing Marlisa, she would have more money than she could spend in her lifetime and the sister that she never had finally in her life. But first things first.

Paula moved quietly about her office. Even after last night's drama, more than likely Callie had still gotten into the office early and was already working diligently. Sometimes the difference between Callie and Marlisa surprised Paula. While it wasn't unusual for Callie to be at work at the crack of dawn, it was odd for Marlisa to even roll out of bed before the crack of noon. That's why Paula had no problem taking everything from Marlisa. She didn't deserve it. She was just reaping the benefits of having Philip Elliot as her father and Callie as her sister. The way Callie had to drag Marlisa's dead weight around in the company had to be exhausting. Paula certainly felt exhausted dealing with Marlisa *and* Alise, for that matter. So, for the moment at least, Paula was just happy to stay out of Callie's way. However, for Paula to get the results she needed to be happy there would have to be destruction to Callie's life. It would be unfortunate in some ways, but collateral damage always is, and Paula could certainly live with it.

It wasn't until Marlisa breezed into the office at 12:15 p.m. that Paula realized she had worked through the entire morning nonstop. Suddenly with Marlisa's presence, the room felt very small. Paula could hardly think with her shuffling papers and flitting around the room making sure every bit of air was filled with her perfume. She could hardly breathe, and she certainly couldn't concentrate. She was just about to leave the office to work in her hotel suite when Marlisa took a call that got her attention.

"Yeah?" Marlisa whispered in her cell phone. She was sitting at her desk and eyeing Paula. While Paula's ears perked up, she kept her head down and pretended not to be listening.

"No, no," Marlisa whispered anxiously, now swiveling in her chair to turn her back on Paula. *"No courier.* Right. The back and give my name. An hour or *sooner."* Marlisa turned around in her chair and busied herself with papers on her desk. Then she got up, grabbed her purse and walked to the office door.

"Where are you going?" Paula asked frowning. "You just got here."

"And now I'm just leaving."

"I wouldn't do that if I were you," Paula said smirking, "her highness has called a meeting with just you.'

"Callie?"

"Who else?"

"When?"

"In the next hour."

"Well, she can call me," Marlisa snapped and continued towards the door.

"She doesn't have to explain anything to you, you know. I mean, when me and Alise met with her last night—"

"What? The three of you met? Where?"

"At Alise's house."

"Why wasn't I invited?"

"That's a question for Callie."

"But I'm asking you! What did you talk about?"

"We talked about a lot of things! Now don't get your butt on your back and start yelling at me! All of this is entirely Callie's call. Since Alise is moving away—"

"Alise is moving?"

"Boy," Paula said smiling, "you really are out of the loop. But the good news is, and there is good news for you, Michael might be up for grabs."

"What does that mean?" Marlisa said walking slowly back to her desk. She put her purse down and turned towards Paula. "Last I heard Callie and Michael were getting back together."

"Last I heard, which was last night at the dinner meeting the three of us had—"

"You were at dinner? At Alise's house? *You?*"

"Look, I know this is weird, but me and Alise are going out of town to look at land. And you and Callie need to talk about some things. It might not be all bad for you if you still really want Michael."

Paula watched Marlisa carefully hoping she would believe the fairytale she had just been told. Although it would have been easy for Marlisa to confirm Callie's request for a meeting, odds were that she would rather wait and see. Paula had long learned simple lies with a little truth are the easiest to control *and* they get the best results. People always say, "Why would this person or that person lie about something so easy to check?" The answer is simple: it's *because* the

173

lie is so easy to check that it's assumed to be true. As long as the lie has a bigger purpose, then it's best to just go with the easy effort rather than the elaborate scheme. In this case, Paula needed to keep Marlisa in the office in order to stop her from meeting whoever it was she was about to meet. She had no doubt that whatever was in the package that was too important for a courier, was worth its weight in gold and Paula wanted to get her hands on it. At this point, Paula felt it was important to monitor Marlisa's every move.

She also instinctually believed that when Marlisa said "in back" to the caller she was referring to the back entrance of the very office building they were sitting in now. It was only used by celebrities and other VIPs to gain access to the studio and private offices without being seen from the street. Cars would drive into the tunnel, check in with the guard at the gate, but they needed clearance. The guard would certainly call Marlisa when her visitor gave her name, and she would approve their entrance on the spot. However, Paula was going to intercept Marlisa's package while Marlisa sat on pins and needles waiting for Callie's call which would never come. Marlisa would stay put, as long as she believed it was a priority and that meant she had to believe the lie.

"So...you think...Michael and Callie are splitting up?"

"I think you need to be clued in on everything that Callie has going on with the business and with Michael."

"You're lying," Marlisa stated and turned away from Paula to grab her purse from the desk again. Paula quickly picked up her cell phone and hit a speed dial number.

"Hello, Alise," Paula was holding her cell phone towards Marlisa. She had it on speaker and smiled at Marlisa's reaction when Alise's voice answered calmly.

"Yeah?"

"I'm going to work at home for the rest of the day, but I just want to confirm that we're off on our adventure early tomorrow morning. You still up for it?"

"Oh, yeah. I've made up my mind about leaving this area. So, I'll pick you up around eight tomorrow morning."

"Ok. I'll be ready." Paula hung up and smiled at Marlisa. "After you close your mouth, you can tell me what I have to gain by lying to you?" Marlisa didn't respond but only looked at her sister dumbfounded.

"If I were you, I would park my behind at that desk," Paula pointed to Marlisa's desk for emphasis, "and wait for Callie to call the meeting so that I could be included in what's going on behind my back."

Marlisa walked back to her desk and sank down in her high back, executive desk chair. She looked so tiny slumped down in such a big chair that Paula almost felt sorry for her until she remembered it was *Marlisa.*

"I, on the other hand," Paula said as she gathered her research documents from her desk and packed up her lap top, "will continue my important work from home."

"What are you working on? I mean, I've never seen you actually working before."

"That is what you're going to find out within the hour."

Marlisa looked sadly at Paula, probably feeling left out again. Growing up as the youngest sister had its drawbacks. Paula sauntered out of the office and waited at the elevators. She was nonchalant until she entered the elevator and the doors closed. Then she dropped her briefcase and frantically pressed repeatedly on the button leading to the private parking garage. Hoping she hadn't missed Marlisa's visitor, Paula hurriedly made her way to the guarded entrance. After drilling the security guard to make sure no visitor had entered the premises in the last fifteen minutes, Paula sat down in the climate controlled booth and waited with the guard.

Within ten minutes the mystery visitor arrived with the package, which Paula easily intercepted. While Paula didn't know exactly what was in the package, she did know Marlisa and took a gamble that everything had been done over the phone. She didn't think Marlisa would have been too willing to show her face while soliciting something that had to be whispered about in her cell phone. So, posing as her youngest sister Paula paid him the requested fee along with a $500 tip to forget about his trip there. She advised him that coming inside would only leave a record of his visit and that was something they both wanted to avoid. He whole heartedly agreed and sped away on his motorcycle.

Paula, happy to have succeeded on her mission was immediately angered when she opened the package. Looking around she went to her car for privacy and emptied the contents on her front seat. There were two discs in clear plastic cases. One case was marked "ORIGINAL" and the other "FINAL." Paula turned her car on and inserted the one marked FINAL in the CD player and listened to it in its entirety. Afterwards, she put in the other disc marked as the original, but she only needed to listen for a few minutes to realize that the conversation between Callie and Stephen took place weeks ago. From what they both said, it had to be the night they were all notified about Anthony.

The new realization of what Marlisa was about to do infuriated Paula. Marlisa could have finished their deal weeks ago, but instead she kept everything going unnecessarily with all intentions of cutting Paula completely out of the plan. She already had what was needed to doctor a recording for Michael. Marlisa had just wanted to spy on Callie and Michael when she forced Paula to give in to her demands to add spyware to Callie's phone. Paula thought about waiting in the stairwell knowing that she only did it for the big payoff that she now knew Marlisa had no intention of giving her. Seething, Paula got out of her car and slammed the door. It was time to make Marlisa say "uncle."

Paula took the next twenty minutes to hide the package, get a bucket from the janitor's closet and fill it with water. Then she went back to the office she shared with Marlisa and stood in the doorway.

"We're going to legal."

Marlisa looked up from her desk. "Legal? What for?"

"So that you can sign over the rest of your ownership in this company to me."

"Nope," Marlisa said leaning back in her chair, "I don't think so. And what's with the bucket of water?"

"You don't need to worry about that. All you need to do is meet me in legal in about ten minutes."

"And why on earth would I do that?" Marlisa asked casually as she leaned further back in her chair and propped her feet on the desk.

"Because you want the package with the fake recording of Stephen and Callie that was just delivered."

"Keep your voice down!" Marlisa said between clenched teeth as she jumped up from her chair. She rushed to the office door and tried to close it, but Paula, who wouldn't move from the doorway, effectively blocked her efforts.

"Where is it?" Marlisa whispered anxiously.

"I have it, the fake one and the original. So if you want them, you'll do as I say," Paula answered calmly.

"I'm not so stupid that I didn't make my own copy. All I have to do is get somebody to fix me up another disc to play for Michael," Marlisa whispered smugly.

"And all I have to do is play the original for Michael proving that you made something fake to fool him. Then I'll tell him how you got the recording in the first place." Marlisa eyes fluttered, but she still held her head up. "And then I'll tell him about Callie's cell phone being bugged. There's no telling what private conversations you heard between them." Paula leaned in closer to Marlisa and added, "He'll *hate* you forever and you know it. All of what you've done would have been for *nothing*."

"Uh…uh…um," Marlisa stuttered weakly.

"Choose," Paula sneered, "your company or Michael. I'm good either way."

"What if I—"

*"Choose!"*

Marlisa stepped back looking defeated as she contemplated her options. They both knew Michael *would* hate her and then what would she be left with? She took a deep breath and grimaced. "Let's go."

"In a minute. I have to talk to Callie about something." Turning decisively, Paula marched down the hall with Marlisa following closely.

"I thought I had the meeting with Callie," Marlisa replied completely confused.

"Nope. Just me."

Still holding on the bucket, Paula she strode past Kelly, who protested loudly as Paula forcefully opened Callie's door.

"Wait…I have to call you back," Callie said hanging up her office phone. "What do you think you're doing barging in here, Paula!

Unceremoniously setting the bucket next to Callie's desk, Paula grabbed Callie's cell phone and dropped it into the container of water. Callie shrieked while Kelly and Marlisa, who were both standing in the doorway, gasped in surprise. As Callie hastily grabbed it out of the bucket of water, Kelly ran to Callie's bathroom.

"Water may not have gotten in everywhere," Kelly said running back with a towel in hand, "So we might be able to save it, if we dry it out really quickly." However, before she could take the phone from Callie, Paula snatched it and dropped in back in the bucket.

"Oops!" Paula yelled, but this time she placed her hand on the phone and held it underwater.

"What are you doing!" Callie screamed trying to pull Paula's hand away.

"I'm getting your phone for you!" Paula answered as she struggled against Callie efforts to retrieve it. The two of them flailed away in the water, with Callie scooping water up and purposely splashing Paula in the face while screaming for her phone.

"Let go, Paula! Let it go!"

"I'm helping you!"

Finally Paula released her hand and stood back. Callie, whose shirt was soaked, gingerly picked her phone out of the water and looked at Paula, who was also drenched.

"What is wrong with you?" Callie screamed as Kelly ran over to retrieve the phone and gently wrap it in the towel.

"It's completely dead, isn't it?" Callie asked Kelly. She was clearly panicked and in shock. "What about all of my contacts?" Turning to Paula she screamed frantically, "Why were you tying to drown my phone! *What is wrong with you?"*

"Let's see what we can do, Callie," Kelly said gently, attempting to reassure Callie again. "I'm sure there's a back up of your contacts that we can download from somewhere. With technology today you never know. We might even be able to download all your apps directly from this phone. When it dries out we—"

Paula had grabbed the phone and threw it against the wall. This time Callie just stood wide-eyed looking.

"Oops, it was an accident," Paula said shrugging her shoulders.

"Paula you cocked your legs like you were throwing a fast ball! I don't know why you've done this, but it has something to do with you being a vile, sneaky, underhanded, deceitful, lying, hateful, old …old Tasmanian devil!"

Paula gasped clearly offended and put her hands on her hips. "How dare you! Who are you calling old?"

"Wait a minute. Out of everything I said you're offended because I called you old?"

"Well, it's not like I haven't been called those other things before."

"Even Tasmanian devil?"

"Yes, once, but so what? I even agree with a few of those names, but *old?* How dare you! I use the best skin treatment money can buy, and I look remarkable! I see myself in the mirror and I look a whole lot younger than you, Callie!"

"Younger than me! You must be smoking crack cocaine if you really believe that! That does it! I'm starting drug testing because here's yet *another* sister acting like she's on drugs!"

"Another sister? Who are you talking about, Callie?" Marlisa yelled from the doorway

"It's not drugs, Callie! It's the *truth*!"

"The truth? First of all, Paula, you couldn't find the truth—"

"What sister, Callie?"

"—with a flashlight if it was buried in your—"

"What sister, Callie?"

"Shut up, Marlisa!" Callie and Paula screamed simultaneously while staring at Marlisa.

"All I wanted to know is what sister is acting like she's on drugs!"

"You, Marlisa!" they responded in unison.

Marlisa stood with her mouth opening looking horrified.

"Hee, hee, hee," Kelly snickered and gave Marlisa an exaggerated grin before walking out the door with the rescued pieces of the cell phone.

Turning back to Callie, Paula shook her finger, "I'm not going to stand here and be insulted like this."

"Then get out! Out of my office and out of my life!"

"I did you a favor, Callie!"

"Not for free!" Marlisa yelled. "She doesn't do anything for free!"

Paula looked at Marlisa and smiled slyly. "You ever notice how Marlisa always rolls in like the fog, hanging around, listening and stuff?" Paula turned back to Callie, "She seems to always know when things are going on. It's almost like your office is bugged."

Marlisa immediately looked at Callie, with eyes growing larger as Callie's eyes narrowed in return. Paula was satisfied with the look that passed between them. Callie would be calling someone to "debug" her office as soon as they left.

"I thought you were leaving, Paula. And if you really want to do me a favor then take that one," Callie pointed to Marlisa, "with you. Both of you have problems that I'm not qualified to deal with."

"Fine then and good luck with your phone!" Paula replied

sarcastically.

"Oh, thanks and you take care of that "magic mirror, mirror on the wall," that makes you look so young, but watch out for the seven dwarfs, Grandma!"

"Why you would think that I was on drugs?"

"Because you're crazier than a bat!" Paula shouted angrily. "And as for you, Callie—"

"I didn't know bats were crazy. I just thought—"

"Oh, Jesus Christ! Get out! Everybody just get out of my office now!"

## Chapter 17

Marlisa sat in her car outside of Michael's office. She finally had what she needed to turn Michael away from Callie, possibly for good, but now she had cold feet. It wasn't that she didn't want to go through with the plan; it was that she was afraid it wouldn't work. What if after all she's done, Michael just doesn't believe her?

She looked at the disc in its new, clear plastic, unmarked cover lying on the passenger seat. Coming up with a story for why she even had a recording was simple and partially true. A while ago Callie had accidently pushed her intercom button and it got stuck. Marlisa had heard all of Callie's movements around her office, even when she cleared her throat. It wasn't until Marlisa alerted Callie that they were connected that Callie corrected the problem. In true Callie fashion, they all got new office phones with a different intercom connection, but that didn't mean it was entirely implausible that it could happen again. This time Marlisa would say, she recorded Callie's blatant infidelity out of her concern for Michael. The falsified version didn't need much in the way of changing the actual conversation Stephen and Callie had, but it did include the sounds of heavy love making. It all sounded very authentic, but Marlisa wasn't sure Michael would believe his own ears, simply because she was the messenger.

Marlisa acknowledge how much she could use Paula's help on this, but getting Paula to do anything else was completely out of the question. After they had signed the paperwork that would transfer the last of her company shares to Paula, Paula had immediately verbally evicted her from the office. Marlisa only had until Paula came back from whatever psycho road trip she was taking with Alise to clear out on her own. If she didn't, Paula had actually threatened to physically evict Marlisa herself.

It bothered Marlisa to completely give up the company, but CM Music Productions was only part of Marlisa's financial holdings. She acknowledged that it was a big part, but even without it she was far from poor. As a matter of fact, she was still very rich; she just wasn't *extremely* rich anymore. Owning the publishing rights to their father's catalog of songs was enough to keep the flow of new money into her bank account even as she gave away money and assets to Paula. Plus she had various profitable international investments that would ensure she would never have to think about money, but that didn't mean she wanted Paula to have it.

Although in the end for Marlisa, unlike Paula, money wasn't the point. Michael was the point. Loving someone until it physically hurt was not easy to live with, and Marlisa had done it for more years than she wanted to count. Everything she had endured had come down to this very moment. She no longer had real relationships with any of her sisters. It was completely over with Paula, but so what and good riddance. However, it hurt her deeply that she had probably lost Alise and, once she crossed this line, Callie would never speak to her again. But what choice did she have? Michael had always been the goal, and now Marlisa realized he might just shoot the messenger or he might forgive Callie. After all, they were separated, but still married.

Marlisa thought about that for a moment and then shook her head. No, he wouldn't forgive Callie for stringing him along while having sex with Stephen behind his back. He might be angry about her wanting to get away from the chaos of her life, but eventually he would understand why she needed to go away. But if she had actually been having sex with another man while he remained faithful as he waited for her to make up her mind about their marriage, then he would see that as a betrayal. Marlisa was sure of it, especially if Callie wasn't sleeping with Michael. From the recording it was clear that Callie wasn't sleeping with Stephen, but as long as she could convince Michael otherwise, the truth didn't actually matter.

Marlisa had to make him believe her version, and she had to do it today. This was her last and only chance at happiness with the man she loved. He would be devastated and Marlisa would be there to pick up the pieces just like before. She would show him how much better off he would be with someone who loved him as much as she did. He just needed to believe she was worthy of his love and that Callie was not. The bogus tape of Callie and Stephen making love would prove he had chosen the wrong sister all those many years ago.

Marlisa summoned her courage and got out of her car. With each step she took, she reassured herself that she was doing the right thing for the right reasons and that he would believe and appreciate it. She marched past Mrs. Taylor, Michael's faithful secretary, before the older woman had a chance to stop her and opened Michael's office door.

"I'm sorry, Michael, but she just rudely ignored me," Harriet Taylor said angrily. She had jumped up from her desk and now stood behind Marlisa glaring. Marlisa knew his secretary didn't like her, but at this point the only thing she could offer Harriet was a number and a place in line…a very long line.

"I'm calling security," Harriet said resolutely and turned quickly to go back to her desk when Michael's voice stopped her.

"No, no, no," he said, "don't worry about it."

"Are you sure?" Harriet asked, turning and glaring at Marlisa.

"Yes, I'm sure."

Slowly Mrs. Taylor stepped back, grabbed the doorknob and rolled her eyes at Marlisa before closing the office door.

"What's going on, Marlisa?" Michael asked impatiently. "I'm a little busy, so…"

"I wouldn't be here if it wasn't important, Michael. I've actually agonized over my decision, but I think you should know."

"Know what?"

"That Callie is planning on leaving you."

Michael, who had been sitting behind his desk, got up and with his back to Marlisa turned to look out of his office window. "And how would you know that?"

"Because I accidently heard a conversation she had with Stephen. I mean, a conversation, among other things."

Michael turned quickly. "Among other things?"

Marlisa swallowed hard and watched as Michael came around to the front of his desk and sat on it. They were only a couple of feet apart and Marlisa felt her heart beat faster. Being so close to him gave her the courage she needed to continue.

"Yeah, Michael. Callie has been having sex with Stephen for a while now." Michael didn't say anything, but she saw his jaw tighten as she continued. "And now she wants to go to Europe with him to spend time together…alone. I just thought you should know."

"I know he's attracted to Callie, but so are a lot of men. I've been dealing with that since before we got married."

"But Callie has never been interested back. She stayed true to you. Until now."

"Yeah, well things have changed a little, but I started that."

"But Callie's been stringing you along, Michael. She's been pretending she's getting back with you, but she's not. She's with Stephen now and has been for awhile."

"How do you know?"

"I told you, I heard them together. Callie must have accidently pushed the intercom button on her office phone. She probably didn't realize that I was even in my office at that hour and that I could hear everything. I decided to record it so that you could hear for yourself what she's been doing behind your back."

"Why now? I mean, why do you need to tell me now if she has supposedly been with him for a while?"

"Because …Michael…it's time you…just listen to the recording."

Marlisa pulled out the disc and offered it to Michael, but he crossed his arms. She laid the disc on his desk beside him.

"Why should I trust you, Marlisa?"

"Don't trust me or believe me! Just listen for yourself!"

"Marlisa, I'm in advertising. I know more than anyone else that you can take bits and pieces of a lot of different things and put them together to create one big illusion. Whatever is on the disc could sound like Callie, and even be Callie, but the context of her words would be something you came up with."

"I would never do that, Michael. Not to you and not to Callie," Marlisa said quietly. She was genuinely hurt at Michael's accusations, while completely disregarding the truth in them. "I wouldn't lie to you about the fact that you being with Callie is a mistake. What happened between me and you is proof that—"

"Marlisa, please," Michael said gently, "What happened between us was a mistake and it was entirely my fault."

"No, Michael, it wasn't your fault. It was *fate!* And now that I can prove Callie doesn't want to be with you—"

"How do you know that?"

"Because she told me."

"So you want me to believe that you're Callie's confidant now?"

"We have been getting along really well, like we used to." Michael scoffed.

"No really, Michael! I think since she's been leaning towards being with Stephen, she's been like her old self with me. Talking to me like she used to—telling me things!"

"Like what?"

"Like how she sees you differently because…" Marlisa trailed off looking embarrassed.

"Because what?"

"Because of ...Raylene."

Michael immediately scowled and stood up. Marlisa took a step backwards.

"What do you know about Raylene?"

"I know what Callie told me."

'What did she supposedly tell you?"

"That you were selfish and unfeeling when you ...told her...to get rid of your baby," Marlisa said softly. She was genuinely embarrassed for Michael and could barely stand the way he stared at her. It was clear that her words both shocked and hurt him. Then suddenly, his eyes flashed with hot anger.

"She did *not* tell you that," he said intensely.

"Michael," Marlisa said walking towards him with a look of complete innocence, "how else would I know?"

Her words hung in the air as Michael absorbed their meaning. They looked at each other for another moment and then Michael walked back to the other side of his desk.

"It's time for you to leave, Marlisa."

"Ok," Marlisa said softly and reached for the disc on the desk.

"Leave it," he snapped.

As she backed up towards the door, Marlisa continued to look at Michael, who had turned his back to her.

"Michael, Callie also said she really wanted you to sign the divorce papers. She wants out for good."

Michael didn't respond, but when he turned to look at her, the hurt on his face was evident. Everything she had given up for him was about to pay off. He would be able to release Callie from his heart, and when he did, Marlisa was ready to take her place. She would give him a little space as he processed the news. Then she would go to him. And then he would be hers.

*Chapter 18*

Callie was absorbed in pressing business matters when Michael stepped into her office. However, she was happy for the distraction. Work was the only thing that could always keep her mind from wandering and lately, with everything around her going crazy, she needed that kind of focus. After what had happened at Alise's house the previous night and today's lunch time performance, with Paula once again starring in the drama, Callie felt as if she was losing her mind. Why had Alise turned against her and sided with Paula? Why do Marlisa and Paula always seem to be putting their heads together, even when they clearly don't want to be working with each other? Paula was the key. None of the chaos in the business and between the sisters started until Paula came to town. Callie always thought she could deal with everything as long as Alise was still in her corner. Now Callie didn't know what to think, so she didn't. She just worked, but now with Michael back in her life where he should be, she could also concentrate on building something solid with him again. Forget the sisters—all of them, at least for now.

"Hey, this is a nice surprise," Callie said smiling, but when she made eye contact with Michael, she immediately saw that something was wrong.

"What is it, Michael? The kids?"

"No, you," he replied in a steely tone.

"What about me?"

"Is this what you want?" he tossed an envelope on her desk. Callie grabbed it recognizing her lawyer's return address. She knew what was originally in the envelope, but hurriedly took a look at its contents to confirm.

"Michael these divorce papers are from a long time ago. I didn't even sign them. You should have just thrown them away." To demonstrate, Callie dropped them in her trash can under her desk. She hesitated only a moment when she realized that Michael had signed them. She tried not to notice that he had also dated it with the current date, but she dismissed it as a misunderstanding that she had just cleared up. However, when she looked back at Michael he was still frowning at her. She couldn't tell if he was angry or hurt or both.

"Honestly, Michael, I decided that I want to work it out with you," Callie said smiling. She wasn't sure what was going on, but Michael's reaction was beginning to alarm her.

"*You* decided."

"Well, I guess we both did. I mean, you waited patiently for me to come around. You said you would wait as long as it took because you loved me. And Michael I appreciated that! You had patience with me when I didn't even have a lot of patience with myself. I was just trying to figure things out."

"You were "figuring things out," huh?" Michael asked sarcastically.

"Yeah," Callie answered tentatively." I don't understand what's going on here."

"No, actually, Callie, it was me who didn't understand exactly what was going on, but now I know. You were planning on running off with Stephen. When were you going to tell me?"

"I hadn't …I didn't know anything really, yet."

"But you were thinking about it?"

"Yes, I was! I needed to get away from looking at your face and then Marlisa's face. Or having to hear Marlisa's voice followed by a conversation with you. *Every, single day!* The both of you are always in my line of sight or hearing or business dealing or family issues or something! It is always the both of you and I need to get away from…from… *both of you!*"

"That's fine, but why do you need to go with Stephen? You could go away alone!"

"Because I don't want to go alone! I want to go with somebody who sees me! *Just me!* Not as a wife, or sister, or mother, or boss, or as some role that I fulfill for them! I just don't want to have to think about who I'm supposed to be or what I'm supposed to do! I just want to be myself!"

"You can't be yourself with me?"

"Not completely, Michael," Callie said dejectedly. "You expect things from me."

"I'm *supposed* to expect things from you! You're my wife!"

"That's what I mean! I'm your wife, fulfilling a role for you!"

"Oh, so you just hate that, huh?"

"No, I love it, Michael, but please try to understand. I've had moments when I've thought I wanted to…oh, I don't know how to explain myself except to say that I'm just being selfish. I know that, but there is a…a sorta *freedom* that is exhilarating when all you have to do is think about what makes you happy from one moment to the next. I feel that with Stephen— young, adventurous, and yes, selfish."

"Ok, Callie. Fine. All I've ever wanted was for you to be happy. Really. And since it's so selfish of me to want my wife, all you have to do is sign the divorce papers, and you can ride off in the sunset with your Stephen."

"That's not what I want."

"Well, Marlisa warned me—"

*"Marlisa!"* Callie snapped as she stood up. "What does Marlisa

have to do with this?"

"Apparently you've been doing a lot of talking to her about your feelings for me and Stephen."

"I have not!" Callie yelled. "How could you even bring her into this? How could you even begin to believe her?"

"Because you told her about what happened with Raylene."

Callie's eyes grew wide in surprise. "Michael, I did not tell her anything. Marlisa, above all people, would be the last person I talked to about you! You should know that!"

"Then how did she know, huh?"

"I don't know," Callie said frantically trying to think, "But the point is *I* didn't tell her! *I* wouldn't do that to you!"

Michael only glared at Callie and she suddenly realized that he didn't believe her. Calming herself down, Callie stared back.

"Do you believe me?" She asked quietly. She wanted to give him a chance to think about it without her yelling and pushing him into an emotional response. She needed to know that he not only believed her words, but believed in his heart that she would never betray his confidence, especially on something so personal. "Michael, either you believe me or you believe Marlisa. She said I told her and I'm telling you that I didn't. One of us has to be lying. So, who do you choose to believe?"

Michael had also calmed down, but she could see the pain on his face. She could see his jawline tighten as he tried to control his emotions. The hurt in his eyes over his belief that she had betrayed him was almost unbearable to watch.

"Only you, me and Raylene knew, but it only got out after I told you."

"And you think I would tell Marlisa? Or that Marlisa would tell you the truth?"

"She was right about your plans to go away. And you didn't say anything, Callie. You were just going to up and leave."

"That's different, Michael."

191

"Not to me," he said so softly that just the tone hurt Callie's heart.

The two of them looked at each other in silence and Callie could feel her eyes tearing up. She didn't want to push him over anything having to do with Raylene, but she needed him to answer her previous question. This wasn't about Raylene anymore. It wasn't even about Marlisa anymore. It was about whether he trusted and believed in her.

"Either Marlisa is telling the truth or I am. So, who do you choose to believe?" Callie watched the sadness in Michael's eyes transform into something that she didn't recognize. In the quiet of her office she thought she could hear her own heart beating as she anxiously waited for his response.

"I choose Marlisa," he said softly before walking out of the office.

Slowly Callie sank back in her chair and stared out of the big glass windows. There would be no more easing her mind with work or anything else. It was now time for her to just have a good cry.

*Chapter 19*

Marlisa tiptoed around in Callie's office trying to be as quiet as possible. She had waited around until both Callie and Kellog left and was fortunate that it hadn't taken all night. While the executive floor cleared out pretty quickly after five, it was not unusual for Callie, Kellog and Marvin, when he was in town, to work late into the evening.

Marlisa couldn't relax after her successful meeting with Michael until she had thoroughly "debugged" Callie's office. She had to do it before the cleaning lady entered Callie's office, but as usual, the trick was not to even be seen in the building. There were only a couple of the cleaning staff allowed in Callie's office, and if she moved anything too far out of place, the cleaning person would correct it and cover her presence. With any luck she would be in and out and the office would be perfect for Callie when she came back in the morning.

Marlisa had parked her car topside and waited in the stairwell, periodically giggling whenever she thought about Paula's mental breakdown as she had waited in that same passageway. To further cover her tracks, Marlisa had immediately unplugged and thrown away anything connected with the office bugs. She was afraid that if she tried to listen in again, Callie would have set a trap for her. With technology as it was and with Marlisa being completely ignorant of it, she didn't want to take a chance that there was some way of backtracking the bugging devices in order to identify who was at the other end listening. In addition, Marlisa had no way of knowing if Callie had already found them or not. She just had to take the chance and remove them tonight to minimize the risk of exposure, although she hoped she was not already too late. It was a matter of timing. Marlisa smiled. Everything was a matter of timing and finally Marlisa had gotten it right with Michael. She was hopeful that this whole bugging situation would also work out in her favor. She couldn't get caught—not now.

Marlisa had removed four of the five bugs from the office, but stood trying to remember where the fifth and final one was. She went through them in her mind as she moved around in the semi-darkness. She was using only the light from Callie's bathroom to illuminate the room and after looking around again, she realized she was stumped. There were five: one on the phone, one in the bookcase by the window, one on the underside of a ridiculously expensive landscape painting hanging on her wall, one on the top of the high arching doorframe and one Marlisa suddenly remembered, was on the underside of Callie's desk.

In the dim light, Marlisa rushed to Callie's desk, quickly pulled out the chair and dropped to her knees. She took out her cell phone and selected the flashlight app to shine a light on the last unethical and illegal bugging device in Callie's office. She had just removed it when she flashed on something in the trash can that caught her eye. Focusing the bright light on the object, she slowly pulled it out of Callie's trash. Upon noticing what it was, Marlisa quickly stood up and turned on the desk lamp. She needed to see the documents clearly and more importantly she needed to see the signature without the trickery of shadows. It was his handwriting. He had signed the divorce papers—but Callie hadn't.

Marlisa slowly sank down in Callie's high back desk chair. The soft leather enveloped her, but Marlisa didn't notice. She was staring at the blank spot above her sister's printed name. Callie Elliot Armstrong. All it needed was her signature or a signature that *looked* like hers.

Marlisa had done it literally hundreds of times. She had perfected her sister's signature years ago and when Callie had her emotional breakdown. Marlisa had sometimes signed both her name and Callie's in the same business document. She managed to sign two different names with two different styles side by side and no one was the wiser. Callie wasn't around and business had to go on, so Marlisa figured out a way to make that happen. She always told everyone the documents were being delivered to and from Callie's home for her signature, but that was only half the time. The other times, Marlisa had just signed her sister's name…perfectly.

Selecting a pen from Callie's desk supply, Marlisa put the tip close to the paper. She hesitated as she thought about how wrong this would be, but then she thought about all the wrong she had already done. She had bugged her sister's office and personal phone, she had staged a suicide attempt, blackmailed, spied, accepted Paula into the company and she had lied so much she barely recognized the truth.

And then there was the initial incident that she had set in motion years ago. Her attempts to be with Michael must have seemed sudden to Callie. However, for Marlisa she had been setting it up for as long as she had known Michael. When she saw her opportunity to be with him, she took it. She finally got her chance to make love to the man she loved, and she wanted— no, needed him more than anything else in the world. After she slept with Michael she had thought everything would finally be as it always should have been, except Michael wasn't ready to accept that Callie wasn't the woman for him. Now he does. Marlisa saw this as a chance to finally fix everything for her and Michael. When he finds out Callie signed and filed the divorce papers he'll be devastated…but free.

Marlisa looked down at the documents with renewed resolve. She was sure it was the right thing to do and after signing the papers, she put them back in the envelope. In the morning she would go to the post office and mail them herself. If Marlisa could keep Callie in the dark about the divorce being processed, while convincing Michael that his wife didn't want him anymore because she signed and filed the papers, he would finally *see* her. Marlisa had to be sure to stand between them until Michael finally realized that she was the only one for him. There was a chance that when Callie found out, she would protest and deny filing the paper, but by then Michael wouldn't want her anymore. Marlisa turned off the light and hugged the envelope to her chest. She was the happiest she had been in a long time. She was finally getting everything she ever wanted and Callie and Michael would thank her later for setting things right.

Getting up quickly, she left her sister's office. She knew Michael was upset about the news she delivered to him today, and she knew she needed to give him a little space, but not too much. Tomorrow, Marlisa decided as she pushed the button for the elevator. She would give him tonight alone, but tomorrow night was hers.

*Chapter 20*

Callie lay on her bed in the dark thinking about the events of the last two days. Alise had turned on her for some reason. Callie knew Alise hadn't been herself because she had lost a child and it's possible she was having PTSD—Post Traumatic Stress Disorder. Alise blamed herself for the death of her own son and that had to push her into a new reality. However, Callie was having a hard time trying to understand what reality for Alise would include Paula. Even if she gave Alise a break on that issue, Callie knew there was still some secret that Alise and Paula shared and it had something to do with Marlisa and her. Of course, Marlisa brings up an entirely different issue that Callie just didn't want to think about anymore. But she couldn't help thinking about the apparent secrets Marlisa was keeping with Paula, too. Again, Paula was the connection.

Callie thought back to last year when they all signed the papers agreeing to share CM Music Productions with Paula and Alise. It was all engineered by Paula. She reappeared in their lives after years, she introduced a problem with the inheritance, she set up DNA tests and then she created a solution that benefited her own interests. Callie remembered that at the first business meeting the sisters had together,

Alise told her that she would set things right soon and she had asked Callie to trust her. Callie did trust Alise, but now…

Callie wasn't sure what was going on entirely, but she knew Paula was at the center of it. She got up, turned on the light and went through her night table drawer. Finally she fished out a business card and looked at it hard. It was emotional remembering, but if she wanted to know what was going on, she had to start from the beginning. Paula's big announcement about the inheritance was the whole reason she came to town. That's when things got confusing, so that was where Callie would start.

*Chapter 21*

Callie touched the doorknob and hesitated. She hadn't been to this office since last Thanksgiving for the DNA test. She went a little lightheaded again remembering how she had demanded that Paula not tell her, but show her the test results in writing. And Paula did. Callie saw it with her own eyes. Phillip Elliot was not her biological father. He had raised all four sisters, but Marlisa was the only one who shared his blood. For Callie, it was a surprise to find out she was a product of her mother's affair with a man no one could even identify. Since her mother was deceased, that secret had gone to the grave with her...until Paula showed up.

Callie sighed and took a step away from the door. She leaned against the wall, slowly and silently counting to ten. She had done a remarkable job at keeping her composure when she read that Marlisa was their father's natural child. She had also done a remarkable job keeping all of her emotions in check since that day. She had practiced forgetting the details, but being at this office was bringing her pain back into sharp focus again. Paula had been happy to start all of this "who's your daddy" mess, rehashing their father's will and demanding DNA tests. It was all about money for Paula, but for Callie it was so much more. She had lost a father and her identity. Now, she was nobody's daughter and she was keeping that a family secret.

Callie had resigned herself to keeping quiet and sitting at the helm of a company that rightfully belonged to Marlisa. She knew in her heart it was wrong, but most days she didn't feel as guilty as had she thought she would. It was, and still is, hard keeping quiet, but Marlisa was not the one who made CM Music Productions a success. Marlisa didn't deserve it.

Callie realized that was something she told herself every day when she went into the office, and every night before she closed her eyes. Marlisa *didn't* deserve it. Still Callie felt her guilt increasing and that's why she worked so hard making sure the company remained a success. Somehow she felt she was earning her place in the company.

However, it wasn't just keeping the company and the inheritance that made her feel ashamed at times. She was keeping Marlisa in the dark about her real father. Callie stopped the truth from getting to Marlisa when she signed off on sharing the business with all of the sisters. She let Paula manipulate her so that they could both claim part of Marlisa's inheritance. Some days Callie thought that Marlisa didn't deserve to know the truth, but deep down she knew better.

Up until she and Marlisa had witnessed that strange, heated argument between Paula and Alise, Callie thought her odd feelings came only from the guilt. But now she knew her instincts had just been trying to tell her that something in this whole sisterly mess was not quite right. Marlisa didn't deserve the company or her friendship or her loyalty as a sister, but she did deserve to know the truth about her father.

She knew Alise was overly emotional and heartbroken after what had happened. It was, and still is, a tragedy that can never be measured, but the things Alise said just didn't make sense. Callie corrected herself – it didn't make sense *to her*, but it seemed to make perfect sense to Paula and Alise. Callie knew Paula had done something, and it must have been big, *and Alise knew*. Callie had a fleeting thought that her real father might be named in the test documents and she wondered if that was the big secret. Maybe her real father was still alive. Callie found her courage again and stood resolutely in front of the door.

She grabbed the doorknob again, took a deep breath and opened the door. She walked into the office and was relieved to see the waiting area empty. Apparently, the need for blood tests was not in high demand, at least not today.

"May I help you?" the receptionist said, appearing seemingly out of nowhere. Her name plate said Carla.

Callie walked up to the desk, or rather a high mantle that came up to the middle of her chest. It was like someone had cut a hole in the wall that separated the two rooms. When the receptionist sat back down, Callie could barely see her. She had to lean across the high mantle that divided them. Peering over to the other side, Callie could see that the young girl had a regular desk and work area that the high wall shielded from the view of anyone in the waiting area. No one could just walk up unnoticed and read the blood test results or whatever other sensitive information that might be laying around. Callie smiled a little when, as her eyes scanned the desk, she realized that was exactly what she was trying to do.

"I called earlier about the results of my DNA test," Callie said smiling. "I wanted to get a copy of the results."

"Do you have ID?"

Callie pulled out her Maryland driver's license and handed it to Carla. She looked at it and went to a file. Pulling out a folder, she walked back to stand in front of her desk.

"I think we're the only office in town that doesn't keep computerized files. They promised they would convert them next year, but some people are fighting it. They don't trust computers."

Carla's eyes flicked towards her right. Callie saw a woman walking out the door leading to the back offices. She had to be eighty years old if she was a day. Callie smiled a little, but looking back at Carla, she

201

grew concerned.

"What's wrong?"

"Well, nothing really. But I think I need to get approval to give you a copy."

"It is my file, isn't it?"

"Yes, but that doesn't mean I can show it to you."

"Really?" Callie said with more attitude than expected.

*No, Callie. Calm down. Getting mad isn't going to help. What would Paula do?*

Callie smiled at Carla and did her best "Paula the manipulator" impression.

"Can you please do your best to get the approval? I mean, I have kids that may have a hereditary disease that skips a generation and…and…I'm so worried…but I can get ahead of this thing if I can just *prove*…"

"I understand," Carla said sympathetically as she put her hand on top of Callie's. "I will see what I can do."

Carla walked out the door to the back offices. Callie looked at the file that lay on the desk and looked around the reception area. She was alone. Carefully she tried to pull herself up onto the mantle in order to reach the file, but it was too high. She took off her heels and backed up. She would need to get a running start.

Callie moved to the center of the room, but then took a few more steps backwards. She wasn't as young as she used to be. Getting a running start, she was able to jump up and then pull her upper body onto the mantle. When she felt herself sliding off, she lifted a leg across the top and was able to balance herself enough to scoot forward on her elbows. With one leg perched on the mantel and the other leg dangling, Callie felt an unnatural breeze as her skirt crept up her backside. The hem of the skirt was almost resting on her waist but she was in too precarious of a position to try to pull it down. It didn't help that her positioning had also caused a giant "wedgie" that converted her regular panties into a thong.

Why did she pick today to put on a pair of her brightly colored novelty panties with the writing on the front? Today's selection was bright green. Callie almost laughed thinking about the poor soul who might come into the office right now. They would certainly get an eyeful, especially since she was probably the only woman in the state wearing stockings and a garter belt instead of pantyhose right now. She just hoped that in return for the bare bottom "show" she'd give them, they would have the decency to "make it rain."

Callie heard voices from the back office and started to panic. She was able to reach the file in her awkward position and she eagerly opened it. Going through the paperwork she was confused. Two sets of test results? Callie looked at the dates. Same date, but different outcomes for both her and Marlisa. Callie looked at the one which matched the paternity between her and her father at 99.9%. It read "office visit" in the details of the blood sample. Callie remembered seeing that on the paperwork Paula showed her for Marlisa. What was on the paperwork for her own results she saw that day? She'll have to check. Callie had been so devastated that she didn't take a closer look. She didn't want to see more. She had seen the only thing that mattered in just one glance.

Callie looked at the zero probability paternity results for her and her father. It read "Sample delivered." Who delivered a sample of her blood and how did they get it? Callie only gave blood once and she certainly didn't have extra blood lying around waiting to be tested. Whose blood was delivered? Realization crept up slowly on Callie. *Two sets of tests results!* Was Paula really capable of doing *that?* Yeah, she was. It seemed complicated, but it was actually very simple. Paula had put together a crude, elementary and effective plan. But did Alise know? What about Marlisa's part in this? Did Paula forge Marlisa's DNA match using this paperwork or did Marlisa have two sets of results, too?

Callie's emotions were morphing into something unfamiliar as she tried to make sense of things, but she hurriedly brushed them aside when she saw the back office doorknob turn. She forcefully pushed herself off the mantle and, misjudging the height, stumbled and fell, landing on her back with her legs in the air. If anyone had walked in now they would see the front side of her panties which read "I love cucumbers" and had a picture of said cucumber winking with a big grin plastered on its cartoon face.

Callie quickly sprang up like a Jack-in-the-Box and surprised the old woman standing on the other side of the desk. It was the same woman Callie had seen earlier. Carla, who was standing behind her, also flinched.

"Oooh! There you are! I didn't see you at first," she said and laughed gruffly. "You startled me."

Callie was also a little startled by the way the old woman looked up close, and the loud, croaky tone coming from her tiny frame. Her voice sounded like it had been exposed to years of cigarette smoking, and by the looks of her, it was probably done while on a stool in a dark, smelly bar.

"I'm sorry, Hon, but we can't give you any information," the woman said firmly. "We have strict instructions that only the administrator can have access to this file. Now if you want, I can give you her information so—"

"That's ok," Callie said trying to ease back into her heels without them noticing her fidgeting or her sudden growth spurt. "I'll figure it out."

"I'm sorry," Carla said compassionately looking at Callie. The old woman and Callie turned to go their separate ways while Carla scribbled on a card. Callie was at the exit door when she heard Carla call out to her.

"Ms. Armstrong?"

"Yes?" Callie turned around and walked back to the receptionist's desk. She looked past Carla, but the older woman was nowhere in sight.

"Take the information anyway. Just in case you change your

mind," she whispered, handing Callie a page from her message pad. Callie looked on the back where Carla had written a name and phone number.

"You should be able to get what you need from her," the receptionist said and smiled weakly.

"Thank you. You've been just great." Callie gave Carla a warm smile. "And you're right. I'm going to make sure I get what I need… one way or another…directly from Ms. Paula Alexander."

"But if you have other questions, let me know," Carla said sympathetically. "I'll do what I can to help you."

Callie thought about sisters Paula, Marlisa and Alise. Then her mind drifted to Michael and Stephen, the two men in her life and she thought about everything that had happened in the last year between them. Looking at the receptionist, Callie smiled sadly.

"Thank you, very much, Carla. But I think I'm on my own now."

*Chapter 22*

All Callie could think about was how totally foolish she had been. She was driving on the Beltway on her way back home, but she didn't want to go home just yet. She bypassed her exit towards Potomac, Maryland and continued north. She didn't need to figure out where she was going. She just needed to keep driving until she knew that she had arrived. At the moment driving was helping her think and calming her down, so she kept straight up I-95 and took in the view. As always, the trees and foliage were beautiful for that time of year. Fall had come slowly, but she was really beginning to feel the coolness in the air. The sun was bright in the sky and on any other day she would have thought about how blessed she was to have so much. Unfortunately, all she felt was alone because she had just proven that she couldn't trust the people around her. Her own family, her sisters, actually thought it was best to lie and steal from her.

Although Callie felt she needed to know the truth, after finding out, she just wasn't sure if she knew what to do with the truth. She had been too trusting of her sisters and even of Michael. As for Stephen, she wasn't clear on where she stood with him, but she still thought about him and wondered. What if she hadn't told him…*that*? What if she had just let their friendship continue the same as it had always been? With Stephen all Callie seemed to have were "what ifs."

After leaving the medical office, Callie went to her safe deposit box at the bank to get the DNA test results she had gotten from Paula and easily confirmed her suspicions. Although the paperwork "proved" she was not related to Philip Elliot and that Marlisa was, Callie knew the documents had been tampered with because of the date discrepancy. Paula had covered her tracks by changing the date and method of delivery for the sample with Callie's name, but she had neglected to falsify the time and date electronically stamped at the bottom of the document. Even though she had gone in on the same day as Marlisa to be tested, Callie's results had a different day on the bottom stamp. Callie had also gone in on an afternoon and the time stamp was clearly for a time in the morning. When comparing the two sets of results it was hard to ignore that the date and time at the bottom of hers did not match its header and yet Marlisa's was a perfect match.

Paula probably missed it because the time was in military format and rather than the American date format of month, day, year it read day, month, and then year. In addition, there were no symbols to distinguish the numbers were dates and times. It was just a bunch of numbers and it actually looked like an official document number had printed on the paper. Callie only caught it because a similar computer time and date stamp prints on her company internal emails.

However, to be completely sure, Callie took things a step further. Using her considerable money and influence, she was able to quickly identify the technician who processed her "results" and discovered that he was not even working at that time. He had already taken off for the Thanksgiving holidays when Callie came in for testing, and he didn't return back to work until the middle of December. Unless someone was authenticating blood samples under a co-workers name and ID, Paula had lied about everything. She must have brought in samples of someone else's blood that would have never matched Philip Elliot and then had both Callie and Marlisa do a legitimate test. With two sets of results, Paula showed Callie the results she needed—Marlisa's real one and the bogus one with Callie's name on it. Paula had scammed her way into the company and now Callie was absolutely sure of it.

Unfortunately, she was also sure that Paula couldn't have done it without her help. Callie had agonized over her decision every day since she went along with Paula's solution. However, it was especially painful now knowing that if she had done the right thing from the beginning, Paula's lies and manipulation would not have worked. She should have followed her instincts and gone with her first decision to challenge Paula, but instead Callie only saw Marlisa walking away with everything. Callie didn't have an excuse for the part she played, but that didn't excuse her sisters' behavior over this last year either.

Callie could easily dismiss Paula, but why would Alise let such a lie stand? And what did Marlisa get out of exchanging shares with Paula? Callie didn't understand any of it except all of her sisters seemed to be teaming up and taking turns stabbing her in the back. Callie's eyes filled with tears as she thought about Alise. She thought back to the fight Alise and Paula had the night they all found out about Anthony. Now it seemed clear to Callie that Alise must have known what Paula was doing. Alise had wanted to say something then, but something stopped her. Callie wanted to know what had stopped her that night, but she also wanted to know what had been stopping Alise in the months before then. She decided that she wasn't going to try to figure out any of her sisters' motives. She was getting tired of thinking about them at all.

Callie pulled up in the parking lot of one of the many restaurants at the Baltimore Inner Harbor. It was a good place to end up on a nice fall day. She loved seafood and the water and the other attractions. She could lose herself just by walking around people watching. Callie smiled as she realized that losing herself now was a good idea if she wanted to keep her sanity. She didn't want to be the woman with three sisters and a husband all deeply betraying her.

"Now that I have arrived, I guess I figured out where I was going," she said getting out of the car.

Suddenly her phone rang and she looked at the caller ID, but it only displayed the number. Callie frowned realizing that it looked familiar, but with her new phone's contact list only partially restored, she didn't know exactly who was calling. She pressed the reject call button and put the phone in her jacket pocket. It was a shame that the only phone numbers she knew by heart were her kids' cell phones and Michael's cell and home. Everybody else was just a speed dial number or a name from a call list. She never paid attention to actual phone numbers anymore. She didn't even know Michael's office number since she didn't usually call it. She promised herself she would do better, but for the moment, that familiar number could be anybody and she wasn't in the mood to talk to just anybody.

Callie ate a nice lunch and spent the afternoon walking around the waterfront and visiting some of the attractions there. She loved the aquarium and as the afternoon turned to evening, the live entertainment really kicked it up a notch. It was already dark because of the change in season, but Callie stayed for dinner after meeting a group of women throwing one of their friends a "divorcee shower." Apparently the sentiment is the same as a bridal shower and baby shower— to celebrate the start of a new direction in life. The women invited Callie to the party and for once, she didn't over think it and simply accepted.

They had a cake and gifts to open and although most of the gifts weren't really appropriate for a family restaurant, Callie enjoyed the message. After the party, Callie felt relaxed enough to head back home, but she decided she would make a quick stop at the office. After getting her head in a good place, she didn't want her evening to turn into a pity party for herself, home all alone. Maya and Ashley were away for the weekend with Michael's parents and Vanessa was interning at a health clinic near her college campus. Catching up on the work she missed while playing hooky would be just what Callie needed to keep her emotions in check. If she didn't think about the situation then, for at least the moment, it was gone and she could function. She knew without a doubt that she didn't want to be home alone with nothing to do except think about all the ways in which her family had hurt her.

Callie had trained herself to remain reserved, cautious and to keep her focus. Even though she knew how to find that delicate balance between trust and suspicion, she still constantly gave people the benefit of the doubt. That didn't mean she couldn't distance herself enough from the situation so as not to be gullible, because she frequently did. She could usually think things through in a sensible manner to see them clearly. However, this time she couldn't really distance herself, keep her focus or see things clearly. She was dealing with her family and she honestly didn't know what she was supposed to do. She was hurt, but she was also very angry at her sisters for keeping secrets. She was even angrier at Michael because he didn't believe in her, and she levied the harshest criticism at herself for depending on all of them so much.

Callie had cried enough and worried enough and became angry enough over the last year to last her a lifetime. She just wanted to be happy and suddenly she realized that being happy was the one thing that she never learned how to do. At that moment, as Callie drove along the interstate, she vowed she would make the kinds of changes in her life that would put an end to tears at night and anxiety during the day. She knew she had to deal with everyone in due time like getting Paula out of the company, but she wasn't ready to stress herself out about it tonight. She needed to get to the bottom of Alise's problem, because there was a *big* problem if she was teaming up with Paula, but Callie didn't have room in her head for somebody else's issues now. Plus she wasn't sure how to come back from what happened between her and Michael. How could she ever "unhear" his voice saying, 'I choose Marlisa.' Callie understood she was officially on her own and that was how she was going to handle all of her problems—on her own, but in due time. First she would teach herself how to happy, and maybe she wouldn't hurt so much.

*Chapter 23*

While driving on the highway, Callie looked at her phone as it rang again with the same number as earlier. As a matter of fact, this was the fourth call over the course of the evening and although she hesitated, she decided to take it. She realized that it could be Marvin since she didn't really know his full number, but the exchange was his. If it was business, she could get caught up on the day's events as she headed back to the office. Answering the phone through the Bluetooth, she smiled when she heard his voice.

"You're screening my calls now?"

"Never," Callie said softly, still smiling. "I've been wondering about you."

"Yeah?"

"Yeah...so…" She trailed off not sure what she should say.

"I'd like to talk," he replied, breaking the awkward pause.

"Ok."

"Can I see you tomorrow?"

"Yeah, sure," Callie answered eagerly. "So you're back?"

"Couldn't stay away, no matter how much I told myself I should."

She could hear the smile in his voice.

"Lunch?" he asked.

"It's a date."

"Sorry, but I'm not dating at the moment."

"Well, excuse me," Callie said laughing, "I certainly didn't mean to jump to any conclusions."

Now it was his turn to laugh and Callie joined in with him. It was turning out to be a really good night to learn the lessons of happiness. She looked out into the darkness of the highway and was actually pleased that she had decided to free herself from all of her self-imposed restraints. What good did it do her anyway? She had nothing but hurt to show for it, and she wanted to be really honest with him now. She had made her decision.

"So what time can we do lunch? I've got—"

"I've missed you, Stephen," she said gently.

"I've missed you too, so we can catch up during—"

"No, Stephen, I don't want to pretend anymore. We need to talk about what happened."

"You mean when you tore my heart out?"

"Is that what I did? Because it was certainly not what I had intended."

"That's what it felt like. And then you wouldn't even talk to me about it."

Callie had pulled up to the building and turned into the parking garage. They both were silent as she parked her car in a space and turned off its engine.

"I'm sorry for that. I was wrong, but I just couldn't handle the way you looked at me— like you hated me."

"So you think you can face me now?"

Callie thought for a moment and slowly nodded her head. She realized she had changed practically overnight. Only family, the people who you loved the most could do that to you. The thing about it is that sometimes the changes can do more harm than good and Callie wasn't sure which way things would go for her. Still nodding her head, she broke the silence.

"Yeah, Stephen, I think I can face anything now."

"Then let me set the agenda." She could hear him take a deep breath before continuing. "I need to have my say."

"Ok," Callie said getting out of the car. She walked briskly inside to the elevator and pushed the button.

"I don't think it was right for you to say that to me and then just walk away."

"At the time, I thought it was best to just leave it alone."

"It wasn't, at least not for me."

Callie flinched at his words as she stepped in the elevator. "I'm getting into the elevator now, so I hope I don't lose you."

Stephen chuckled. "If you do lose me, you know I'll end up coming back. Sad, but true."

Callie grinned broadly and hit the button for the floor she wanted. As Stephen continued speaking, Callie watched the display showing each floor as she passed by. At this time of night there were no other riders, so she reached the top pretty quickly. She knew he had to purge a little so she just listened, but as she stepped out of the elevator, she was taken aback by what he had just requested.

"I don't understand, Stephen."

"I know that you said you had chosen to stay with Michael and I can handle that, as a matter of fact it was expected. But I need you to take back what you said before you dumped me. It was ...hurtful." His voice broke and she was momentarily stunned. "So before we meet tomorrow, Callie, tell me that what you said to me was a lie."

"I can't do that, because it's true and as far as choosing Michael, I mean, you and I had too many things that would get in our way and you know that."

"I do know that."

"We were ...*are* just, I don't know...different. We're in different places in our lives, different types of—"

"Just take it back, Callie. Tell me you didn't mean what you said or …or else say it again so that I know I understood you correctly. Either way I'm fine."

"Stephen, please."

"You know maybe I won't ever really be fine because you can't say things like that and then expect us to be friends. I don't know how it will work out for us, yet." Stephen took a deep breath as Callie remained silent on the line. "Listen, I know you have work to do, but Callie, this has been bothering me more than you can even imagine."

"I don't think—"

"Please."

"Ok," she paused and then she spoke her next words very softly, "if you think it will help."

"It will."

"Then maybe I should come over. Do you want to see me?"

Stephen hesitated before responding slowly. "Yes, I want to see you. Come over ….if you think it will help."

"It will," Callie answered calmly, "but let me get this straight, you want me to take what I said back, like I didn't mean it."

"We can forget you said it," Stephen said while Callie nodded. She had frequently wished she hadn't said it.

"Then we can go on like normal," Stephen continued speaking unable to see Callie nodding her head in agreement. "I hope you want to forget it too…I mean, if you didn't mean it. Because it hurt, Callie, if it was true."

"It's true, so now you just want me to confirm what I said."

"Only if it's still true."

"It's true," Callie said softly.

"Then I get to have my say. You can't just walk away from me again."

"No, I won't do that again," Callie said quietly, "So, open the door."

"What?"

"Open your door."

Callie heard movement inside and then he was standing there looking at her. She felt her heart beat faster and her knees go a little weak. She had no idea she would be so overwhelmed at the mere sight of him again. They both still had their cell phones to their ears and Stephen looked so vulnerable that Callie wanted to run to him, but she didn't. She couldn't, not knowing how he would react to seeing her.

"Take it back," he whispered in the phone.

"I can't because it's true."

"Then say it again to my face. I need to hear it."

They both stood looking into each other's eyes while Callie got up the nerve to tell him what she knew he needed to hear.

"Say it."

"I'm in love with you, Stephen."

While still making eye contact with Stephen, Callie slowly pulled the phone away from her ear and hung up. They stood looking at each other until Stephen dropped his cell phone and reaching out, pulled Callie to him. He began kissing her passionately as he backed up into the foyer. Closing the door with his foot, he pushed her up against the wall. Callie had dropped her purse and, while ardently returning Stephen's kisses, was trying to maneuver out of her jacket.

"I hope you know I'm not going to stop you this time," Stephen whispered between kisses.

"I hope you know, you wouldn't be able to," Callie responded breathlessly, as she returned every kiss. Suddenly she stopped and put her hand on his chest. "I also hope you know it's been a while, so I might hurt you."

Stephen grinned broadly."That is *so sexy.*"

He quickly picked her up, strode purposely into the bedroom and closed the door behind them.

*Chapter 24*

2:00 a.m. Callie opened her eyes and found herself looking directly into Stephen's open eyes. There was just enough light streaming in through the curtains for her to make out the serious look on his face. Without a word, he pulled her to him and began to gently kiss her lips. Their first time had been powerful, almost frenzied sex, but now feeling his gentleness, Callie knew their love making would be different—and she was right.

4:30 a.m. Callie stood looking out of the hotel suite's window into the night. She was wearing one of Stephen's cotton undershirts she had taken out of his bureau's top drawer and it only came to her thighs. Normally at this time she would almost be ready to go into work, even on a Saturday. However, work was the furthest thing from her mind as she smiled to herself.

"Nice view," Stephen said groggily from the bed.

"The city's always beautiful from up here."

"I wasn't talking about the city."

Callie smiled and sauntered back to stand next to the bed. She stood over him as he lay on his back with his eyes just about closed.

Suddenly, she put one knee at his side on the mattress and swiftly flung her other knee over his body, straddling him. He quickly pulled her to him and whispered, "I love you" in her ear. Callie nibbled his ear and then pushed herself back on him. "I love you too," she replied right before she arched her back and let a little sigh escaped from her lips.

6:48 a.m. Callie felt Stephen kissing her neck and caressing her breasts even before she opened her eyes.

"Is this how they do wake-up calls in this hotel," Callie murmured, "by rubbing breasts?"

"Well, for men, I think they might rub something a little different"

Callie laughed as Stephen brushed his tongue against her nipple.

"*Stephen,*" Callie said giggling, "what are you, a baby? You need a little something every two hours?"

Stephen smiled and then let his tongue trail down her stomach.

"Waaah," he said, imitating a baby's cry, just before his head disappeared under the cover.

10:30 a.m. Callie cracked one eye open and found Stephen standing over her with a breakfast tray.

"I think I willed you awake," he said as she sat up and positioned herself comfortably against the pillows.

"How long have you been standing there?"

"About thirty- five minutes."

"Oh, you have not."

"Well, it was close to that."

"Thirty-five minutes?"

"Either thirty-five or one, I don't remember which."

After he carefully set the tray across her lap, he kissed her on the forehead.

"So you were watching me sleep?" Callie asked chewing on a piece of bacon.

"Yep."

"That's a little creepy, you know."

"I know. If I were you, I would watch out for me."

"That's good advice."

Stephen sat on the bed across from Callie and drank coffee as she ate. He was wearing sweat pants and a white cotton undershirt like the one of his that Callie was still wearing. They chatted comfortably about politics, the stock market and other items from the newspaper Stephen had put on the breakfast tray.

Before drifting off to sleep the first time, they had talked about her reasons for being there, although she did leave out a lot of details. She didn't tell him about Raylene or give him too many details about Marlisa's role. She didn't want to talk about Paula's scam or about Alise's transformation, as she would be talking about all of that soon enough. For the time being, she only wanted to focus on him and her in their moment. So she told him how she was tired of all of the emotional turmoil and that being with him made he feel safe. She also told him that he was right to push away her previous sexual advances. Because although she didn't want to admit it, she was in a hurry to use her "cheat card" that Michael had handed her when he cheated first.

After Michaels' infidelity, Callie felt she could sleep with anyone of her choosing without any real protests from Michael. Callie had chosen Stephen and maybe, subconsciously, she had chosen him from the very first time they met. She had wanted him because he excited her, but after sleeping with him, Callie knew she would have tried to bury her true feelings. Eventually, she realized now, she would have teetered between wanting more of Stephen and punishing herself for wanting him at all. Stephen was probably right when he said her "buyer's remorse" would have made her turn completely away from him. Callie marveled at how well Stephen knew her, but it also saddened her because it highlighted how little Michael knew her anymore. It was also sobering to realize that maybe she didn't know Michael as well as she thought she did anymore, either.

Michael protected Marlisa because she was emotionally needy and wanted him to be her knight in shining armor. Although it was not his job, he did it anyway. Callie just now understood that maybe *he* needed to be somebody's hero, and Callie never gave him a chance to be hers. She was never the type of woman to pretend to be weaker or dumber just so that the man in her life could feel stronger and smarter. He always told her how strong she was and Callie always thought that he had admired that quality in her, but maybe over time…

Callie still couldn't excuse the fact that Michael sided with Marlisa and chose to place the blame for his embarrassment and shame over what happened with Raylene on her. Callie believed either she or Michael or both of them had been bugged by Marlisa. Why else would Paula bring that up out of the clear blue sky? And Marlisa's reaction was classic Marlisa. Ever since she was a little girl, she couldn't effectively mask her emotions. However, Marlisa's actions didn't really matter, because Callie wasn't married to her. It was Michael's reaction that mattered most and he had surprised her. She shouldn't have to defend herself against her husband as he sides with any woman who he let crawl into their "marriage bed." Now Callie felt it was time to put her own wants and desires first. This may be her first time, at least in a very long time, that she was throwing caution to the wind and so far she liked it a lot.

"You know," Stephen said taking a sip of coffee, "I was thinking about that trip to Paris we talked about. Do you still want to go?"

"Yes," Callie said without hesitation.

"That was too quick to be an official Callie Armstrong answer."

"So ask me again."

"Do you—"

"Yes."Callie smiled at Stephen who seemed a little puzzled.

"No regrets, Stephen."

"I was hoping you would say that," he replied. He slowly smiled and Callie felt a little tingly watching his lips. He was really a sexy man.

"I have a private jet so, how about we go today?"

"Today?" Callie frowned as she thought about such a spur of the moment trip.

"Aw, now that's the Callie I know and love—the thinker."

"But how could we prepare in time? I mean, I have to pack and that alone could take a week."

"I can buy you whatever you need when we get there."

"But there are certain things that I want to bring with me, like stuff for my hair, the body wash I like, my lotions and make-up and—"

"Ok, how about you pack an overnight bag with your personal stuff, a couple of changes in clothes and, then when we get there, I take you shopping for anything else you want."

Callie stared at Stephen. This was something she would have never considered before, but now she was really contemplating it.

"I have to take care of things at work."

"You have Marvin and Kelly."

"Even so, I'll be getting a million phone calls a day for everything and the kids—"

"We give them a new, private number to my answering service. The only people that will have it will be your kids, Marvin and my secretary to be used for emergencies only. The service will know how to contact us and you can call back whoever you feel like talking to. Of course, the kids can call anytime day or night, but for everybody else, you only return the calls you want."

"So if a sister gets the number from one of my kids and calls…"

"She'll have to leave a message and if you don't want to talk," Stephen said shrugging his shoulders, "don't return the call. It's not like you're going to run into her in front of the Eiffel Tower later."

"We'll have privacy."

"We'll have privacy."

"In Europe."

"In Europe."

Callie nodded. "Let's do it."

221

*Chapter 25*

Alise reached over and turned off the CD player in her car. It was already a long drive and Paula's "singing" was making her contemplate giving her sister a swift karate chop to the neck. Paula stared at Alise from the passenger seat, seeming a little put off.

"Why did you turn that off? It was coming to my favorite part."

"Because I wanted to hear my favorite part. You hear that?"

"What?" Paula said frowning in concentration. "I don't hear anything."

"Yeah, that's my favorite part. Silence."

"Well, if you don't put the music back on, I'll just do this little a cappella number that I'm *writing*. I haven't quite worked out the melody or all lyrics yet, but I'll practice it now since I'm in the mood for music."

Paula waited for Alise to turn on the player again, but Alise kept both hands planted firmly on the steering wheel.

"Suit yourself," Paula said shrugging her shoulders. "And a one and a two… *My Jesus ooh, my Lordy in heaaaaaven,*—"

"Oh, for heaven's sake, Paula!" Alise said reaching to turn the player back on. "You are so immature! You know all your hollering sounds like a bullfrog being strangled! I'll turn it back on, but no more religious music!" Alise pushed the setting and switched the disc to an old Jeffrey Osborne album that had been re-mastered for a CD.

"Should I be insulted that you're banning religious music from my ears?"

"*And* your mouth. You have no idea what it's like for me to have to sit here and listen to the devil's wife lift her voice in praise and worship."

"What? I hope you know that I'm an ordained pastor."

"You're an ordained liar, and I do not want the Lord Himself reaching down here from his throne to silence you. I'll look up and you'll just be a puff of smoke over there. Now, don't get it twisted, I won't mind the puff of smoke, 'cause I'll just roll the window down. My concern will be the burn stain that you'll leave on my leather seats. I'm not sure if I could ever get you out."

"Yeah, well that's probably true." Paula said it so seriously that Alise couldn't help herself and burst out laughing. Paula laughed too and their laughter helped ease the tension that had been periodically building since they left Maryland.

Paula had been buoyant for the whole trip and Alise knew why. She had agreed to go visit the cities that Paula had marked on the map. Although they looked promising *if* what Paula told her was actually true, the reason for Paula's glee had nothing to do with them visiting those cities. Alise knew she was just happy about the one area they weren't visiting and that was any place near Charlotte, North Carolina. However, Alise also knew her merriment would disappear in just under an hour.

The idea was for them to drive to the most southern city on their route and work their way backwards. Alise had told Paula that she didn't want to make an impulsive purchase which would be easier to do if she was closer to home. However, if she was at the place furthest from home and knew she had to drive back and pass all the other cities anyway, she would force herself to wait until she got back home to make any final decisions. Unless, of course, there was some property that she just couldn't pass up, but that was a wild card to be dealt with if necessary. Paula had agreed and even though Alise had wanted to end this whole thing the previous day, she couldn't get everything and everyone in place quickly enough.

So, Alise had to stall for an entire day, which meant spending more time with Paula thaen she had since she was a teenager. They started off leisurely driving south, on a beautiful Friday morning, stopping for an early lunch and shopping before they even got out of Maryland. Then Alise feigned dizziness and nausea, which forced them to stop for medicine and a short rest. Soon after a little more scenic driving, they stopped for dinner and shortly after that it made sense to get a couple of rooms for the night and start again in the morning.

Alise had made a reservation at a luxury spa and resort near Chapel Hill, although Paula was told they got lucky with two rooms for the night. The resort boasted beautiful gardens, lovely boutiques and English bed and breakfast style rooms in a luxury setting. Alise knew the spa alone would keep Paula occupied long enough for her to do a few follow up phone calls. Franklin had already alerted her that the best he could do was have everything set up for Saturday morning. Alise had told him to make it at noon and he had agreed.

*"You know, I spoke with the grandson of Mary and Frank Arrington. Frank had passed away shortly after they lost their savings to Paula's uh…"*

*"Scam, Franklin," Alise said firmly, "it was a scam."*

*"Well, Mary has struggled financially ever since and now the grandson wants to talk to you personally. He wants some type of guarantee first that this is not another type of thing to uh…"*

*"Swindle, Franklin," Alise interjected again, "or if you prefer rip-off, cheat, hoodwink, defraud, double-cross or con. No matter what you call it Franklin, it is what it is and we both know Paula did it."*

*"I know. So, will you talk with him?"*

*"Yeah, give me the number."*

Alise had talked with the grandson and made her promises and guarantees. Then she spoke with Annie again to confirm her arrival. Annie was the woman Paula had lived with and who was Pastor Paula's staunchest supporter. She had been so happy to hear from Alise and was able to help Franklin with all of Alise's requests.

However, as the time came closer, Alise now felt a little uncomfortable knowing how this could turn out for Paula. It wasn't that Paula didn't deserve it, but Alise couldn't help but imagine how their mother would have felt about it all. Perhaps it was going through North Carolina, a place that held close family ties for their mother, that was making Alise feel a little reflective. Their mother thought family should always be protected from outsiders because that's how she was raised and that's how she had raised the sisters. Although that lesson did not stick with Paula, and Marlisa had problems with it too, Alise had taken it to heart. She shot a glance at Paula who was humming along to the song that was playing and looking out the window at the countryside as it flew past her window. Maybe their mother was right. She should try to fix as much as she could and keep it just between the sisters. Alise thought it was worth a try as she took the next comfort exit off I-85.

"What now?"

"We need gas and we should probably eat something."

"You're hungry again? It's a wonder that you're not as big as a house. Well, maybe your butt is."

"Keep it up, Paula, and you're going to need to check the bus schedules."

"Oh, please, I'm not ever riding a poor house on wheels again. I'll fly back first."

They got out of the car and Alise topped off her gas tank while Paula went to the bathroom. Once they finished at the gas station, Alise drove across the street to the fast food restaurant and parked.

"Aren't we doing the drive through?"

"I don't want to eat and drive."

"Fine, be picky then," Paula said grabbing the door handle to get out," but if I get grease stains on any of my clothes from walking in there," she pointed to the building, "you are paying the dry cleaning bill. No wait, I'll probably just throw the clothes away, so prepare to buy me a completely new outfit. I swear they have grease just floating in the air like soot in these places." Paula pulled on the handle, but before she could open the door, Alise stopped her.

"I've been thinking."

"Oh, Lord," Paula said loudly while rolling her eyes and crossing her arms over her chest.

Alise just stared at her frowning.

"What?" Paula asked innocently.

"Are you finished?"

"Finished what?"

"Being rude."

"Oh that? You are way too sensitive, Alise."

"Maybe I am, but that's because I had to play the role as the responsible one in the family because you were too busy thinking about yourself."

"Hey, that was your choice."

"I'm sure that's how you see it and I'm sure you think that "every man for himself" is the philosophy we should all live by, but—"

"Survival of the fittest is—"

"*But*, I just couldn't look out for myself with two younger sisters, a father who traveled all the time and a mother who had problems. I was the only one who could look after our mother, and in turn make sure the younger ones didn't suffer. You know what happened with Mom, Paula."

Paula was silent and sat looking at her hands. Alise waited for some type of response, but none came.

"You don't know how hard that was to be left alone and you never even checked on her."

"I did."

"When?"

"Don't worry about it. That was between me and my mother."

"Well, good, if you're not lying." Alise paused. "I've been thinking about her lately and that's probably because we've been talking a lot about North Carolina. But it reminded me of how important it was to her that we be a family. That's what she wanted for her girls.

"Now it seems like my whole life we've been on opposite sides. I've always tried to do what's right and you've …well, you know what side you've been on. But in this moment I want to try to do what our mother would have wanted us to do. We both know she just wanted all of her girls to get along. She would want us to put aside the backstabbing and lying and to cancel this Elliot versus Alexander feud that you've been practically waging alone. What you did to Callie and Marlisa is inexcusable, but maybe you can make it right by talking to them. You need to tell them the truth. You need to give them back their father. I mean, they may have a different father than ours, but in the end they're still family. *Our family.* Because family isn't just about blood."

Paula was silent. Then she looked up at Alise and stared at her for a moment before speaking.

"So that's what you really think?" Paula asked pensively.

"Yeah, I do," Alise answered, feeling a surge of hope. It felt like she was finally getting through to her sister.

"Well, if you believe that…" Paula trailed off while still watching Alise, "…you have learned nothing in our time together."

"*What?*"

"Don't 'what' me. What was that last thing that you just said?"

"Uh…,"Alise frowned thinking back, "I said family isn't about blood."

"The hell it ain't! You think I would be sitting here listening to

227

your sentimental jibber-jabber if we weren't sisters? Let me think, the answer to that is, uh–*no*! You would be talking to the back of my head as I walked into that grease spot of a restaurant if we didn't have the same blood! And you know what? I probably would have strapped Marlisa to a raft and set her afloat in the Atlantic Ocean if we didn't have the same mother. But as far as those Elliot sisters go, I know you will eventually tell them the truth, but I'm still not giving back the money or my ties in the company. Tell them and "give them their daddy," but I'm here to stay and I want a check."

Paula reached for the door handle again just as Alise put the child lock on the doors, locking Paula in the car.

"Let's just go. Suddenly, I've lost my appetite."

"Me too," Paula said pursing her lips to make a smacking sound as she settled back in her seat. As Paula reclined the seat, Alise put her sunglasses on and, more determined than ever, she headed towards Charlotte.

## Chapter 26

Alise looked over at Paula who was sleeping peacefully in the passenger seat. They had only been back on the road for about twenty minutes when Paula had drifted off as if she hadn't a care in the world. She was able to blackmail, lie, cheat, steal and God only knows what else, without fretting, even in her dreams. Alise had done what she thought was best and offered Paula a way to redeem herself, but Paula was satisfied with the way things had turned out—so far.

Alise opened up the compartment between the two front seats, and keeping her eyes on the road, rummaged a bit before her hand found the small spray bottle of leather conditioner. Pulling it out from under a notepad, she positioned it directly over Paula so that the mist from the container would land evenly on her face. Alise pumped the trigger several times and then quickly put the bottle back in the compartment.

"Huh...whaa...what?" Paula mumbled as she waved her hand in front of her face.

"Oh, good, you're awake," Alise said cheerfully. "Looks like you've been slobbering though. Anyway, I decided to take a detour. Now it wasn't on our list, but you know, I think it might work out best of all, so I'm a little excited."

"What detour?" Paula asked groggily as she sat up just in time to see the sign announcing the city.

"*Char-ra-lotte!*" she screamed.

"Wow, you said that just like a real southerner," Alise said grinning. "It's like you added an extra syllable or—"

"What are we doing here?" Paula snapped.

"I got a tip on a property that may end up being exactly what I'm looking for!"

"I thought you wanted somewhere more spacious. This entire Charlotte area is a little saturated, isn't it?" Paula asked as she rummaged through her purse. Finding what she was looking for, she put her purse back down on the floor in front of her. Then she put on both the sunglasses and the brightly multicolored, silk scarf that she had just fished out of her bag.

"Yeah, but I'm thinking of living on the outskirts of the city anyway. Get a little small town, country living. I just got a tip on a place that might be perfect. The land is being auctioned off now."

"Who gave you this tip?" Paula asked as she adjusted the scarf over hair and securely tied a bow under her neck.

"Marlisa. She called while you were sleeping so I took a detour."

Paula's blinked rapidly and her mouth hung open, but she didn't say anything. She only sank lower in her seat and pulled the scarf tighter around her head.

"What's with the psychedelic scarf? You look like a Quaker on acid."

"Oh, uh, too much air," Paula answered absentmindedly, looking out the passenger side window. As Alise took a side road away from the heart of the city, Paula suddenly sank down further in her seat so that the top of her head was on par with the dashboard.

"Too much air? What air?"

"Huh?"

"You said it's too much air. What air are you—"

"The air around here!" Paula replied impatiently while waving one

230

hand around in front of her, but using the other hand to firmly hold the scarf in place.

"Well the windows are up and there's nothing really blowing from the vent, it's too cold outside to put on the air conditioner and—"

"There's still air already inside!" Paula said tersely as she continued to peep out of the window.

"But there's no air blowing."

"Of course, it's blowing!"

"Well, I don't know what *you* feel, but I—"

"Your breath, Alise! Ok? It's your breath that I feel blowing and that's the problem!"

Alise stifled a laugh and tried to recover by coughing. She had to force herself not to look at Paula again if she wanted to keep her composure. It was clear that Paula was completely panicked. However, Alise made herself focus on the task at hand and it was not over by a long shot. It wasn't long before Alise pulled up into a middle school parking lot and after finding a spot, she turned off the car engine.

"Let's go," she said to Paula as she got out of the car. Walking around to the passenger side Alise grabbed the door handle to open the passenger door, but Paula had locked it.

"I'm not going," Paula yelled through the glass

"Yes, you are, Paula. I might need a backup in there, like a witness to my auction purchase."

Alise hit the unlock button on her key chain setting off the familiar beeping and the flashing of the car's lights. However, before she had a chance to open the door, Paula had manually locked it again.

"You don't need a backup!" Paula yelled looking up at Alise through the pane of glass.

"Yes, I do!" Alise yelled back. She hit the unlock button again, but this time was faster than Paula and opened the door.

"Alise, no!"

"Listen, Paula all I want you to do is to sit all the way in the front.

No one will even notice you and I don't want anyone to even know we're together. But sometimes if it's a good deal, people try to out play each other in their bids. I need a second pair of eyes in front of me to see who is doing the sneaky bids."

"I don't know anything about auctions."

*Neither do I,* Alise thought. She just needed to say something plausible to get Paula inside and sitting in one of the front chairs. Alise's phone beeped and as she stood in the open door so that Paula could not shut it again, she pulled the phone out of her purse and checked the message

*We're ready*

*Franklin*

"Who was that?"

"Franklin," Alise answered and then decided to improvise a little more, "he has the papers ready for me to sign. I'm cashing out of the company."

"Oh?" Paula said perking up. Alise stepped back a little as Paula sat all the way up. "Who are you selling to?"

"I was going to sell it to Callie, but…if you be my backup in there now or if I get something out of this trip you planned, then I'll sell it to you. I mean, it doesn't matter to me one way or the other."

"Then what was all your Mother Teresa talk about sisters back there?"

"I was trying to free your conscious for the sake of our mother. Don't get me wrong, I love Callie, but I'm tired of looking after her. I've done it my whole life and now honestly, I'm tired. Mom would be proud of what I've already done, so my conscious is clear."

During the time that Alise had been talking, Paula had put one and then the other foot on the ground. Alise now stood behind the door ready to close it quickly once Paula stood up and moved out of its path.

"Well, I suppose I can help you if you remember me later."

"Believe me, Paula, I couldn't forget you if I tried. And I have tried—a lot."

"Alright, I get it. Let's just do this quickly and get out of here. It's a little *Deliverance* feeling around here if you ask me."

"Actually, I kind of like the atmosphere. It's like one of those towns that no matter where you go, you always seem to run into people that you know."

Paula slowed her walking and, keeping her head down, hunched her shoulder even further inward. Alise had to grab her arm to force her to pick up the pace and since Paula was about to be in for a real shock, Alise also wanted to keep her from turning and running. She tightened her grip on Paula's arm as they walked through the door of the cafeteria where everyone was already waiting.

The cafeteria was of average size. The walls were painted off-white and decorated with a variety of colorful student posters on a host of subjects ranging from anti-drugs to school spirit. The linoleum floors were also off white with flecks of brown and gold. Lining the walls were the brown, portable lunch tables with the little seats permanently connected underneath and small wheels attached at the end of each table leg. Once folded the entire table could be easily rolled to any location and set back up again. Although it was clear that the room was used daily as a lunch room, because of the portability of the tables and the stage at the far end, the space also seemed to be multi-purpose.

Today it was being used for a makeshift town meeting for all contributing members of the church building fund that Pastor Paula chaired. Fold up chairs had been neatly lined up in two sections so as to create an aisle in the middle between them. A podium had been set up in the center of the stage. The room was fairly crowded and as Alise walked in with Paula, she could see that most of the seats were taken. She felt Paula tense up and then pull away, so she turned her body to block Paula's path to the exit. Then, so as not to cause a scene, but to ensure Paula's attendance, Alise quickly called out to one of the guests.

"Hi, Annie," Alise said cheerfully, waving with her free hand, "I'm Alise, Pastor Paula's sister!"

"Oh, hi!" Annie's voice rang out as she made her way towards them.

"Paula, you can either quietly make your way to the seat on the end of the first row next to Franklin," Alise whispered in Paula's ear, "or you can stay and say 'Hello' to Annie and the other people you cheated right now. It's your choice, but she'll be here in about fifteen seconds...fourteen...thirteen..."

Paula snatched away from Alise, and still hunched and covering her face, she quickly walked up the outside aisle next to the wall and took the seat beside Franklin. Alise exchanged pleasantries with Annie while still keeping an eye on Paula, who sat rigidly in her chair. When Alise finished chatting, she quickly made her way up the same aisle and sat directly behind Paula. Leaning forward Alise began the first of the two meetings she would conduct in the room. The second would be the public one that was about to be called to order. However, the first meeting was going to be very private with just three in attendance: Alise, Paula and Franklin.

"This is the deal, Paula; you are going to give back what you stole from these people with interest. Compared to what you make with your share of the company, it's really a drop in the bucket, but to some of these people it was their life savings. Nod if you understand."

Paula nodded curtly. Franklin pushed a set of documents in front of Paula who signed them without a verbal protest. However, her foot was tapping and Alise knew this was a sign that Paula was seriously irritated. Franklin did something on his phone and nodded to Alise. She had asked that he and the accountant set up an immediate bank transfer from Paula's account into a new account set up just to house the funds for this purpose. Franklin and the accountant would then distribute payments to each person submitting a valid claim as one of Pastor Paula's contributors. Annie helped get the list together from church records, but they were also able to verify participants and amounts through bank and other church documents.

"Next," Alise continued, "you're going to sign a statement which unequivocally names both Callie and Marlisa as the true and only heirs of Philip Elliot's estate. As the executor of the will, you are officially putting that issue to rest. Understand?"

Paula did another quick nod and Franklin slid more documents in front of her to sign.

"And finally, Pastor Paula, you're going to sign over all the shares you own of CM Music Production. They are the product of… what's the term again, Franklin? Oh, "ill-gotten gains" so they do not belong to you."

This time Paula didn't nod, she turned around and took off her sunglasses to look Alise in the eyes.

"Sorry, Alise, I know how much you like wearing your Wonder Woman cape, but your little extortion game ends now. You've gone too far and I don't feel like playing anymore." She looked around the room and then back at Alise. "Tell them, what do I care? I'll just announce that I'm here to bring back their money. I never told them I was dead. It was in the letter that *you* wrote, remember?"

"You know I didn't write any letter, that was all your doing," Alise whispered angrily, barely moving her lips.

"You and I know that, but they don't."

"Oh, Paula," Alise said and sighed. "You know I didn't think that you would rollover that easily when it came to money, don't you? I had hoped it wouldn't come to this, but you're going to sign those papers one way or another."

"Really?" Paula said smirking. She put her sunglasses back on, turned around in her chair and folded her arms. Alise stared at the back of her head and worked at regaining her composure.

"Yes, *really,* Paula," Alise replied calmly. "You see, I spoke with the grandson of Frank and Mary Arrington, you remember them, don't you? They were the retired couple that almost, literally gave away their farm to you because they believed in you so much. It seems like after the harsh economic down turn, this elderly couple didn't have enough savings to fall back on. Now Frank has passed away and his grandson thinks it was caused by the stress and humiliation of what you did. And poor Mary, well she barely has enough to live on at all. Richard, that's the grandson, now has to financially help out his grandmother, who raised him to be the man that he is today."

"That's all very interesting Alise, but what's your point?"

"My point is, Richard the grandson, is very upset with you and he wanted my personal guarantee that we would give back the money, which I gave him because we will. Then he wanted me to personally give him information on you because he doesn't believe that you're dead, especially when I told him that I didn't write that letter."

"So what? He'll just need to stand in the "I'm upset with Pastor Paula" line with everybody else."

"No, actually he gets to go to the front of the line, Paula, because you committed federal crimes with your mail and bank fraud." Alise watched as Paula tensed up, but Paula still showed no sign of backing down.

"And?" Paula finally said defiantly.

"*And* he's with the FBI *and* he has a grudge *and* he's ready to take you out of here in handcuffs right now. All I have to do is point you out to him." Alise leaned in closer to her ear before continuing the conversation. "He already has the proof, Paula. So, you can either sign over your shares and walk out of here a free woman, or you can be escorted out of here by someone who wants to see great harm come to you. I invited the Sheriff here today, but it's Richard who will make sure you get the book thrown at you. *You will go to prison.* But it's your choice."

"What about the money still in my bank account?"

"You keep that Paula and your investments. I mean, at least for now. It all depends on if Callie and Marlisa want to pursue anything."

Paula turned her head in profile to Alise and whispered through clenched teeth, "You're going to pay for this, Alise. Mark my words, one day you are going to pay."

"Maybe, but it ain't today, is it? *Now sign.*"

Franklin pushed more documents in front of Paula and as she was signing Alise frowned.

"What a minute," she said to Franklin, "I thought the shares she was signing over would be split between Callie and Marlisa."

"They will be."

"But…it says she's giving twenty-four percent *each*?"

"Yeah, there was a new shuffle just a couple of days ago. Marlisa signed over all of her ownership shares to Paula."

"*What?*" Alise said jumping up from her seat. She hurriedly came around to stand in front of Paula and Franklin.

"Why did she do that, Paula?"

"What does it matter anyway?"

"It matters."

Paula crossed her arms and pressed her lips together so tightly that her jaw clenched.

"Oh, hi. Richard Arrington, isn't it?" Alise said smiling at someone behind Paula. "I'll be over in a minute," she added looking at Paula.

"*Alright, Alise,*" Paula spat and then she shrugged her shoulders, "No need of me protecting Marlisa anyway. I helped her bug Callie's cell phone." Alise's jaw dropped open in surprise. "She said she wanted to get enough conversation on tape to prove to Michael that Callie and Stephen were having an affair."

"But they weren't!"

"Didn't matter. You can doctor a recording to prove anything you want, but Marlisa already had what she needed from the bug in Callie's office." Alise let out an exasperated sigh and shook her head from side to side as Paula continued. "She just wanted to listen in on Callie and Michael with the cell phone bug. Then she had planned to double-cross me, but I found out."

"And forced her to pay Paula style?"

"Yep. And now *you* want to cheat me out of what I earned."

Alise looked at Paula and shook her head again. It was no use. She didn't believe she could ever get through to Paula.

"Do you have what you need, Franklin?" Alise said looking at the lawyer again.

"Yeah, I'll fax it to the office right now and courier the original. Kim is in the office waiting for it just like you asked. She'll text me when she gets it," Franklin said as he put the documents in his briefcase and stood up.

"Let me know immediately, too."

He nodded and walked back down the outside aisle to the exit.

"Well I'm going, too. There's no need for me to hang around here with the likes of you."

"You're not going anywhere yet. Not until Franklin gives me the ok that Kim has the fax. Then I want to give him a head start to get the originals sent off."

"What do you think I'm going to do, run him off the road?"

"Maybe or maybe you'll get one of your flying monkeys to do it. I don't know what kind of plan you might have already concocted, but I'm not stupid enough to give you the benefit of the doubt."

"You can't force me to stay," Paula said standing up.

"Ladies and gentlemen, thank you all for coming," Alise announced loudly, "Please, everyone take a seat. Annie and Richard how about you sit right up front?" Alise said smiling. She eyed Paula who had sat down quickly and turned her face away from Annie sitting only three seats away. Alise went up to take her place behind the podium and started the meeting.

After Alise explained the purpose of the meeting and the procedure for putting in the claims to recover each contributor's lost funds, she took a few questions to wrap everything up. She had managed to dodge every Pastor Paula question effectively until the very last one. It was asked by Richard Arrington, who stood up to address Alise.

"We are glad you've come to rectify things, since many people lost much of their savings and we all appreciate you taking this step. But I haven't been able to tell from the answers you've given if Pastor Paula scammed these good, trusting people or if she, too, was a victim of fraud."

"Well, like I said before—"

"Excuse me, Ms. Elliot, but that's not my question."

"Oh?"

"My question is: where *exactly* is Pastor Paula right now?"

"She's…"

Alise paused willing herself not to look at Paula. She wanted Paula to pay for all of her lies in one way or another, but she wasn't sure she could send her own sister to jail. At this point everything will be reset. The money from the scam will be repaid with interest, but that didn't change what these people had to go through because of Paula's greed. What about Frank Arrington, who suffered in ways that could never be repaid? Alise stared blankly at Richard.

"Well?" he asked.

"She's…" Alise started again and then thought about the damage Paula had done even in her own family. Callie and Marlisa would have their company back as a partnership since Alise had already signed over her interest in it too. With the even split of Paula's ownership, Callie actually owned most of the company she had worked so hard to build, which is probably the way it should be. Marlisa was left with twenty-four percent, but that was more than she had when she woke up. Besides it served her right to lose so much after all the deal making she had done with Paula. Snakes bite and Marlisa knew Paula was a snake when she embraced her.

But what about the emotional turmoil Paula created for Callie and Marlisa with her paternity scam? Their identity was stolen because of Paula's jealousy and greed. How do they get repaid for not knowing who their father was for a whole year?

Alise looked around the room at the people watching her expectantly. They begin to murmur to each other and then suddenly, they were yelling at her for answers.

"You know she ain't dead!" Mr. Robinson, a gruff, elderly man wearing jeans and a flannel shirt that tightly squeezed his pot belly, spoke up first. "I didn't believe it when I first heard it!"

"We don't know that!" Annie said speaking up for Pastor Paula as she had done since Paula disappeared.

"I'm just glad to be restored by God, that's all. I didn't lose faith, so I don't care where she is," Mrs. Griffin, another elderly attendee, said. "I just want to praise him!" she added as she raised her hands and rocked back and forth.

"I didn't lose faith in God, either. I just lost faith in that criminal!"

Alise continued to look around the room as it erupted in voices speculating on the whereabouts of their former pastor. Finally, Alise looked at Paula who was as still as a statue. She was scared. Alise didn't see it often, but she knew her sister was afraid of what was going to happen next. However, in the din of the chaos, Alise felt like she was in a trance and could only hear one voice clearly and it belonged to her mother.

*You don't do that to family.*

"Where is she, Miz. Elliot?"

*Family's all you got.*

"Do you know where her grave is?"

*Family should look out for each other.*

"She ain't in the damn grave. She's in Acapulco!"

*You're sisters, Alise. Remember that.*

"Can you give Ms Elliot a chance to talk, please!"

Alise looked up sharply at the voice. He was a young man with kind eyes and he smiled at her as she slowly looked him over from head to toe. He was brown skinned like Anthony had been and of a similar build, but it was the marine fatigues that made Alise catch her breath. She smiled at him, but she was seeing her own son, at ten blowing out his birthday cake, at five on his first day at kindergarten, as an infant when the nurse first put him in her arms. She wondered, like she had every day since she had learned the news, why she just didn't do the right thing. She knew she would never stop feeling responsible for his death. She would never stop wishing that she had done things differently. Dropping her head she closed her eyes and felt a single tear roll down her cheek. Annie ran up to the stage and put her arms around Alise.

"All y'all pushing done stressed her out. We all just need to quiet down," Annie announced in the microphone.

The room went silent as Alise gathered her thoughts. She had been hearing her mother's voice during the entire ride down. She heard her mother's voice while she tried to talk Paula into doing the right thing and as she stood in front of the people who needed honesty from her now. However, when she looked back at the young marine, with his cap tucked under his arm, waiting respectfully for her to speak, all she could hear was Anthony's voice in their last conversation.

*"You're proud of me, huh, Mom?'*

"Always," she had answered then and she repeated it quietly now as she stood behind the podium.

"So, where can we find her?" Richard asked again, more gently in the quiet of the room.

"She's…"

*You're proud of me, huh Mom?'*

"She's…" Alise looked over at Paula.

*"I love you, Mom."*

"She's right there," Alise said pointing.

The room erupted again, but this time the focus was on the women in the front row wearing the bright, multicolored scarf. Richard Arrington strode over quickly to Paula and within seconds of Paula's scarf and sunglasses being removed, he had handcuffed her. Now there was an even bigger stir as the reality of what just happened swept across the room.

241

"I told she wasn't dead! See there? I done told you!" Mr. Robinson's shouts were then followed by an excited "I told you" so chuckle.

"As I live and breathe," Annie whispered. She was still standing with her arms around Alise, but in a matter of seconds her whole body went slack as she fainted. Alise made sure Annie was tended to and then focused on getting out of the noise and the chaos. Paula and Richard were surrounded by the townspeople while the Sheriff and others who had been in the meeting tried to maintain order.

"Alise, get me a lawyer!" Paula screamed to Alise, who was busy trying to move forward through the crowd to get out the room.

"Get your own lawyer!"

"You have to help me, Alise!"

"Survival of the fittest, remember?"

"How could you do this to family?"

"How could you do the things you did!" Alise yelled back stopping her progress just for a moment to look at Paula.

"Alise! Alise!" Paula continued to call out to her, but rather than respond, Alise just focused on getting to the exit.

"Your mother must be so proud!" Paula yelled just as Alise pushed her way through the door.

Once outside, Alise immediately thought about Callie and the last time they spoke. She cringed when she thought about the things she said to her younger sister and best friend. She had to make it right as soon as possible. Running to her car, she quickly got in and started it up. She didn't want to see Richard Arrington or the Sheriff bringing Paula out in handcuffs. Alise told herself that turning Paula in was the right thing to do. Simply "resetting the table" was not the same as Paula being held accountable for the things she did or the pain she caused in the aftermath. Alise told herself that again and again as she drove towards I-85, but she could still feel the sting of Paula's words. Her mother would not be proud at all and Alise did not know what she was going to do with that thought.

*Chapter 27*

Marlisa stood in the doorway of Michael's bedroom watching him sleep. He was bare-chested and lying on top of the covers in his boxer briefs. She couldn't stop smiling as she played with the buttons of the shirt she was wearing. It was the dress shirt Michael had been wearing the night before and Marlisa had quickly picked up the discarded garment on her way to the master bathroom. It smelled like him and she had already decided it was coming home with her when she went. Now she wore it over her undergarments and couldn't help but smile knowing that she was so close to finally having her dreams come true.

Walking slowly to his bed, Marlisa stood above him, marveling in his beauty. He was finally hers, once and for all. Callie couldn't stop the inevitable now that Michael sees the truth. He understands that Callie is all wrong for him because she can't see how he needs a woman to stand by him and give her her full attention. Marlisa knew all along that Callie couldn't do that and now Michael knows that, too. He had told her himself just last night, although he may not remember it.

He had already been drinking when Marlisa came by and he was glad to see her—sort of. He wanted someone to talk to, just like she thought he would. The kids were away with his parents for the weekend, Callie had betrayed his trust and he felt lost. Marlisa didn't think the technicality of Callie not exactly betraying him actually mattered. If not this time, then she surely would the next time. Plus, while Marlisa knew Callie had not slept with Stephen that night like Michael thought she had, it wasn't because Callie didn't try. It was because Stephen was too much of a gentleman to let her do it. Callie wanted to and that was all that really mattered. She "lusted in her heart" and Michael deserved better. If he had to think that Callie was having an ongoing affair behind his back while misleading him, then so be it.

Although Marlisa knew it was the Raylene thing that really made Michael turn away from Callie, he would never know the truth because he would never look for it. It would be Callie's word against Michael's own common sense, and there was no way he would be able to find out the truth about Callie's phone being monitored. There was no profit in it for Paula to tell and she was the only other person who knew.

Marlisa reached out to touch him in order to wake him, but her hand froze. Since he was sleeping, she decided she would use the time to snoop around a little first. She had never even been in his bathroom before and she thought that would be a good place to start. She had no idea what kind of body wash or brand of razors that he used and she felt it was important for her to get to know as many intimate details about him as she could. Such knowledge would come in handy with the holidays fast approaching.

Marlisa practically skipped down the short hallway towards the bathroom, but then suddenly stopped at the entrance to his dressing room. His dress shirts took up an entire wall and his dress shoes were all shined and lined up on what looked like a custom designed shoe rack. Marlisa carefully touched each shirt with her fingertips as she walked by them for the entire length of the room. Then she closed her eyes and just breathed in the air, smiling as she realized that the entire room smelled like Michael. She was finally home.

Opening her eyes she told herself she had to snap out of it. Although everything she had worked for was close, there was still more to do. First, she had to convince Michael that Callie couldn't forgive him and that she didn't know how to tell him since she still loved him in *some* ways. Callie has had her moments of going soft just because she couldn't find the words to decline or because she didn't want to hurt someone's feelings. Michael knew that about Callie. He would believe she couldn't face him with the hurtful truth. So, if Marlisa could also convince Michael that Callie's love for him had changed then Michael would want to get out of Callie's way, especially with another man in the picture. Callie's attachment to Stephen had already laid the groundwork for that storyline. Michael would never force Callie to come back to him. He would wait for her to come back on her own.

The next step for Marlisa would be to make sure Callie believed Michael was still sleeping with her because then Callie would never voluntarily go back to back to him. She would need Michael to come and get her. Marlisa knew it didn't matter whether she was sleeping with Michael or not, as long as Callie thought she was, then the plan would work. She would emotionally paralyze them both and use that time and separation to stand between them. If she had learned nothing else from Paula, she had learned that a simple lie or two and a little misdirection can be more effective than the biggest elaborate scheme around.

Marlisa headed out of the dressing room and had just entered the bathroom when she heard the house phone ring and Michael stir. Pushing the door nearly closed, Marlisa stood behind it and listened. She first heard a little commotion, like things falling, and then Michael's sleepy voice answering the call. He had it on speaker and Marlisa's ears really perked up when she heard Alise's voice.

"Michael, thank goodness I got you on this line. I've been calling your cell phone for the last hour."

"Mmmm…," Michael grunted.

"Have you seen Callie?"

"No."

"You haven't talked to her, either?"

"Not since…uh…Thursday, yeah, Thursday."

"So, you don't know where she is? I've been calling all of her numbers: cell, office home, but all I keep getting is her voicemail. Where are the kids?"

"With my parents for the weekend."

"And you don't know where Callie is?" Alise was now very alarmed

"*Noooo, Alise, I don't.*"

"You sound terrible."

"I feel terrible."

Alise let out a long sigh. "I really need to talk to Callie, like *now.*"

Marlisa took that as her cue to enter the conversation. Rushing out of the bathroom she was suddenly standing in front of Michael, who was now sitting on the side of the bed barely able to hold his head up.

"I think Callie might have gone off with Stephen."

Michael looked up at Marlisa with a look of surprise. "Is that my shirt?"

"Is that *Marlisa*?" Alise asked in disbelief. "Oh, Michael, please tell me you haven't done anything stupid again. Not after—"

"Alise, please. Not today. I have a terrible headache."

"Did she spend the night?" Alise sounded worried.

"Not that I know of."

"Did she drug you?"

"Not that I know of."

"Oh, Alise, please just stop it! Michael and Callie have broken up for good, so you just need to get used to me and Michael being together."

"*What?*" Michael and Alise said simultaneously.

Marlisa immediately realized she was showing her hand too soon.

"I meant that we're friends. Always have been. Besides, Michael," Marlisa said, feeling a little hurt by his reaction, "I thought you said you and Callie were over."

"That has nothing to do with you!" Alise yelled through the phone.

"Then why am I here?"

"Yeah, why is she there, Michael?" Alise asked now directing her yelling at Michael.

"*I don't know!*" Michael sighed. "I can't even think right now, Alise. It's just that it was a long night with a lot of liquor. I needed to talk and Marlisa was good company."

Marlisa smiled with that acknowledgement and turning towards the phone she smugly lifted her chin as if Alise could see her "I told you so" look.

"While you were doing all of this talking, did your "company" tell you that she bugged Callie's office *and* her cell phone to listen in on *your* private conversations with your wife?"

Michael slowly lifted his head to look at Marlisa, who swallowed hard and took a quick step backwards. Michael eyes bore into her and he was frowning in a way that actually scared Marlisa a little.

"When? When exactly did she put the bug in the phone?"

"I don't know exactly when, but—"

"She's lying, Michael!" Marlisa yelled not able to control the panic rising in her voice. "That's not true!"

"I'm not lying, Marlisa! I'm so tired of all of the lies that I don't know what do! Paula confessed to helping her and to receiving all of Marlisa's ownership in the company as a payment for it. There was something about making a fake recording to give to you. I don't know all the details. I just know you cannot trust Marlisa!"

"That's not true, Michael!" Marlisa pleaded. "You can trust me! It's that Paula that can't be trusted. If she told that to Alise, then maybe *she* did it! But I had nothing to do with that kind of carrying on!"

"Get out, Marlisa," Michael said calmly. He was no longer looking

247

at her, but was staring at the picture on his bedside table. It was a wedding photo of him and Callie. "Get out now, Marlisa."

"But Michael, you've got to listen—"

"*Please do not make me say it again*."

"Oh...oh...ok, Michael," Marlisa stuttered. "I know you're upset, so I'll leave now."

"Yeah, get out!" Alise chimed in from the speaker phone.

"Oh, and Marlisa?"

"Yes, Michael?" Marlisa answered hopefully.

"Leave the shirt."

Marlisa darted out of the door, but then slipped off quickly to the side to stand and listen to the rest of the conversation from outside of the open bedroom door.

"Is she gone?"

"I guess, I mean she left the room, but I don't care about that," Michael signed deeply. "Alise, I've got to find Callie. I may have made the biggest mistake of my life."

"Bigger than ...you know...the whole Marlisa thing?"

"Yeah, at this point...I think so in some ways."

"Well, I need to find her too. Same reasons."

"I'll call Vanessa."

"I already have. She said Callie gave them, meaning the kids, a private number to reach her."

"Well, what is it?"

"Doesn't matter. It's a service and she has to want to return your call. She won't want to return mine."

"Or mine, but it's still worth a try. I won't be able to rest just sitting here. Where could she be?"

"I know." Marlisa had stepped back into the room.

"It's that Marlisa again? She's like a human boomerang. You throw her out and then damn, her behind comes right back."

"Do you want to know or not?" Marlisa snapped and then looking at Michael her voice immediately turned softer. "Do you want to know?"

"Yes, Marlisa," Michael replied impatiently.

"She's with Stephen." Both Michael and Alise were silent. "They're going away. I heard them talking."

"Yeah, you sure did," Alise said.

"Where, Marlisa?" Michael asked evenly.

Marlisa thought for a moment about the answer to that question. She knew they had planned on going to Paris and that was on the recording she had given to Michael. But if Michael didn't know that, then it's possible that he hadn't listened to the recording at all. That meant he had only listened to her! She forced herself to remain somber on the outside, but on the inside she was giddy. He had dumped Callie because of what she had told him. He didn't even need the proof! Marlisa would have to find a way to get the recording back so that he wouldn't know the answer she was about to give was not a mistake, but an outright lie.

Marlisa then thought ahead to her nest steps. She had to get to Callie first and poison her against anything Michael had to say. Marlisa would tell Callie that Michael had ran back into her arms as soon as he had a reason. He did it the first time, which caused the separation and he did it again, rather than go back into their marriage. Callie wouldn't be willing to listen to anything Michael said to win her back if she believed Michael betrayed her again. She would have her excuse to stay wrapped in Stephen's arms. Then Marlisa knew Michael would come back once again to lick his wounds in her arms. Marlisa knew it would be the last time because he would finally realize that she, not Callie, was the one woman that truly loved him. Then they could all start over as a family.

"Marlisa? Snap out of it! Where is Callie?" Michael asked again.

"With Stephen."

"Where?"

This time Marlisa didn't hesitate, but answered confidently. "In Rome."

"Thank you, Marlisa. Now get out again."

"Yeah, get out again," Alise added.

"But Michael—"

"Marlisa, please!" Michael shouted as he glared at her. "I just can't do this right now!"

Marlisa scurried out of the room again, but this time she hastily ran to the guest bedroom and changed back into her clothes. Hesitating for only a moment, she stuffed Michael's shirt into her bag and headed towards the front door. However, before leaving she decided to make a quick detour. She needed to know what Michael and Alise were planning.

"...to get my parents to look after the kids. I'm going to get my wife back, once and for all." Michael voice sounded determined. "And then," he continued, "I'm going to have to have to have some words with Stephen."

"I'm going with you," Alise said. "I won't be able to rest until I've undid all the damage I caused by waiting for the right moment to do the right thing. There is no *right* moment. There's only right now."

"I'll make reservations for both of us."

"I'm not back yet. I'm still on the road."

"Then I'll meet you there because I'm getting on the first plane out."

"What if she hasn't left yet? Or what if Marlisa is lying?"

"She's not lying about Callie going away. She admitted she had thought about it, but the things I said probably pushed her into it. I'll keep trying to reach her, but I'm not going to wait. I'm going as soon as I can make arrangements."

"Me too."

"I'll text you the details."

"Ok, I guess I'll see you in Rome."

"Yeah, see you in Rome."

Marlisa tiptoed to the front door and after grabbing the doorknob she yelled her goodbyes, but Michael didn't respond.

"He probably didn't hear me," she said aloud to herself.

Once in the car, Marlisa called her travel service to make arrangements for her flight out. She would have liked to have retrieved the recording of Stephen and Callie, but there was no time for that now. Besides, if and when Michael finds out he's in the wrong country, Marlisa hoped her mission would have already been completed. She smiled. It will definitely work, especially when she makes sure Callie "accidentally" finds Michael's shirt in her bag. Michael won't stand a chance after that discovery. It's going to take some maneuvering, but compared to the last year, this final little step is a piece of cake. She would have Michael all to herself for the very first time and then they would be able to concentrate on just each other. She wasn't going to lose him to Callie this time

She had learned in a seminar on positive thinking to always visualize and take action towards your final goal. Marlisa had been doing that with Michael, and it always helped calm her down. She again imagined her wedding to Michael and she had already decided on her bridal gown. Coincidentally enough, it was being designed and made in Paris.

"That's a sure sign," Marlisa said to herself as she reached the corner of Michael's street. She went over the arrangements she had to make before flying out to find her sister in Paris. She knew they would be staying at one of Stephen's properties, but figuring out the exact location would be a more difficult task, especially if they decided to travel around the country. However, Marlisa wasn't deterred. The way things were working out for her now, she wouldn't be surprised if she just bumped into Callie in front of the Eiffel Tower.

*Chapter 28*

Callie snuggled down in the soft leather seat of Stephen's private plane. She had gotten things together quicker than she thought. Then again, she was only carrying a couple of suitcases. She liked the idea of spontaneity, but in actuality, packing just an overnight bag like Stephen had suggested would have been next to impossible. As it was now, packing only the two suitcases, in addition to her overnight bag, was still winging it for her.

She was able to get a hold of Vanessa and give her a general rundown, but she was waiting for Vanessa's return call so that she could speak with all of the girls. Because they were with Ursula, there would have been too many questions being thrown at her daughters from their grandmother. Callie didn't want to put them in that position, plus she wanted to make sure they were ok with her long trip. They were her only concern and Vanessa was going to call back as soon as she could make sure it was just the three of them alone.

Callie had told Stephen she had to speak with each of her daughters before they took off, and he was more than understanding. Now as she sat with her cell phone on the table waiting, her phone buzzed, but Callie selected the reject button rather than answer it. She had already ignored about fifteen calls from Alise alone. Although Alise had left several messages, Callie had only listened to the first, in which she asked Callie to call her back as soon as possible. However, Callie couldn't bring herself to return the call. What would she say to the one sister that hurt her the most?

Besides, Callie didn't want to get tangled up in another sister drama and possibly put off her trip. She knew it would be an easy thing to do because she had been doing it all of her life. Besides, she and Stephen had decided on a no drama, all play and no work trip. The last time she spoke with Alise there was more drama than she could handle. But Callie felt herself giving in as Alise's number appeared on the screen again. What if she was calling to apologize? It would be nice, but Callie wasn't sure it she wanted it. Not this time. She wasn't about to ignore the fact that her sisters seemed to be doing whatever was in their own best interest. They were in it for themselves, so it was time for her to only think of herself, too. Whatever Alise wanted, Callie would deal with in due time.

Callie looked down as the phone vibrated again. This time it was Michael. She immediately rejected it.

"Not this time," she said aloud.

"What does that mean?" Stephen asked puzzled. He looked up from his reading and Callie shook her head from side to side.

"I thought there was no work on this trip?"

"We haven't started yet," he said grinning.

"That's sort of cheating."

"Yeah, a little, but I know how to turn it off, you don't."

Callie was about to protest, but then realized he was right.

"Ok," she nodded, "I have to agree with you."

"Well, if you're that easy then this is really going to be a fun trip."

"Oh, you have no idea," Callie said as she winked at him.

Just then her phone vibrated and it was finally the call she had been waiting for.

"Vanessa, hi honey."

"Hey, Mom, ok, we're all here. I told them you were going away and explained that the phone number I gave them for you is only for their use."

"Even if they gave it out, I won't return any calls except to you three anyway."

"I know. I told them and I thought it was weird until I talked to Aunt Alise."

"Oh?"

"Yeah. Did you know she had gone out of town with Aunt Paula? They went looking for property to buy together."

"What?" Callie said it with such surprise that Stephen looked up.

"Anything wrong?"

Callie shook her head and smiled and he went back to his reading.

"Do you know what that's about, Mom? I mean she's hanging out with Aunt Paula now?"

Callie thought about her last visit with Alise and how she had talked about the Elliot sisters like she and Marlisa were a plague. She felt the sting of hurt and humiliation all over again as she remembered how Paula had closed the door in her face as Alise stood by and watched. Then Callie thought about how Alise knew what Paula had done this whole time. Maybe Alise would explain everything and maybe it would even make sense. Unfortunately, Callie just wasn't sure if she could forgive Alise or if she would even *want* to forgive her at all. Alise had always been the one she could count on. The one she could trust. If that wasn't who Alise was anymore, then Callie didn't want to know that, at least not now. She couldn't handle it now.

"Why would Aunt Alise be traveling with Aunt Paula?"

"I don't know."

"And that's why I think getting away from everyone is the best thing for you now, Mom. I mean, now that Aunt Alise doesn't seem to be in your corner and Aunt Paula never was. Then there's the whole thing with Aunt Marisa and Dad …"

"Ain't family great?" Callie asked quietly.

"They're supposed to be, but I think...well, it doesn't matter what I think. Just take care of yourself Mom, ok? Don't worry about us. I'm interning a lot, and with school I'll be busy, but I'll check in on Ashley and Maya. That's why I decided to come for this weekend outing at the last minute. I thought I had to buffer Maya against Grandma Ursula."

"What do you mean?" Callie asked with the beginnings of a smile.

"What do you mean, what do I mean? Have you *met* Grandma Ursula? She won't let Maya use her cell phone because putting it to her ear might give her brain cancer. She can't watch television because that filth rots the mind. And she can't listen to her iPod because when Grandma Ursula checked it Maya had some rap loaded on it. Nothing bad, but we all know that *all* rap is the music the devil invented because it's only about sex."

Callie thought about some of the rap songs on her iPod and grinned.

"Well, just do what you can to keep the peace and thank you for understanding, Vanessa."

"I'm always on your side," Vanessa said softly.

"I know. I love you."

"I love you, too, Mom. Here's Ashley."

"Hey, Mom. Have a good trip. It's important that you just "do you" and not worry about us. Oh, and can you put some money in my account? Senior stuff, you know."

"Ok, my little Ashley. I'll see you soon. I love you."

"Love you too. Here's Maya. Don't take too long Maya Ang-e-*no*."

"You're such a child, Ashley." Maya said with a grown up tone as the phone exchanged hands between them. "Just because I like poetry doesn't mean you have to make me the butt of your stupid jokes."

"No, you're just the butt. So hurry up. Mom has to go."

"You're not the boss of me," Maya said, still maintaining her mature voice.

"Oh Maya, Maya, Maya," Ashley said condescendingly, "I'm older than you, so of course I'm your boss. Now get over it, shrimp boat!"

"Mom! Make Ashley stop!" The grownup pretense was now gone and she was back to being a nine year-old fighting with her sister. As the two argued, both Callie and Vanessa tried to interfere. Finally Vanessa forced Ashley out of the room, but not before she tossed Maya a parting shot.

"I'm leaving because you're such a big baby, Maya."

"And you're such a big ass!" Maya yelled back.

Callie's mouth dropped open, but before she had a chance to scold her youngest, Vanessa had forced an apology out of Maya.

"Say it louder, Maya! You shouldn't be talking like that in front of Mom!"

"I'm sorry, Mom, but I'm under stress dealing with Ashley *and* Ursula."

"Oh, so it's Ursula now?"

"Yeah. "Grandma" is just one of those titles that bind us all unnecessarily."

Callie grinned broadly at her little philosopher and poet at work again, but she managed to keep the smile out of her voice.

"I think you're right," she replied seriously to her daughter, keeping her amusement under control.

"Yeah," Maya said pensively. "Anyway, love you, Mom. Have a good trip."

"I will. I love you, too."

Callie had thought Vanessa was coming back on the line, but Maya had just hung up. Callie smiled as she looked at Stephen.

"I was a little worried, but I think the kids will be just fine without me."

"So we're ready to go?" he asked putting down the documents he had been reading.

"Yeah, I think we are."

"I'll go talk to the pilot."

Stephen got up and Callie looked down at her phone. The phone had been constantly beeping for almost the entire time she was on the phone with the girls. Now checking her missed calls she saw that the incoming numbers had been from Michael, Alise and…Marlisa?

Callie frowned as she thought about calling Marlisa back. What could she possibly want to talk to her about? Just as Callie, driven by curiosity, was about to push the call back button for the missed call from Marlisa, Stephen slid in the seat next to her and pulled her close.

"I finally have you all to myself," he said as he gently kissed her lips.

Callie smiled and then seeing some of her lipstick on his lips, she tenderly began to wipe it off with her thumb. Stephen stared at her as she concentrated on removing all traces of the color "Soft Blossom" from his lips.

"You better watch out, girl" Stephen said with the deep southern drawl he reserved for charming women, "'Cause you giving me ideas."

"Well, it is a long flight."

Just then Callie's phone, which was still in her hand, began to vibrate. She looked at the caller ID for a moment and then turned her phone off and dropped it into her bag. She looked back at Stephen, smiled and nuzzled his neck.

"Mmmm, honeysuckle," he whispered as he breathed in the scent of her hair.

Callie pulled back and looked at him. That's what Michael always used to say, but he wasn't Michael. He was someone different. There were a lot of things different now and would continue to be different in the future. Everyone would see that soon. Sighing, she allowed herself to relax completely in his arms, knowing that she had to use this time away from her sisters to heal emotionally. Callie knew that when she saw them again, she was going to deal with each and every one of them—once and for all.

## An Interview with the Author

**Clearly there is a book three planned. What can readers expect in the sisters' final chapters?**

I think readers will like that the next book offers a lot of hope for the sisters' relationship. Reconciliation? Maybe, but not necessarily. However, readers will definitely have a better understanding of Paula's behavior.

**Will Callie ultimately chose Stephen or Michael?**
Hmmm....we'll see.

**Are there any parallels with theses sisters and people in your real life?**

I think all writers find parallels between their characters and real life experiences. One similar character connection is the sisters' father and my father. As I was growing up, my father wrote songs, performed and recorded with a lot of people. I've also performed, so the music connection is a part of my real life that seems to seep through in my writings.


**Contact newrelease@juaniabooks to be alerted to upcoming release dates.**